COUNTER-CLOCK WORLD

Philip K. Dick was born in Chicago in 1928 and lived in California for most of his life. He attended college for a year at Berkeley. Apart from writing, his main interest was music. He won the Hugo Award for his classic novel of alternative history, *The Man in the High Castle* (1962). He was married five times and had three children. He died in March 1982. His novel *Do Androids Dream of Electric Sheep?* was adapted into the world famous film *Blade Runner* in the same year.

'The fact that what Dick is writing about is reality and madness, time and death, sin and salvation – this has escaped most critics. Nobody notices that we have our own homegrown Borges, and had him for thirty years . . .'

Ursula K. Le Guin

'No other writer of his generation had such a powerful intellectual presence. He has stamped himself not only on our memories but in our imaginations'
Brian W. Aldiss

BY THE SAME AUTHOR

Novels

Solar Lottery
Eye in the Sky
Vulcan's Hammer
The Man Who Japed
The Cosmic Puppets
The World Jones Made
Time Out of Joint
Dr Futurity
The Man in the High Castle
The Game Players of Titan
Clans of the Alphane Moon
Flow My Tears, the Policeman
   Said
The Penultimate Truth
The Simulacra
Martian Time-Slip
Dr Bloodmoney, or How We
   Got Along After The Bomb
The Zap Gun
Now Wait for Last Year
Counter-Clock World
Blade Runner (also published
   as Do Androids Dream of
   Electric Sheep?)
Ubik
Our Friends from Frolix 8
Galactic Pot-Healer
The Three Stigmata of
   Palmer Eldritch
A Scanner Darkly
Valis
The Divine Invasion
The Transmigration of
   Timothy Archer
Confessions of a Crap Artist
The Ganymede Takeover
   (with Ray Nelson)

Deus Irae
   (with Roger Zelazny)
A Maze of Death
Lies, Inc.
   (The Unteleported Man)
The Man Whose Teeth Were
   All Exactly Alike
In Milton Lumky Territory
Puttering About in a
   Small Land
Humpty Dumpty in Oakland
Radio Free Albemuth
We Can Build You
The Broken Bubble

Short Stories

A Handful of Darkness
I Hope I Shall Arrive Soon
The Variable Man
The Book of Philip K. Dick
The Golden Man
The Preserving Machine
Collected Stories 1:
   Beyond Lies the Web
Collected Stories 2:
   Second Variety
Collected Stories 3:
   The Father-Thing
Collected Stories 4:
   The Days of Perky Pat
Collected Stories 5: We Can
   Remember It For You
   Wholesale

PHILIP K. DICK

Counter-Clock World

HarperVoyager
An imprint of HarperCollins*Publishers*
1 London Bridge Street
London SE1 9GF

www.harpercollins.co.uk

This paperback edition 2008

Previously published in paperback by Grafton 1990 and Voyager 2002

First published in Great Britain
by Sphere Books Ltd 1968

A catalogue record for this book is
available from the British Library

ISBN-13: 978 0 00 712770 2

Set in Times

Printed by CPI Group (UK) Ltd, Croydon CR0 4YY

MIX
Paper from
responsible sources
FSC™   FSC™ C007454
www.fsc.org

FSC is a non-profit international organisation established
to promote the responsible management of the world's forests.
Products carrying the FSC label are independently certified
to assure consumers that they come from forests that are managed
to meet the social, economic and ecological needs
of present and future generations.

Find out more about HarperCollins and the environment at
www.harpercollins.co.uk/green

Chapter 1

Place there is none; we go backward and forward, and there is
no place.   – St Augustine

As he glided by the extremely small, out-of-the-way
cemetery in his airborne prowl car, late at night, Officer
Joseph Tinbane heard unfortunate and familiar sounds.
A voice. At once he sent his prowl car up over the spiked
iron poles of the badly maintained cemetery fence,
descended on the far side, listened.

The voice said, muffled and faint, 'My name is Mrs
Tilly M. Benton, and I want to get out. Can anybody
hear me?'

Officer Tinbane flashed his light. The voice came from
beneath the grass. As he had expected: Mrs Tilly M.
Benton was underground.

Snapping on the microphone of his car radio Tinbane
said, 'I'm at Forest Knolls Cemetery – I think it's called
– and I have a 1206, here. Better send an ambulance out
with a digging crew; from the sound of her voice it's
urgent.'

'Chang,' the radio said in answer. 'Our digging crew
will be out before morning. Can you sink a temporary
emergency shaft to give her adequate air? Until our crew
gets there – say nine or ten A.M.'

'I'll do the best I can,' Tinbane said, and sighed. It
meant for him an all-night vigil. And the dim, feeble
voice from below begging in its senile way for him to
hurry. Begging on and on. Unceasingly.

5

This part of his job he liked least. The cries of the dead; he hated the sound, and he had heard them, the cries, so much, and so many times. Men and women, mostly old but some not so old, sometimes children. And it always took the digging crew so long to get there.

Again pressing his mike button, Officer Tinbane said, 'I'm fed up with this. I'd like to be reassigned. I'm serious; this is a formal request.'

Distantly, from beneath the ground, the impotent, ancient female voice called, 'Please, somebody; I want to get out. Can you hear me? I know somebody's up there; I can hear you talking.'

Leaning his head out the open window of his prowl car, Officer Tinbane yelled, 'We'll get you out any time now, lady. Just try to be patient.'

'What year is this?' the elderly voice called back. 'How much time has passed? Is it still 1974? I have to know; please tell me, sir.'

Tinbane said, 'It's 1998.'

'Oh dear.' Dismay. 'Well, I suppose I must get used to it.'

'I guess,' Tinbane said, 'you'll have to.' He picked a cigarette butt from the car's ashtray, lit it and pondered. Then, once again, he pressed his mike button. 'I'd like permission to contact a private vitarium.'

'Permission denied,' his radio said. 'Too late at night.'

'But,' he said, 'one might happen along anyhow. Several of the bigger ones keep their scout-ambulances heading back and forth all through the night.' He had one vitarium in particular in mind, a small one, old-fashioned. Decent in its sales methods.

'So late at night it's unlikely – '

'This man can use the business.' Tinbane picked up the vidphone receiver mounted on the car's dashboard. 'I want to talk to a Mr Sebastian Hermes,' he told the operator. 'You find him; I'll wait. First of all try his place of business, the Flask of Hermes Vitarium; he probably has an all-night relay to his residence.' If the poor guy can currently afford it, Tinbane thought. 'Call me back as soon as you've located him.' He hung up, then, and sat smoking his cigarette.

The Flask of Hermes Vitarium consisted primarily of Sebastian Hermes himself, with the help of a meager assortment of five employees. No one got hired at the establishment and no one got fired. As far as Sebastian was concerned these people constituted his family. He had no other, being old, heavy set, and not very likable. They, another, earlier vitarium, had dug him up only ten years ago, and he still felt on him, in the dreary part of the night, the coldness of the grave. Perhaps it was that which made him sympathetic to the plight of the old-born.

The firm occupied a small, wooden, rented building which had survived World War Three and even portions of World War Four. However, he was, at this late hour, of course home in bed, asleep in the arms of Lotta, his wife. She had such attractive clinging arms, always bare, always young arms; Lotta was much younger than he: twenty-two years by the non-Hobart Phase method of reckoning, which she went by, not having died and been reborn, as he, so much older, had.

The vidphone beside his bed clanged; he reached, by reflex of his profession, to acknowledge it.

'A call from Officer Tinbane, Mr Hermes,' his answering girl said brightly.

'Yes,' he said, listening in the dark, watching the dull little gray screen.

A controlled young man's face appeared, familiar to him. 'Mr Hermes, I have a live one at a hell of a third rate place called Forest Knolls; she's crying out to be let out. Can you make it here right away, or should I begin to drill an air vent myself? I have the equipment in my car, of course.'

Sebastian said, 'I'll round up my crew and get there. Give me half an hour. Can she hold out that long?' He switched on a bedside light, groped for pen and paper, trying to recall if he had ever heard of Forest Knolls. 'The name.'

'Mrs Tilly M. Benton, she says.'

'Okay,' he said, and rang off.

Stirring beside him, Lotta said drowsily, 'A job call?'

'Yes.' He dialed the number of Bob Lindy, his engineer.

'Want me to fix you some hot sogum?' Lotta asked; she had already gotten out of bed and was stumbling, half-asleep, toward the kitchen.

'Fine,' he said. 'Thanks.' The screen glowed, and thereon formed the glum and grumpy, thin and rubbery face of his company's sole technician. 'Meet me at a place called Forest Knolls,' Sebastian said. 'As soon as you can. Will you have to go by the shop for gear, or – '

'I've got it all with me,' Lindy grumbled, irritably. 'In my own car. Chang.' He nodded, broke the connection.

Padding back from the kitchen, Lotta said, 'The sogum pipe is on. Can I come along?' She found her brush and began expertly combing her mane of heavy dark-brown hair; it hung almost to her waist, and its intense color matched that of her eyes. 'I always like to see them brought up. It's such a miracle. I think it's the most marvelous sight I've ever watched; it seems to me it fulfills what St Paul says in the Bible, about "Grave,

8

where is thy victory?"' She waited hopefully, then, finished with her hair, searched in the bureau drawers for her blue and white ski sweater which she always wore.

'We'll see,' Sebastian said. 'If I can't get all the crew we won't be handling this one at all; we'll have to leave it to the police, or wait for morning and then hope we're first.' He dialed Dr Sign's number.

'Sign residence,' a groggy middle-aged familiar female voice said. 'Oh, Mr Hermes. Another job so soon? Can't it wait until morning?'

'We'll lose it if we wait,' Sebastian said. 'I'm sorry to get him out of bed, but we need the business.' He gave her the name of the cemetery and the name of the old-born individual.

'Here's your sogum,' Lotta said, coming from the kitchen with a ceramic container and ornamented intake tube; she now had her big ski sweater on over her pajamas.

He had only one more call to make, this one to the company's pastor, Father Jeramy Faine. Placing the call, he sat precariously on the edge of the bed, dialing with one hand, using the other to hold in place the container of sogum. 'You can come with me,' he said to Lotta. 'Having a woman along might make the old lady – I assume she's old – more comfortable.'

The vidscreen lit; elderly, dwarfish Father Faine blinked owlishly, as if surprised in the act of nocturnal debauchery. 'Yes, Sebastian,' he said, sounding, as always, fully awake; of Sebastian's five employees, Father Faine alone seemed perpetually prepared for a call. 'Do you know which denomination this old-born is?'

'The cop didn't say,' Sebastian said. As far as he himself was concerned it didn't much matter; the company's pastor sufficed for all religions, including Jewish

9

and Udi. Although the Uditi, in particular, did not much share this view. Anyhow, Father Faine was what they got, like it or not.

'It's settled, then?' Lotta asked. 'We're going?'

'Yes,' he said. 'We've got everyone we need.' Bob Lindy to sink the air shaft, put digging tools to work; Dr Sign to provide prompt – and vital – medical attention; Father Faine to perform the Sacrament of Miraculous Rebirth . . . and then tomorrow during business hours, Cheryl Vale to do the intricate paper work, and the company's salesman, R.C. Buckley, to take the order and set about finding a buyer.

That part – the selling end of the business – did not much appeal to him; he reflected on this as he dressed in the vast suit which he customarily wore for cold nights. R.C., however, seemed to get a bang out of it; he had a philosophy which he called 'placement location,' a dignified term for managing to pawn off an old-born individual on somebody. It was R.C.'s line that he placed the old-borns only in 'specially viable, selected environments of proven background,' but in fact he sold wherever he could – as long as the price was sufficient to guarantee him his five percent commission.

Lotta, trailing after him as he got his greatcoat from the closet, said, 'Did you ever read that part of First Corinthians in the NEB translation? I know it's getting out of date, but I've always liked it.'

'Better get finished dressing,' he said gently.

'Okay.' She nodded dutifully, trotted off to get work-pants and the high soft-leather boots which she cherished so much. 'I'm in the process of memorizing it, because after all I am your wife and it pertains so directly to the work we – I mean you – do. Listen. That's how it starts, I mean; I'm quoting. "Listen. I will unfold a mystery: we

10

shall not all die, but we shall be changed in a flash, in the twinkling of an eye, at the last trumpet call."'

'A call,' Sebastian said meditatively as he waited patiently for her to finish dressing, 'that came one day in June of the year 1986.' Much, he thought, to everyone's surprise – except of course for Alex Hobart himself, who had predicted it, and after whom the anti-time effect had been named.

'I'm ready,' Lotta said proudly; she had on her boots, workpants, sweater, and, he knew, her pajamas under it all; he smiled, thinking of that: she had done it to save time, so as not to detain him.

Together, they left their conapt; they ascended by the building's express elevator to the roof-field and their parked aircar.

'Myself,' he said to her as he wiped the midnight moisture from the windows of the car, 'I prefer the old King James translation.'

'I've never read that,' she said, childish candor in her voice, as if meaning, But I'll read it; I promise.

Sebastian said, 'As I recall, in that translation the passage goes, "Behold! I tell you a mystery. We shall not all sleep; we shall be changed – " and so on. Something like that. But I remember the "behold." I like that better than "listen."' He started up the motor of the aircar, and they ascended.

'Maybe you're right,' Lotta said, always agreeable, always willing to look up to him – he was, after all, so much older than she – as an authority. That perpetually pleased him. And it seemed to please her, too. Seated beside her, he patted her on the knee, feeling affection; she thereupon patted him, too, as always: their love for each other passed back and forth between them, without

11

resistance, without difficulty; it was an effortless two-way flow.

Young, dedicated Officer Tinbane met them inside the dilapidated spiked iron-pole fence of the cemetery. 'Evening, sir,' he said to Sebastian, and saluted; for Tinbane every act done while wearing his uniform was official, not to mention impersonal. 'Your engineer got here a couple of minutes ago and he's sinking a temporary air shaft. It was lucky I passed by.' The policeman greeted Lotta, seeing her now. 'Good evening, Mrs Hermes. Sorry it's so cold; you want to sit in the squad car? The heater's on.'

'I'm fine,' Lotta said; craning her neck, she strove to catch sight of Bob Lindy at work. 'Is she still talking?' she asked Officer Tinbane.

'Chattering away,' Tinbane said; he led her and Sebastian, by means of his flashlight, toward the zone of illumination where Bob Lindy already toiled. 'First to me; now to your engineer.'

On his hands and knees, Lindy studied the gauges of the tube-boring rig; he did not look up or greet them, although he evidently was aware of their presence. For Lindy, work came first; socializing ran a late last.

'She has relatives, she claims,' Officer Tinbane said to Sebastian. 'Here; I wrote down what she's been saying; their names and addresses. In Pasadena. But she's senile; she seems confused.' He glanced around. 'Is your doctor coming for sure? I think he'll be needed; Mrs Benton said something about Bright's disease; that's evidently what she died of. So possibly he'll need to attach an artificial kidney.'

Its landing lights on, an aircar set down. Dr Sign stepped from it, wearing his plastic, heat-enclosing,

12

modern, stylish suit. 'So you think you've got a live one,' he said to Officer Tinbane; he knelt over the grave of Mrs Tilly Benton, cocked an ear, then called, 'Mrs Benton, can you hear me? Are you able to breathe?'

The faint, indistinct, wavering voice drifted up to them, as Lindy momentarily ceased his drilling. 'It's so stuffy, and it's dark and I'm really very much afraid; I'd like to be released to go home as soon as I can. Are you going to rescue me?'

Cupping his hands to his mouth, Dr Sign shouted back, 'We're drilling now, Mrs Benton; just hang on and don't worry; it'll only be another minute or so.' To Lindy he said, 'Didn't you bother to yell down to her?'

Lindy growled, 'I have my work. Talking's up to you guys and Father Faine.' He resumed the drilling. It was almost complete, Sebastian noted; he walked a short distance away, listening, sensing the cemetery and the dead beneath the headstones, the corruptible, as Paul had called them, who, one day, like Mrs Benton, would put on incorruption. And this mortal, he thought, must put on immortality. And then the saying that is written, he thought, will come to pass. Death is swallowed up in victory. Grave, where is thy victory? Oh death, where is thy sting? And so forth. He roamed on, using his flashlight to avoid tripping over headstones; he moved very slowly, and always hearing – but not exactly; not literally, with his ears, but rather inside him – the dim stirrings underground. Others, he thought, who one day soon will be old-born; their flesh and particles are migrating back already, finding their way to their onetime places; he sensed the eternal process, the unending complex activity of the graveyard, and it gave him a thrill of enthusiasm, and of great excitement. Nothing was more good, than this re-forming of bodies which had, as Paul put it,

13

corrupted away, and now, with the Hobart Phase at work, reversing the corruption.

Paul's only error, he reflected, had been to anticipate it in his own lifetime.

Those who were presently being old-born had been the last to die: final mortalities before June of 1986. But, according to Alex Hobart, the reversal of time would continue to move backwards, continually sweeping out a great span; earlier and still earlier deaths would be reversed . . . and, in two thousand years from now, Paul himself would no longer 'sleep,' as he himself had put it.

But by then – long, long before then – Sebastian Hermes and everyone else alive would have dwindled back into waiting wombs, and the mothers who possessed those wombs would have dwindled, too, and soon; assuming, of course, that Hobart was right. That the Phase was not temporary, short in duration, but rather one of the most vast of sidereal processes, occurring every few billion years.

One final aircar now sputtered to a landing; from it strode short little Father Faine, with his religious books in his briefcase. He nodded pleasantly to Officer Tinbane and said, 'Commendable, your hearing her; I hope now you won't have to stand around in the cold any longer.' He noted the presence of Lindy at work and Dr Sign waiting with his black medical bag, and of course Sebastian Hermes. 'We can take over now,' he informed Officer Tinbane. 'Thank you.'

'Good evening, Father,' Tinbane said. 'Good evening, Mr and Mrs Hermes, and you too, Doctor.' He glanced then at sour, taciturn Bob Lindy, and did not include him; turning, he walked off in the direction of his squad car. And was quickly off into the night, to patrol the rest of his beat.

Coming up to Father Faine, Sebastian said, 'You know something? I – hear another one. Somebody very near to being reborn. A matter of days, possibly even hours.' I catch a terrific, strong emanation, he said to himself. What must be a uniquely vital personality very close by.

'I've got air down to her,' Lindy declared; he ceased drilling, shut off the portable, much-depended-on rig, turned now to excavation equipment. 'Get ready, Sign.' He tapped the earphones which he had put on, the better to hear the person below. 'She's very ill, this one. Chronic and acute.' He snapped the automatic scoops on, and they at once began to toss dirt from their exhaust.

As the coffin was lifted up by Sebastian, Dr Sign and Bob Lindy, Father Faine read aloud from his prayer book, in a suitable commanding and clear voice, so as to be audible to the person within the coffin. '"The Lord rewarded me after my righteous dealing, according to the cleanness of my hands did he recompense me. Because I have kept the ways of the Lord, and have not forsaken my God, as the wicked doth. For I have an eye unto all his laws, and will not cast out his commandments from me. I was also uncorrupt before him, and eschewed mine own wickedness. Therefore the Lord rewarded me after my righteous dealing, and according unto the cleanness of my hands in his eyesight. With the holy thou shalt be holy – "' On and on Father Faine read, as the work progressed. They all knew the psalm by heart, even Bob Lindy; it was their priest's favorite on these occasions, being sometimes replaced, as for example by psalm nine, but always returning.

Bob Lindy rapidly unscrewed the lid of the coffin; it was cheap synthetic pine, lightweight, and the lid came right off. Instantly Dr Sign moved forward, bent over the old lady with his stethoscope, listening, talking to her in

15

a low voice. Bob Lindy started up the hot fan, keeping a stream of constant heat on Mrs Tilly M. Benton; this was vital, this transfer of heat: the old-born were always terribly cold; had, in fact, an inevitable phobia about cold which, as in Sebastian's case, often lasted for years after their rebirth.

His part of the job temporarily over, Sebastian once again moved about the cemetery, among the graves, listening. Lotta this time tagged after him and insisted on talking. 'Isn't it mystical?' she said breathlessly, in her little girl's awed voice. 'I want to paint it; I wish I could get that expression they have when they first see, when the lid of the coffin is opened. That look. Not joy, not relief; no one particular thing, but a deeper and more – '

'Listen,' he said, interrupting her.

'To what?' She obligingly listened, obviously hearing nothing. Not sensing what he sensed: the enormous *presence* nearby.

Sebastian said, 'We're going to have to keep a watch on this strange little place. And I want a complete list – absolutely complete – of everyone buried here.' Sometimes, studying the inventory list, he could fathom which it was; he had a virtually psionic gift, this ability to sense in advance a forthcoming old-birth. 'Remind me,' he said to his wife, 'to call the authorities who operate this place and find out exactly who they have.' This invaluably rich storehouse of life, he thought. This onetime graveyard which has become instead a reservoir of reawakening souls.

One grave – and one alone – had an especially ornate monument placed above it; he shone his flashlight on the monument, found the name.

THOMAS PEAK
1921–1971
Sic igitur magni quoque circum
moenia mundi expugnata dabunt
labem putresque ruinas.

His Latin was not good enough for him to translate the epitaph; he could only guess. A statement about the great things of the earth, all of which fell eventually into corruption and ruin. Well, he thought, that is no longer true, that epitaph. Not about the great things with souls; them especially. I have a hunch, he said to himself, that Thomas Peak – and he evidently had been somebody, to judge by the size and stone-quality of the monument – is the person I sense to be about to return, the person we should watch for.

'Peak,' he said aloud, to Lotta.

'I've read about him,' she said. 'In a course I took on Oriental Philosophy. You know who he is – was?'

He said, 'Was he related to the Anarch by that name?'

'Udi,' Lotta said.

'That Negro cult? That's overrun the Free Negro Municipality? Run by that demagogue Raymond Roberts? The *Uditi*? This Thomas Peak buried here?'

She examined the dates, nodded. 'But it wasn't a racket, in those days, my teacher told us. There really is a Udi experience, I believe. Anyhow, so we were taught at San Jose State. Everyone merges; there's no you and no – '

'I know what Udi is,' he said testily. 'God, now that I know who he is I'm not so sure I want to help bring this one back.'

'But when the Anarch Peak comes back,' Lotta said, 'he'll resume his position as head of Udi and it'll stop being a racket.'

17

Behind them Bob Lindy said, 'You could probably make a fortune by *not* bringing him back to an unwilling, unwaiting world.' He explained, 'I'm now done with your job-call, here; Sign is inserting one of those hand-me-down electric kidneys and getting her on a stretcher and into his car.' He lit a cigarette butt, stood smoking and shivering and meditating. 'You think this fella Peak's about to return, Seb?'

'Yes,' he said. 'You know my intimations.' Our firm operates at a profit because of them, he meditated; they're what keep us ahead of the big outfits, make it possible in fact to get any business at all . . . anything, anyhow, above and beyond what the city police throw to us.

Lindy said somberly, 'Wait'll R.C. Buckley hears about this. He'll really go into action on this one; in fact, I suggest you call him right now. The sooner he knows, the sooner he can formulate one of those wild rizzle-drizzle promotion campaigns he concocts.' He laughed sharply. 'Our man in the graveyard,' he said.

'I'm going to plant a bug here on Peak's grave,' Sebastian said after a thoughtful pause. 'One that'll both pick up cardiac activity and will transmit a notifying coded signal to us.'

'You're that sure,' Lindy said, nervously. 'I mean, it's illegal; if the LA police find it, you know – maybe a suspension of our license to operate.' His innate Swedish caution emerged, now, and his dubiousness regarding Sebastian's psionic intimations. 'Forget it,' he said. 'You're getting as bad as Lotta.' He plomped her friend-lily on the back, meaning well. 'I always say, I'm not going to let the atmosphere of these places get to me; it's a technical job having to do with exact location, adequate air supply, digging accurately so you don't saw it in half,

18

then raising it up, getting Dr Sign to patch its busted parts together.' To Lotta he said, 'You're too metaphysical about this, kid. Forget it.'

Lotta said, 'I'm married to a man who lay dead down below, once. When I was born, Sebastian was dead, and he remained dead until I was twelve years old.' Her voice – odd for her – was unyielding.

'So?' Lindy demanded.

'This process,' she said, 'has given me the only man in the world or on Mars or on Venus that I love or *could* love. It has been the greatest force in my life.' She put her arm around Sebastian, then, and hugged him, hugged his big bulk against her.

'Tomorrow,' Sebastian said to her, 'I want you to pay a visit to Section B of the People's Topical Library. Get all the information you can about the Anarch Thomas Peak. Most of it has probably gone into erad by now, but they may have a few terminal typescript manuscripts.'

'Was he really that important?' Bob Lindy asked.

Lotta said, 'Yes. But – ' She hesitated. 'I'm scared of the Library, Seb; I really am. You know I am. It's so – oh the hell with it. I'll go.' Her voice sank.

'There I agree with you,' Bob Lindy said. 'I don't like that place. And I've been there exactly once.'

'It's the Hobart Phase,' Sebastian said. 'The same force at work that operates here.' He turned to Lotta again. 'Avoid the Head Librarian, Mavis McGuire.' He had run into her several times in the past, and he had been repelled; she had struck him as bitchy, hostile, and mean. 'Go right to Section B,' he said.

God help Lotta, he thought, if she gets fouled up and runs into that McGuire woman. Maybe I should go . . . No, he decided; she can ask for someone else; it'll work out all right. I'll just have to take the chance.

19

Chapter 2

Man is most correctly defined as a certain intellectual notion
eternally made in the divine mind.   – Erigena

Sunlight ascended and a penetrating mechanical voice
declared, 'All right, Appleford. Time to get up and show
'em who you are and what you can do. Big man, that
Douglas Appleford; everybody acknowledges it – I hear
them talking. Big man, big talent, big job. Much admired
by the public at large.' It paused. 'You awake, now?'

Appleford, from his bed, said, 'Yes.' He sat up, batted
the sharp-voiced alarm clock at his bedside into nullifica-
tion. 'Good morning,' he said to the silent apartment.
'Slept well; I hope you did, too.'

A press of problems tumbled about his disordered
mind as he got grouchily from the bed, wandered to the
closet for clothing adequately dirty. Supposed to nail
down Ludwig Eng, he said to himself. The tasks of
tomorrow became the worst tasks of today. Reveal to
Eng that only one copy of his great-selling book is left in
all the world; the time is coming soon for him to act, to
do the job only he can do. How would Eng feel? After
all, sometimes inventors refused to sit down and do their
job. Well, he decided, that actually consisted of an Erad
Council problem; theirs, not his. He found a stained,
rumpled red shirt; removing his pajama top he got into
it. The trousers were not so easy; he had to root through
the hamper.

And then the packet of whiskers.

20

My ambition, Appleford mused as he padded to the bathroom with the whisker packet, is to cross the WUS by streetcar. Whee. At the bowl he washed his face, then lathered on foam-glue, opened the packet and with adroit slappings managed to convey the whiskers evenly to his chin, jowls, neck; in a moment he had expertly gotten the whiskers to adhere. I'm fit now, he decided as he reviewed his countenance in the mirror, to take that streetcar ride; at least as soon as I process my share of sogum.

Switching on the automatic sogum pipe – very modern – he accepted a good masculine bundle, sighed contentedly as he glanced over the sports section of the Los Angeles *Times*. Then at last walked to the kitchen and began to lay out soiled dishes. In no time at all he faced a bowl of soup, lamb chops, green peas, Martian blue moss with egg sauce and a cup of hot coffee. These he gathered up, slid the dishes from beneath and around them – of course first checking the windows of the room to be sure no one saw him – and briskly placed the assorted foods in their proper receptacles, which he placed on shelves of the cupboard and in the refrigerator. The time was eight-thirty; he still had fifteen minutes in which to get to work. No need to dwindle himself hurrying; the People's Topical Library Section B would be there when he arrived.

It had taken him years to work up to B. And now, as a reward, he had to deal tête-à-tête with a bewildering variety of surly, boorish inventors who balked at their assigned – and according to the Erads mandatory – final cleaning of the sole remaining typescript copy of whatever work their name had become associated with – linked by a process which neither he nor the assortment of inventors completely understood. The Council presumably

21

understood why a particular given inventor got stuck with a particular assignment and not some other assignment entirely. For instance, Eng and HOW I MADE MY OWN SWABBLE OUT OF CONVENTIONAL HOUSEHOLD OBJECTS IN MY BASEMENT DURING MY SPARE TIME. Appleford reflected as he glanced over the remainder of the 'pape. Think of the responsibility. After Eng finished, no more swabbles in all the world, unless those untrustworthy rogues in the FNM had a couple illicitly tucked away. In fact, even though the ter-cop, the terminal copy, of Eng's book still remained, he already found it difficult to recall what a swabble did and what it looked like. Square? Small? Or round and huge? Hmm. He put down the 'pape and rubbed his forehead while he attempted to recall – tried to conjure up an accurate mental image of the device while it was still theoretically possible to do so. Because as soon as Eng reduced the ter-cop to a heavily inked silk ribbon, half a ream of bond paper, and a folio of fresh carbon paper there existed no chance for him or for anyone else to recall either the book or the mechanism – up to now quite useful – which the book described.

That task, however, would probably occupy Eng the rest of the year. Cleaning of the ter-cop had to progress line by line, word by word; it could not be handled as were the assembled heaps of printed copies. So easy, up until the terminal typescript copy, and then . . . well, to make it worth it to Eng, a really huge salary would be paid him, plus –

By his elbow on the small kitchen table the receiver of the vidphone hopped from its mooring onto the table, and from it came a distant tiny shrill voice. 'Goodbye, Doug.' A woman's voice.

Lifting the receiver to his ear he said, 'Goodbye.'

'I love you, Doug,' Charise McFadden stated in her breathless, emotion-saturated voice. 'Do you love me?'

'Yes, I love you, too,' he said. 'When have I seen you last? I hope it won't be long. Tell me it won't be long.'

'Most probably tonight,' Charise said. 'After work. There's someone I want you to meet, a virtually unknown inventor who's desperately eager to get official eradication for his thesis on, ahem, the psychogenic origins of death by meteor strike. I said that because you're in Section B – '

'Tell him to eradicate his thesis himself. At his own expense.'

'There's no prestige in that.' Her face on the vidscreen earnest, Charise pleaded, 'It's really a dreadful piece of theorizing, Doug; it's as nutty as the day is long. This oaf, this Lance Arbuthnot – '

'That's his name?' It almost persuaded him. But not quite. In the course of a single day he received many such requests, and every one, without exception, came represented as a socially dangerous piece by a crank inventor with a goofy name. He had held his chair at Section B too long to be easily snared. But still – he had to investigate this: his ethical structure, his responsibility to society, insisted on it. He sighed.

'I hear you groaning,' Charise said brightly.

Appleford said, 'As long as he's not from the FNM.'

'Well – he is.' She looked – and sounded – guilty. 'I think they threw him out, though. That's why he's here in Los Angeles and not there.'

Rising to his feet, Douglas Appleford said stiffly, 'Hello, Charise. I must leave now for work; I will not and cannot discuss this trivial matter further.' And that, as far as he was concerned, ended that.

He hoped.

23

Arriving home to his conapt at the end of his shift, Officer Joe Tinbane found his wife sitting at the breakfast table. Embarrassed, he averted his gaze until she noticed him and rapidly finished filling her cup with hot, dark coffee.

'Shame,' Bethel said reprovingly. 'You should have knocked on the kitchen door.' With haughty dignity she carefully placed the orange-juice bottle in the refrigerator, carried the now nearly full box of Happy-Oats to its concealment in the cupboard. 'I'll be out of your way in a minute. My victual momentum is now just about complete.' However, she took her time.

'I'm tired,' he said, at last seating himself.

Bethel placed empty bowls, a glass, a cup, and a plate before him. 'Guess what the 'pape says this morning,' she said as she retired discreetly to the living room so that he, too, could disgorge. 'That thug fanatic is coming here, that Raymond Roberts person. On a pilg.'

'Hmm,' he said, enjoying the hot, liquid taste of coffee as he ruminated it up into his weary mouth.

'The Los Angeles chief of police estimates that four *million* people will turn out to see him; he's performing the sacrament of Divine Unification in Dodger Stadium, and of course it'll all be on TV until we're ready to go clear out of our minds. All day long – that's what the 'pape says; I'm not making it up.'

'Four million,' Tinbane echoed, thinking, professionally, how many peace officers it would take to handle crowd control when the crowd consisted of that many. Everybody on the force, including Skyway Patrol and special deputies. What a job. He groaned inwardly.

'They use those drugs,' Bethel said, 'for that unification they practice; there's a long article on it, here. The drug's a derivative from DNT; it's illegal here, but when he goes

24

to perform the sacrament they'll let him – them all – use it that one time. Because the California law states – '

'I know what it states,' Tinbane said. 'It states that a psychedelic drug can be used in a bona fide religious ceremony.' God knew he had had this drummed into him by his superiors.

Bethel said, 'I have half a mind to go there. And participate. It's the only time, unless we want to fly, to ugh, the FNM. And I frankly don't feel much like doing *that*.'

'You do that,' he said, happily disgorging cereal, sliced peaches and milk and sugar, in that order.

'Want to come? It'll be exciting. Just think: thousands of people unified into one entity. The Udi, he calls it. Which is everyone and no one. Possessing absolute knowledge because it has no single, limiting viewpoint.' She came to the kitchen door, eyes shut. 'Well?'

'No thanks,' Tinbane said, his mouth embarrassingly full. 'And don't watch me; you know how I can't stand to have anyone around when I'm having victual momentum, even if they can't see me. They might hear me – chewing.'

He could feel her there; he sensed her resentment.

'You never take me anywhere,' Bethel said presently.

'Okay,' he agreed, 'I never take you anywhere.' He added, 'And if I did, it wouldn't be there, to hear about religion.' We have enough religious nuts in Los Angeles anyhow, he thought. I wonder why Roberts didn't think of making a pilg here a long time ago. I wonder why just now . . . of all possible times.

Earnestly, Bethel said, 'Do you think he's a fake? That there's no such state as Udi?'

He shrugged. 'DNT is a potent drug.' Maybe it was so. In any case it didn't matter; not to him, anyhow. 'Another unexpected rebirth,' he said to his wife. 'At Forest Knolls, naturally. They're never watching those minor cemeteries; they know we'll handle it – with city equipment.' Anyhow, Tilly M. Benton was safely at the LA receiving hospital, thanks to Seb Hermes. Within a week she would be disgorging like the rest of them.

'Eerie,' Bethel said, still at the doorway to the kitchen.

'How do you know? You never saw it happen.'

'You and your damn job,' Bethel said. 'Don't take it out on me, just because you can't stand it. If it's awful, quit. Fish or cut bait, as the Romans said.'

'I can handle the job; matter of fact, I've already put in for a reassignment.' What's hard, he thought, is you. 'Let me disgorge in private, will you?' he said angrily. 'Go off; read the 'pape.'

'Will you be affected?' Bethel asked. 'By Ray Roberts coming here to the Coast?'

'Probably not,' he said. He did, after all, have a regular beat. Nothing ever seemed to change *that*.

'They won't have you out with your popgun protecting him?'

'Protecting him?' he said. 'I'd shoot him.'

'Oh dear,' Bethel said mockingly. 'Such ambition. And then you could go down in history.'

'I'll go down in history anyhow,' Tinbane said.

'What for? What have you done? And what in the future do you intend to do? Keep on digging up old ladies out at Forest Knolls Cemetery?' Her tone lacerated him. 'Or for being married to me?'

'That's right; for being married to you.' His tone was equally scathing; he had learned it from her, over the long, dead months of their alleged marriage.

26

Bethel returned, then, to the living room. Left alone, he continued to disgorge, now left in peace. He appreciated it.

Anyhow, he thought gloomily, Tilly M. Benton of South Pasadena likes me.

Chapter 3

Eternity is a kind of measure. But to be measured belongs not to God. Therefore it does not belong to Him to be eternal.
— St Thomas Aquinas

It had always been difficult for Officer Joe Tinbane to determine precisely what official rank George Gore held in the Los Angeles Police Department; he wore an ordinary citizen's cape, natty turned-up Italian shoes and a bright, fashionable shirt which looked even a bit gaudy. Gore was a relatively slender man, tall, in his mid-forties, Tinbane guessed. He came directly to the point, as the two of them sat facing each other in Gore's office.

'Since Ray Roberts is arriving in town, we've been asked by the Governor to provide a personal bodyguard ... which we planned to do anyway. Four or possibly five men; we're in agreement on that, too. You asked to be reassigned, so you're one.' Gore shuffled some documents on his desk; Tinbane saw that they pertained to him. 'Okay?' Gore said.

'If you say so,' Tinbane said, feeling sullen – and surprised. 'You don't mean for crowd control; you mean all the time. Around the clock.' In proximity, he realized. By personal they meant personal.

Gore said, 'You'll eat with him – excuse the expression; sorry – and sleep with him in the same room; all that. He has no bodyguard, normally. But we have a lot of people out here holding deep grudges toward the Uditi. Not that they don't in the FNM, but that's not our problem.' He added, 'Roberts hasn't asked for this, but we're not about to consult him. Whether he likes it or not he's going to get twenty-four-hour protection while he's in our jurisdiction.' Gore's tone was bureaucratic and stony.

'I gather we won't be relieved.'

'You'll stagger your wake-sleep cycle, the four of you. But no; except for that you'll be with him all the time. It's only for forty-eight or seventy-two hours; whichever he chooses. He hasn't decided. But you probably know that; you read the 'papes.'

Tinbane said, 'I don't like him.'

'Too bad for you. But that's not going to affect Roberts much; I doubt if he cares. He's got plenty of followers out here, and he'll get the curiosity crowd. He can survive your opinion. Anyhow, what do you know about him? You've never met him.'

'My wife likes him.'

Gore grinned. 'Well, he can probably endure that, too. I get your point, though. It is a fact that a major part of his following are women. That seems to be generally the case. I have our file on Ray Roberts; I think you should read it over before he shows up. You can do it on your own time. You'll be interested; there're some strange things in there, things he's said and done, what Udi believes. We're allowing that communal drug experience, you know, even though it's technically illegal. That's what it is: a drug orgy; the religious aspect is just fabrication, just window-dressing. He's a weird and violent man – at least so we view him. I guess his followers don't find him so. Or maybe they do and they like it.' Gore tapped a locked green metal box at the far edge of his desk. 'You'll see when you've read this – all the crimes he's sanctioned for those gunsels of his, those Offspring of Might, to do.' He pushed the box toward

29

Tinbane. 'And after this, I want you to go to the People's Topical Library, Section A or B. For more.'

Accepting the locked file, Tinbane said, 'Give me the key and I'll read this – on my own time.'

Gore produced the key. 'One thing, Officer. Don't fall for the 'pape stereotype view of Ray Roberts. A lot's been said about him, but most of it is fictitious, and what actually is true hasn't been said . . . but it's in there, and when you've read it you'll understand what I'm referring to. In particular I mean the violence.' He leaned toward Joe Tinbane. 'Look; I'll give you a choice. After you've read the material on Roberts, come back and see me; give me your decision then. Frankly I think you'll take the job; it's officially a promotion, a step up in your career.'

Standing, Tinbane picked up the key and the locked box. I don't agree, he thought to himself. But he said, 'Okay, Mr Gore. I have how long?'

'Call me by five,' Gore said. And continued to grin his acid, knowing grin.

In Section B of the People's Topical Library, Officer Joe Tinbane warily stood at the chief librarian's desk; something about the Library intimidated him – and he did not know what it was or why.

Several persons were ahead of him; he waited restlessly, glancing about and wondering as always about his marriage with Bethel and about his career with the police department, and then about the purpose of life and the meaning – if any – of it, what the old-borns experienced while they lay in the ground, and what it would be like, someday, to dwindle away as he eventually would, and enter a nearby womb.

As he stood there a familiar person came up beside him; small, in a long cloth coat, with her dark, extensive

30

brown hair tumbling: a pretty, but married girl, Lotta Hermes.

''Bye,' he said, pleased to run into her.

Her face white, Lotta whispered, 'I – can't stand it in here. But I have to look up some information for Seb.' Her discomfort was palpable; her whole body was held rigidly, awkwardly, so that its natural lines were warped; her fear made her misshapen.

'Take it easy,' he said, surprised at her apprehension; he wanted at once to make her feel better and he took her by the arm, led her away from the chief librarian's desk, out of the immense, dully booming room and into the relatively stress-free corridor.

'Oh god,' she said miserably. 'I just can't do it, go in there and face that woman, that awful Mrs McGuire. Seb told me to ask for someone else, but I don't know anyone. And when I get scared I can't think.' She gazed up at him miserably, appealing to him for help.

Tinbane said, 'This place gets a lot of people down.' His arm around her waist, he steered her down the corridor toward the exit.

'I can't leave,' she said frantically, pulling away. 'Seb said I have to find out about the Anarch Peak.'

'Oh?' Tinbane said. He wondered why. Did Sebastian expect the Anarch to be old-born in the near future?

That would shed a somewhat different light on the pilg by Ray Roberts; in fact an entirely new light: it would explain why now and why Los Angeles.

'Douglas Appleford,' Tinbane decided. He knew the man; a stuffy, formal, but reasonably helpful person; certainly far more easily dealt with than Mavis McGuire. 'I'll take you to his office,' he said to the frightened girl, 'and introduce you to him. As a matter of fact I'm here

31

doing research myself. On Ray Roberts. So I need assistance, too.'

Lotta said, gratefully, 'You know just about everybody.' She looked much better, now; the twisted, hunched posture had left her, and again she struck him as vital and attractive. Hmm, he thought, and guided her down the hall, toward Douglas Appleford's offices.

When Douglas Appleford arrived at his office in Section B of the Library that morning he found his secretary Miss Tomsen trying to rid herself – and him, too – of a tall, sloppily dressed middle-aged Negro gentleman with a briefcase under his arm.

'Ah, Mr Appleford,' the individual said in a dry, hollow voice as he made out Appleford, obviously recognizing him at once; he approached, hand extended. 'How nice to meet you, sir. Goodbye, goodbye. As the Phase has taught us to say.' He smiled a flashbulb instantly vanishing smile at Appleford, who did not return it.

'I'm quite a busy man,' Appleford said, and continued on past Miss Tomsen's desk to open the inner door to his especially private office. 'If you wish to see me you'll have to make a regular appointment. Hello.' He started to shut the door after him.

'This concerns the Anarch Peak,' the tall Negro with the briefcase said. 'Whom I have reason to believe you're interested in.'

'Why do you say that?' He paused, irritated. 'I don't recall ever having felt or expressed my interest in a religious fanatic fortunately laid in his grave for two decades.' With sudden suspicion and aversion he said, 'Peak isn't about to be reborn, is he?'

Again the tall Negro smiled his mechanical smile – and mechanical it was; Doug Appleford now perceived the

32

small but brilliant yellow stripe sewed on the tall man's coat sleeve. This person was a robot, required by law to wear the identifying swath so as not to deceive. Realizing this, Appleford's irritation grew; he had a strict, deeply imbedded prejudice against robies which he could not rid himself of; which he did not want to rid himself of, as a matter of fact.

'Come in,' Appleford said, holding the door to his absolutely pin-neat office open. The roby represented some human principal; it had not dispatched itself: that was the law. He wondered who had sent it. Some functionary of a European syndicate? Possibly. In any case, better to hear the thing out and then tell it to leave.

Together, in this central work chamber of his suite of chambers, the two of them faced each other.

'My card,' the roby said, extending its hand.

Appleford read the card, scowling.

Carl Gantrix
Attorney-At-Law, WUS

'My employer,' the roby said. 'So now you know my name. You may address me as Carl; that would be satisfactory.' Now that the door had shut, with Miss Tomsen on the other side, the roby's voice had acquired a sudden and surprising authoritative tone.

'I prefer,' Appleford said cautiously, 'to address you in the more familiar mode as Carl Junior. If that doesn't offend you.' He made his own voice even more authoritative. 'You know I seldom grant audiences to robots. A quirk, perhaps, but one concerning which I am notoriously consistent.'

'Until now,' the robot Carl Junior murmured; it retrieved its card and placed it back in its wallet, a thrifty, robotish move. Then, seating itself, it began to unzip its briefcase. 'Being in charge of Section B of the Library, you are of course an expert on the Hobart Phase. At least so Mr Gantrix assumes. Is he correct, sir?' The robot glanced up keenly.

'Well, I deal with it constantly.' Appleford affected a vacant cavalier tone; it was always better to show a superior attitude when dealing with a roby. Constantly necessary to remind them in this particular fashion – as well as in countless others – of their place.

'So Mr Gantrix realizes. And it is to his everlasting credit that via such a profound realization he has inferred that you have, over the years, become something of an authority on the advantages, sir, the uses and also the manifold disadvantages, of the Hobart reverse- or the anti-time field. True? Not true? Choose one.'

Appleford pondered. 'I choose the first. Although you must take into account the fact that my knowledge is pragmatic, not theoretical. But I can correctly deal with the vagaries of the Phase without being appalled. And it is appalling, Junior, the things that pop into being under the Phase. Such as the deaders. That really doesn't appeal all that much to me; that, in my opinion, is one of the greater disadvantages. The rest of them I can stand.'

'Certainly.' The roby Carl Junior nodded its thermoplastic quite humanoid head. 'Very good, Mr Appleford. Now down to business. His Mightiness, the Very Honorable Ray Roberts, is preparing to come out here to the WUS, as you may have read in your morning 'pape. It will be a major public event, of course; that goes without saying. His Mightiness, who is in charge of the activities of Mr Gantrix, has asked me to come to Section B of your Library and, if you will cooperate, sequester all manuscripts still extant dealing with the Anarch Peak.

34

Will you cooperate? In exchange, Mr Gantrix is willing to make a sizable donation to assist your Library in prospering in forthcoming years.'

'That is indeed gratifying,' Appleford acknowledged, 'but I'm afraid I would have to know *why* your principal wishes to sequester the documents pertaining to the Anarch.' He felt tense; something about the roby put his psychological defenses into operation.

The roby rose to its metal feet; leaning forward, it deposited a host of documents on Appleford's desk. 'In answer to your query I respectfully insist that you examine those.'

Carl Gantrix, by means of the video circuit of the robot's system, treated himself to a leisurely inspection of the assistant librarian Douglas Appleford as that individual plowed through the wearying stack of deliberately obscure pseudo-documents which the robot had presented.

The bureaucrat in Appleford had been ensnared by the bait; his attention distracted, the librarian had become oblivious to the robot and to its actions. Therefore, as Appleford read, the robot expertly slid its chair back and to the left side, close to a reference card case of impressive proportions. Lengthening its right arm, the robot crept its manual grippers of fingeroid shape into the nearest file of the case; this Appleford did of course not see, and so the robot then continued with its assigned task. It placed a miniaturized nest of embryonic robots, no larger than pinheads, within the card file, then a tiny find-circuit transmitter behind a subsequent card, then at last a potent detonating device set on a three-day command circuit.

Watching, Gantrix grinned. Only one construct

remained in the robot's possession, and this now appeared briefly as the robot, eyeing Appleford sideways and cautiously, edged its extensor once more toward the file, transferring this last bit of sophisticated hardware from its possession to the Library's.

'Purp,' Appleford said, without raising his eyes.

The code signal, received by the aud chamber of the file, activated an emergency release; the file closed in upon itself in the manner of a bivalve seeking safety. Collapsing, the file retreated into the wall, burying itself out of sight. And at the same time it rejected the constructs which the robot had placed inside it; the objects, expelled with electronic neatness, bounced in a trajectory which deposited them at the robot's feet, where they lay in clear view.

'Good heavens,' the robot said involuntarily, taken aback.

Appleford said, 'Leave my office immediately.' He raised his eyes from the pseudo-documents, and his expression was cold. As the robot reached down to retrieve the now-exposed artifacts he added, 'And leave those items here; I want them subjected to lab analysis regarding purpose and source.' He reached into the top drawer of his desk, and when his hand emerged it held a weapon.

In Carl Gantrix's ears the phone-cable voice of the robot buzzed. 'What should I do, sir?'

'Leave presently.' Gantrix no longer felt amused; the fuddyduddy librarian was equal to the probe, was capable in fact of nullifying it. The contact with Appleford would have to be made in the open, and with that in mind Gantrix reluctantly picked up the receiver of the vidphone closest to him and dialed the Library's exchange.

A moment later he saw, through the video scanner of

the robot, the librarian Douglas Appleford picking up his own phone in answer.

'We have a problem,' Gantrix said. 'Common to us both. Why, then, shouldn't we work together?'

Appleford answered, 'I'm aware of no problem.' His voice held ultimate calmness; the attempt by the robot to plant hostile hardware in his work area had not ruffled him. 'If you want to work together,' he added, 'you're off to a bad start.'

'Admittedly,' Gantrix said. 'But we've had difficulty in the past with you librarians.' *Your exalted position,* he thought; *protected by the Erads and all.* But he did not say it. 'There is, in the wealth of material – accurate and inaccurate – one particular piece of info that we lack, that we are particularly anxious to acquire. The rest . . .' He hesitated, then gambled. 'I'll put you in mind of that fact, and perhaps you can direct us to a source by which to verify it. *Where is the Anarch Peak buried?*'

'God only knows,' Appleford said.

'Somewhere in your books, articles, religious pamphlets, city records – '

'Our job here at the Library,' Appleford said, 'is not to study and/or memorize data; it is to expunge it.'

There was silence.

'Well,' Gantrix admitted, 'you've stated your position with clarity and admirable brevity. So we're to assume that that fact, the location of the Anarch's body, has been expunged; as a fact it no longer exists.'

'It has undoubtedly been unwritten,' Appleford said. 'Or at least such is a reasonable presumption . . . and in accord with Library policy.'

Gantrix said, 'And you won't even check. You won't research it, even for a sizable donation.' *Bureaucracy,* he thought; *it maddened him; it was insane.*

'Good day, Mr Gantrix,' the librarian said, and hung up.

For a time Carl Gantrix sat in silence, keeping himself inert. Controlling his emotions.

He at last picked up the vidphone receiver once more and this time dialed the Free Negro Municipality. 'I want to speak to the Very Honorable Ray Roberts,' he told the operator in Chicago.

'That party can only be reached by – '

'I have the necessary code,' Gantrix said, and thereupon divested himself of it. He felt weary and defeated . . . and he dreaded Ray Roberts' reaction. But we can't give up, he realized. We knew from the start that that bureaucrat Appleford wouldn't research the matter for us; we knew we'd have to break into the Library and do it ourselves.

That fact is there in the Library somewhere, he said to himself. That's probably the *only* place it is, the only source from which we can get that information.

And there was not much time left, according to Ray Roberts' arcane calculations. The Anarch Peak would be returning to life any day, now.

It was a highly dangerous situation.

Chapter 4

If, therefore, God existed, there would be no evil discoverable; but there is evil in the world. Therefore God does not exist.
– St Thomas Aquinas

As soon as the roby Carl Gantrix Junior had cleared out of his office, Doug Appleford pressed the intercom button which connected him with his superior, Chief Librarian Mavis McGuire.

'You know what just now happened?' he said. 'Someone representing that Udi cult got a robot in here and began planting hostile hardware all over my office. It has left.' He added, 'Possibly I should have called the city police. Technically, I still could; the scanner I keep in here recorded the incident, so we have the evidence if we want to seek recourse.'

Mavis had her usual accosting, bleak expression, the dead-calm quality which generally preceded a tirade. Especially at this time of day – early in the morning – she was most irritable.

Over the years Appleford had learned to live with her, so to speak. As an administrator she was superb. She had energy; she was accurate; he had never known Mavis to pass the poscred back, when it was handed to her . . . as in this case. Never in his most distorted dreams had he envisioned trying to supplant her; he knew, rationally and coldly, that he did not possess her ability; he had enough talent to act as her subordinate – and do the job well – but that was all. He respected her and he was afraid of her, a lethal combination in regard to any aspirations he might have had to seek a rung higher in the Library's hierarchy. Mavis McGuire was the boss and he liked it that way; he liked it now, being able to drop this into her lap.

Mavis said, her mouth twisting, 'Udi. That abomination. Yes; I realize Ray Roberts is making a pile out here; I expected they'd come sniffing around here. I assume you expelled the hostile hardware.'

'Absolutely,' Appleford assured her. It still lay on the carpeted floor of his office, where the file had ejected it.

'What specifically,' Mavis said in her low, near-whisper voice, 'were they after?'

'The burial site of the Anarch Peak.'

'Do we have that information?'

Appleford said, 'I didn't bother to look it up.'

'I'll check with the Council of Erads,' Mavis said, 'and find out if they want that fact released; I'll check on their policy regarding this. Right now I have other business; you'll excuse me.' She then rang off.

Miss Tomsen buzzed him. 'A Mrs Hermes and an Officer Tinbane to see you, sir. They have no appointment.'

'Tinbane,' he echoed. He had always liked the young police officer. A man as honestly, reputably intent on his tasks as was Appleford: they had something in common. Mrs Hermes; he did not know her. Possibly it involved someone refusing to turn over a book to the Library; Tinbane had tracked such cupidity down in past times. 'Send them in,' he decided. Possibly Mrs Hermes was a Hoarder – someone who refused to give up a book whose time had come.

Officer Tinbane, in uniform, entered, and with him appeared a sweet-looking girl with astonishingly long dark hair. She seemed ill-at-ease and dependent on the police officer.

'Goodbye,' Appleford greeted them graciously. 'Please sit down.' He rose to offer Mrs Hermes a chair.

'Mrs Hermes,' Tinbane said, 'is after information about Anarch Peak. You have anything not yet eradicated that would help her?'

'Probably,' Appleford said. This seems to be the topic of the day, he reflected. But these two people, in contradistinction to Carl Gantrix, appeared to have no connection with Roberts, and this altered his attitude. 'Anything in particular?' he asked the girl in a kindly fashion, wanting to reassure her; she was obviously easily intimidated.

The girl said in a soft little voice, 'My husband just wanted me to find out all I could.'

'My suggestion,' Appleford told her, 'is that rather than plowing through manuscripts and books you consult an expert in contemporary religious history.' A man who, by the way, enjoyed an attractive woman – as Appleford did. He toyed with a ballpoint pen, for dramatic emphasis. 'As a matter of fact I personally know more than a little about the late Anarch.' He leaned back in his swivel chair, folded his hands, observed the inlaid ceiling of his office.

'Whatever you can tell me would be appreciated,' Mrs Hermes said in her shy way.

Shrugging, with a smile, pleased in fact to be encouraged, Doug Appleford began his oration. Both Mrs Hermes and Officer Tinbane listened with obedient attention, and this pleased him, too.

At the time of his death the Anarch had been fifty years old. He had led an interesting – and unusual – life. In his college days, as a brilliant student, he had studied

41

at Cambridge; he had in fact become a Rhodes scholar, majoring in classic languages: Hebrew, Sanskrit, Attic Greek and Latin. Then, at twenty-two, he had abruptly abandoned his academic career – and his country; he had migrated to the United States to study jazz with the then great jazz performer, Herbie Mann. After a time he had formed his own jazz combo, he himself playing the flute.

In connection with this he had lived on the West Coast, in San Francisco. At that time, the late 'sixties, the Episcopal Bishop of the Diocese of California, James Pike, had been arranging to have jazz masses performed at Grace Cathedral, and one of the groups he had called on was Thomas Peak's combo. At this point, Peak had turned composer; he had written a lengthy jazz mass and it had been a success. Pike's Peak, the local newspaper columnist Herb Caen had dubbed him, then; that had been in 1968. Bishop Pike himself had been an interesting person, too. A former lawyer, active in the ACLU, one of the most brilliant and radical clerical figures of his time, he had become involved in what had been called 'social action,' the issues of the day: in particular, Negro rights. He had for instance been at Selma with Dr Martin Luther King. From all this, Thomas Peak had learned. He, too, had become involved in the issues of the day – on a much smaller scale than Bishop Pike, of course. At Bishop Pike's suggestion he had entered seminary school, had become at last an ordained Episcopal priest – and, like James Pike, his bishop, quite radical for those times, although now the doctrines which he advocated had become more or less accepted. It was a case of being ahead of his time.

Peak had, in fact, been charged in a heresy trial, had been booted out of the Episcopal Church; whereupon he had gone on and founded his own. And, when the Free

Negro Municipality had been born, he had headed that way; he had made its capital the place of origin for his cult.

There was not much resemblance between Peak's new cult and the Episcopal Church which he had left. The experience of Udi, the group mind, comprised the central – if not the sole – sacrament, and it was for this that the congregation gathered. Without the hallucinogenic drug employed, the sacrament could not take place; hence, like the North American Indian cult which it resembled, Peak's church depended on the availability, not to mention the legality, of the drug. So a curious relationship between the cult and cooperative authorities had to exist.

As to the Udi experience, the most enlightened reports, based on first-hand testimony of undercover agents, stated categorically that the group-mind fusion was real, not imaginary.

'And what is more – ' Appleford churned on, but at this point he was interrupted. Hesitantly, but with determination, Mrs Hermes spoke up.

'Do you think it would be to the advantage of Ray Roberts to have the Anarch reborn?'

For a time Appleford pondered that; it was a good question, and it showed him that despite her reticence and shyness Mrs Hermes had a good deal on the ball.

'Because of the Hobart Phase,' he said finally, 'the tide of history is with the Anarch and against Ray Roberts. The Anarch died in late middle-age; he will be that when he's reborn, and he will develop progressively into greater and greater vitality and creativity – for thirty years, anyhow. Ray Roberts is only twenty-six. The Hobart Phase is carrying him back to adolescence; when Peak is at his prime, Roberts will be a child, searching for a handy womb. *All Peak has to do is wait*. No,' he decided,

43

'it wouldn't be to Roberts' advantage.' And that, he said to himself, Carl Gantrix had abundantly demonstrated . . . by his avid desire to know where the Anarch's body lay.

'My husband,' Mrs Hermes said in her sweet, earnest voice, 'is the owner of a vitarium.' She glanced at Officer Tinbane, as if asking him whether she should continue.

Tinbane cleared his throat and said, 'I gather that the Flask of Hermes Vitarium anticipates Peak's rebirth momentarily or anyhow within a reasonably short time-period. Technically, it would be incumbent on any vitarium that gets him to offer Peak to the Uditi. But, as we both gather from Mrs Hermes' question, there is some doubt – and on good grounds – as to whether that would be in the Anarch's best interest.'

'If I understand the way the vitaria operate,' Appleford said, 'they generally list who they have, and the highest bidder gets it. Is that the case, Mrs Hermes?'

She ducked her head, nodding yes.

'It's really not up to you,' Appleford said, 'or your husband, to moralize. You're in business; you locate deaders ready to be reborn, and you sell your product for what the market will carry. Once you start poking into the issue of which *morally* is the best customer – '

'Our salesman, R.C. Buckley, always looks into the morality,' Mrs Hermes said, with sincerity.

'Or so he says,' Tinbane said.

'Oh,' she assured him, 'I'm positive he does; he spends a lot of his time studying the customers' backgrounds; he really does.'

There was an appropriate interval of silence.

'You do not,' Appleford said to Mrs Hermes, 'want to know where the Anarch's body lies buried? That's not – '

44

'Oh, we know that,' Mrs Hermes said in her grave, honest little voice; Tinbane started visibly and looked annoyed.

Appleford said to her, 'Mrs Hermes, you probably shouldn't tell anyone you know that.'

'Oh,' she said, and flushed. 'I'm sorry.'

Appleford went on, 'Someone from the Uditi was in here just prior to you, trying to find that out. If anyone approaches you – ' He leaned toward her, speaking slowly, so as to impress it on her. ' – don't tell them. Don't even tell me.'

'Or me,' Tinbane said.

Mrs Hermes, looking as if she was about to cry, said chokingly, 'I'm sorry; I guess I screwed everything up. I always do.'

To Mrs Hermes, Officer Tinbane said, 'Have you told anybody else, Lotta?'

She shook her head, wordlessly, no.

'Okay.' Tinbane nodded to Appleford in shared agreement. 'Probably no harm done yet. But they'll be trying to find out. They may canvass all the vitariums; you better discuss this with Seb and with your employees. You understand, Lotta?'

Again she nodded, this time yes; her large dark eyes glinted with repressed tears.

Chapter 5

Love is the end and quiet cessation of the natural motion of all
moving things, beyond which no motion continues.   – Erigena

At three in the afternoon Officer Tinbane reported to his
superior, George Gore.

'Well,' Gore said, leaning back and picking his teeth,
meanwhile eyeing Tinbane critically, 'did you learn a lot
about Ray Roberts?'

'Nothing that changes my mind. He's a fanatic; he'd do
anything to keep his power; and he's potentially a killer.'
He was thinking about the Anarch Peak, but about that
he said nothing; that was strictly between him and Lotta
Hermes . . . or so he viewed it. In any case it was a
complex problem. He would play it by ear.

Gore said, 'A modern Malcolm X. Remember reading
about him? He preached violence; got violence in return.
Like the Bible says.' He continued to scrutinize Tinbane.
'Want my theory? I checked into the date that Anarch
Peak died, and he's about due to be reborn. I think Ray
Roberts is here because of that. Peak's rebirth would end
Roberts' political career. I think he'd cheerfully kill Peak
– if he could find him in time. If he waits – ' Gore made
a slicing motion with the side of his hand. 'Too late. Once
Peak is re-established he'll stay that way; he was a canny
bastard himself, but without the violence. The critical
time will be the week or ten days – whatever it is –
between the time Peak is dug up and the time he leaves
the hospital. Peak was very ill, the last months of his life;

46

toxemia, I understand. He'll have to lie in a hospital bed, waiting for that to go away, before he can effectively regain control of Udi.'

'Would it be to Peak's advantage,' Tinbane said, 'if a police team could locate him?'

'Oh yes; *hell* yes. We could protect him, if we dig him up. But if one of those private vitariums gets hold of him – they can't shield him from assassination; they're just not equipped for it. For instance, they use regular city hospitals . . . we of course have our own. This, as you know, isn't the first time this has cropped up, somebody having a vested interest in an old-born individual staying dead. This is simply more public, on a bigger scale.'

Tinbane said thoughtfully, 'But on the other hand, owning Anarch Peak, having him to sell, would be a financial asset to a vitarium. Peddled properly to the right party, he could bring in a medium-sized fortune.' He was thinking what a sale like that would mean to a concern as small as the Flask of Hermes Vitarium; it could stabilize them financially for virtually an indefinite period. Confiscation of Peak by the police would be a disaster to Sebastian Hermes . . . this was, after all, the first, the one, the really great break for Sebastian. In the entire life span of his flea-bag enterprise.

Can I take that away from him? Tinbane asked himself. God, what a thing to do, to take cold, professional advantage of Lotta's blurting it out there in Appleford's office.

Of course Appleford might do it, might sell the information to Ray Roberts – at a good price. But he doubted it; Appleford did not strike him as that sort of man.

On the other hand, for the Anarch's own good –

But if the police seized the Anarch, Sebastian would know how they found out; he would track it, with no

47

difficulty, to Lotta. I must consider that, he realized, in view of any plans I might have in her direction. As regards my relationship – or potential relationship – to her.

Just who am I trying to aid? he asked himself. Sebastian? Or Lotta? Or – myself?

I can blackmail her, he found himself thinking, and was horrified; yet the thought had been clearly there. Simply tell her, when I can manage to get her off alone for a few minutes, that – she has no choice. She can be –

Hell, he thought. That's terrible! Blackmailing her into becoming my mistress; what kind of person am I?

On the other hand, in the final analysis it didn't matter what you thought; it was what you did.

What I ought to do, he decided, is talk to some clergyman about this; *somebody's* got to know how to deal with difficult matters.

Father Faine, he thought. I could talk to him.

As soon as he left George Gore's office he shot off in his squad car for the Flask of Hermes Vitarium.

The frail old wooden building always amused him; it seemed perpetually about to fall, and yet it never had. What a variety of enterprises had been transacted, over the decades, on these faded premises. Before becoming a vitarium, Sebastian had told him, the building had housed a small cheese factory, employing nine girls. And before that, Sebastian believed, it had housed a television repair establishment.

He landed his squad car, walked through the doorway. There at the typewriter, behind the counter, sat Cheryl Vale, the obliging, thirtyish receptionist and bookkeeper of the firm; at the moment she was on the phone, and so he passed on through the back doorway, into the employees' portion of the premises. There he found their sole salesman, R. C. Buckley, reading a dog-eared copy of *Playboy*, the eternal salesman's choice and obsession.

'Hi, Officer,' R.C. greeted him, with a toothy smile. 'Out fixing tickets as usual?' He laughed a salesman's laugh.

Tinbane said, 'Is Father Faine here?' He looked around, but did not see him.

'Out with the rest of them,' R.C. said. 'They zeroed in on another live one at Cedar Halls Cemetery in San Fernando. Should be back in a half hour. Want some sogum?' He indicated a nearly full sogum tank, the establishment's pastime when there was nothing else to do.

'Do you think,' Officer Tinbane said earnestly, seating himself on one of Bob Lindy's tall workbench stools, 'that it's what you do, or is it what you think? I mean ideas that come to you that you mull over but never put into action . . . do they count, too?'

R.C.'s forehead wrinkled. 'I don't get you.'

'Look at it this way.' Tinbane gestured, trying to convey what he had on his mind; it was difficult, and R.C. was not the person he would have picked. But at least it was better than mulling. 'Like what you dream,' he said; a way of conveying it had come to him. 'Suppose you're married. You are, aren't you?'

'Oh sure, yeah,' R.C. said.

'Okay, so am I. Now, for instance, say you love your wife. I'm assuming you do; I love mine. Now, suppose you have a dream, you dream you're making out with another woman.'

'What other woman?'

'Any. Just another woman. You're frankly in bed with her. In your dream, I mean. Okay. Is this a sin?'

49

'It is,' R.C. decided, 'if after you wake up you think back to it, the dream, and you enjoy thinking about it.'

Tinbane continued, 'Okay, suppose the idea comes into your head as to how you could hurt another person, take advantage of him; and you don't do it, naturally, because he's your friend, you see what I mean? I mean, you don't do that to someone you like; that's axiomatic. But isn't there something wrong if you have the idea, just the idea?'

'You've got the wrong man to talk to,' R.C. said. 'Wait until Father Faine gets back; ask him.'

'Yeah, but you're here and he's not.' And he felt the urgency of the problem; it probed at him, making him move and talk, forcing him to follow – not his own logic – but its logic.

'Everybody,' R.C. said, 'has hostile impulses, toward everybody, at some time or another. Like sometimes I feel like taking a swing at Seb, or more often Bob Lindy; Lindy really gets my goat. And then even sometimes – ' R.C. lowered his voice. 'You know, Seb's wife Lotta; she comes in here a lot of times. Not for any reason but just to – you know; sort of hang around and talk. She's sweet, but goddam it, sometimes she drives me nuts. Sometimes she can be a real pest.'

Tinbane said, 'She's nice.'

'Sure she's nice. They don't come any nicer. But isn't that the point you were trying to make? Okay; a nice person like that and I feel like bouncing an ashtray off her head because she's so – ' He gesticulated. 'Dependent. Hanging on Seb all the time. And he's so goddam much older than her. And with this anti-time, this Hobart Phase, she's getting younger and younger; pretty soon she'll be a teen-ager and then she'll be in grammar school, and about the time he's back to his prime of say around my age she'll be a baby. A baby!' he stared at Officer Tinbane.

'That's a point,' Tinbane conceded.

'She was older, of course, when he married her. More mature. You didn't know her then; you weren't on this beat. She was full-grown, fully like a real woman; hell, she was a real woman. But now – ' He shrugged. 'You can see what that damn Hobart Phase does.'

Tinbane said, 'Are you sure? I thought you had to be already dead and be reborn to get younger.'

'Christ,' R.C. said, 'don't you understand anti-time at all? Listen; I knew her. She was older. *I* was older; we all were. I think – you know what I think? You've got a mental block against facing it, because you're young now, too young, in fact; *you, too, can't afford to get any younger. You* can't be a cop if you do.'

'You're full of food.' He felt terrific anger, swift and terrible. 'Maybe anti-time affects you a little if you haven't died, maybe sort of stabilizing you, but it's not like the deaders, like Seb was. Sure, I admit he's growing younger, but not Lotta. I've known her for – ' He calculated mentally. 'Almost a year. She's matured.'

An aircar landed on the roof above them; down the stairs came Bob Lindy, Sebastian Hermes, and Father Faine. 'A good job,' Sebastian said, seeing Officer Tinbane. 'By Dr Sign. He's with him – the old-born – at Citizens' Emergency.' He sighed. 'I'm beat.' Seating himself on a cane-bottomed chair he picked a cigarette butt from a nearby ashtray, lit it and began puffing smoke into it. 'Well, Joe Tinbane; what's the good word? Any new unkillings?' He laughed; they all did.

Tinbane said, 'I wanted to talk to Father Faine about a – religious matter. Personal.' To Father Faine he said,

'Can you come out with me to the squad car so we can sit and I can consult you?'

'Yes indeed,' Father Faine said; he followed Tinbane back into the front room of the establishment, past Cheryl Vale, who was still talking on the phone, and out where Tinbane had parked the squad car.

For a moment they sat in silence. Then Father Faine said, 'Does it have to do with adultery?' Like Seb he, too, was undoubtedly slightly psionic.

'Hell no,' Tinbane said. 'It has to do with certain thoughts I've had, not like any I ever had before. You see – there's this situation I can profit from. But at someone else's expense. Now, whose good should come first? If theirs, then why? Why not mine? I'm a person, too. I don't get it.' He lapsed into brooding stillness again. 'Okay, so it does have to do with a woman, but the adultery part isn't the part I'm talking about; it's about hurting her, this girl. I've got a hold over her where I think – I just think; I don't know – I could make her go to bed with me.' He wondered if Father Faine's mild telepathic ability would enable him to distinguish the image of Lotta Hermes; he hoped to hell not . . . but then of course the pastor was pledged to silence. Still, it would be awkward.

'Do you love her?' Father Faine asked.

That stopped him. Cold. 'Yes,' he said finally. It was true; he did. It had never entered his conscious thoughts, but there it was. So this was the spur goading him; from this came the baffling thought-processes.

'Is she married?'

'No,' he said. Just to play it safe.

Father Faine said presently, 'But she doesn't love you.'

'Oh hell no; she loves her husband.' He realized, then, instantly, what he had said, and how easily Father Faine

52

could decipher why he had said she wasn't married; he would know it had to be Lotta. 'And he's a good friend of mine,' he said. 'I don't want to hurt him.' But I do really love her, he thought. And that hurts; that's what's making me feel the way I do; when you love someone you want to be with her, you want to have her as your wife or girl friend. It's natural; it's biologic.

Father Faine said, 'Be careful that you don't tell me the names. I don't know how much you know about the rite of confession, but it is always obligatory not to mention names.'

'I'm not confessing!' He felt indignation. 'I'm just asking for your professional opinion.' Was he confessing – a sin? In a sense, yes; he was asking for help but he was also requesting absolution. Forgiveness for what he had thought, for what he might do; forgiveness for being what he was in essence; this was his essence talking, this part of him that longed for Lotta Hermes and was willing to navigate any difficult series of maneuverings to acquire her, like a salmon flopping and flapping its way against the tidal currents.

'Man,' Father Faine said, 'is on the one hand an animal, with animal passions. It's not our fault, not your fault for having illicit yearnings that transgress God's moral law.'

'Yes, but I have a higher nature,' he said, bitingly. But it doesn't get in the way, he thought; that's not the real conflict. *There really is no part of me rejecting this.*

What I want, he realized, is not advice on what is right, or even absolution. I want a blueprint by which this thing can be brought about!

'I can't help you there,' Father Faine said. Somewhat sadly.

Startled, aware of the near-psionic reading of his mind,

53

he said, 'You sure can figure out what a person's thinking.' He wished, now, to terminate the discussion; Father Faine, however, was not ready to let him go: he had, he realized, to pay the price of consulting him.

Father Faine said, 'You're not afraid of doing wrong; you're afraid of trying to do wrong and failing, and having everyone know. The girl you want, her husband; you're afraid you'll fail and there they'll be, a united front against you, shutting you out.' His tone was critical and upbraiding. 'You have, you say, a certain hold over this girl; suppose you make the try and she jumps the wrong way, gets frightened and huddles up to her husband – which isn't so unnatural – and you're a – ' He gestured. 'I think the phrase is, "a horse's mouth."'

Over the radio of the squad car the police announcer babbled briefly to another team in another part of Los Angeles. Tinbane, however, said, 'That's for me; I have to get moving.' He opened the door of the car, and Father Faine got out. 'Thanks a lot, Father,' he said, formally and correctly.

The door closed; Father Faine departed, back into the building.

Tinbane roared up into the sky, away from the Flask of Hermes Vitarium. For the time being.

Seeing Father Faine re-enter the store, Sebastian Hermes noted his troubled, dour expression and said, 'He must have some problem.'

'We all do,' Father Faine said vaguely, opaque in his thoughts.

'Let's get down to business,' Sebastian said, to him and to Bob Lindy at work at his bench. 'I've been monitoring the bug I put on the Anarch Peak's grave and I believe I've picked up heartbeats. Very faint and irregular, but my intuition tells me there's something there; we're very close.'

'Ought to be worth a million poscreds,' Lindy said.

Sebastian said, 'Lotta picked up a good deal of info at the Library. She did us a good job.' He had wondered, in fact, how, given her timidity, she had managed. 'I know about all there is to know regarding this Anarch Peak. He was a really great man. Nothing like this Ray Roberts; the complete opposite, actually. We'll be doing the world a service and in particular the population of the Free Negro Municipality.' He inhaled the cigarette smoke vigorously, in agitation; the cigarette in his hand grew longer and longer. 'The trouble is,' he declared, 'she's got to go back to the Library again; this time I want all she can get on that nut Ray Roberts.'

'Why?' Bob Lindy asked.

Sebastian gestured for complete attention. 'Roberts is both a threat and at the same time potentially our greatest buyer.' He turned to the expert, R.C. Buckley. 'Aren't I right?'

R.C. digested the subject in his mind for a time. 'Like you say, we'll know better if Lotta can get us more background on him; a lot of what you read in the 'papes about TV stars and politicians and religious figures just ain't so. But yes; I think you're right. The Anarch founded the Udi Cult; it's reasonable that nobody'll want him as badly as they.' He concluded, 'Of course, as you point out they may kill him again right away.'

'Is that our worry?' Lindy said. 'What they do with the Anarch after they get him isn't our affair; our responsibility ends when we transfer ownership and collect the fee.'

Cheryl Vale, listening, said, 'That's awful. The Anarch was such a good man.'

55

'Wait, wait,' Sebastian said. 'Wait for what Lotta brings back from the Library. Maybe Roberts isn't that bad. Maybe we can do perfectly legal, ethical business with him.' His instinct – that they had on their hands a possibly monumental strike – remained undimmed.

Father Faine said, 'Lotta isn't going to enjoy that, having to go back to the Library again. That place has traumatized her.'

'She did it once,' Sebastian said. 'And it didn't kill her.' But underneath he felt guilt; maybe he should go himself. But – the Library baffled him, too. Perhaps, he reflected moodily, that was why he had dispatched his wife to do the research job in the first instance . . . his job actually. And Lotta would know it; yet still she went.

That quality in her made her appealing. And yet it offered a way by which to take advantage of her, a way he had to guard against and decline. The decision lay with him, not with her. Sometimes he declined successfully and other times, as in the case of the Library, he yielded to his own fears; he spared himself and let her suffer. And for this he periodically hated himself . . . as, to a certain extent, he did now.

'One thing,' Father Faine was saying, 'that may not have occurred to you, Sebastian. Allowing for human jealousies, Ray Roberts may resent the rebirth of Anarch Peak, but in his organization there may be those joyfully anticipating Peak's return.'

'A splinter group,' Sebastian said, mulling.

'Through your police buddy, Officer Tinbane, perhaps you can get in touch with them.' To R.C. Buckley, Father Faine said, 'It seems to me that's your job; that's what we pay you for.'

'Sure, sure,' R.C. agreed, nodding vigorously; he got out his notebook, made a few jottings. 'I'll look into it.'

Bob Lindy, wearing the earphones of the monitoring device which Sebastian had installed at the Anarch's grave, said suddenly, 'Hey, I think you're right. I do pick up heartbeats; like you say, irregular and weak, but they're getting stronger.'

'Let me listen,' R.C. Buckley said, going over to Lindy impatiently. He, too, like Sebastian, scented the quarry. 'Yep,' he agreed, after a time; he removed the earphones, offered them to Father Faine.

Sebastian said abruptly, 'Let's go dig him up; let's not wait.'

'It's against the law,' Father Faine reminded him, 'to do any excavating prior to hearing the actual and perfect very voice.'

'Laws,' R.C. said disgustedly. 'Okay, Father, if you want to obey the letter of the law then let's contact Ray Roberts; according to law we have the right to sell to the highest bidder. That's established business practice, in this business.'

At the store's vidphone, Cheryl Vale called to Sebastian. 'Mr Hermes, I have a long distance call for you personally.' She put her hand over the receiver. 'I don't know who it is. All I know is that the call originated in Italy.'

'Italy,' Sebastian said, puzzled. To R.C. Buckley he said, 'Take a look in our inventory card-file and see if we own anybody of Italian extraction.' He walked over beside Miss Vale and took the receiver from her. 'This is Sebastian Hermes,' he said. 'Who am I speaking to?'

To him, as to Cheryl Vale, the face on the small screen was unfamiliar. A Caucasian with long, neatly waved black hair and an intense, thorough gaze. 'You don't know me, Mr Hermes,' the man said, 'and up to now I have never had the pleasure of speaking to you.' He had

57

a mild Italian accent and his speech was formal, measured. 'Nice talking to you, sir.'

'Nice talking to you, too,' Sebastian said. 'You are Signor – '

'Tony,' the dark-haired Italian said. 'Never mind my last name; at the moment it isn't important. We understand, Mr Hermes, that you own rights to the late Anarch Peak. Or the *formerly* late Anarch Peak, if that's the case. Which is it, Mr Hermes?'

Sebastian hesitated, then said, 'Yes, my firm owns the rights to the individual in question. Are you in the market for him?'

'Very much so,' Tony said.

'May I ask whom you represent?'

'An interested principal,' Tony said. 'Not connected with Udi. And that's important. You understand, don't you, that Ray Roberts is a killer and it is essential to keep the Anarch Peak out of his hands? That there is a law both in the Western United States and in Italy which makes it a felony to transfer ownership of an old-born to anyone you reasonably anticipate might harm him? Are you conscious of this, Mr Hermes?'

'I'll let you talk to Mr Buckley,' Sebastian said, nettled; this part of the enterprise was not his pipe of sogum. 'He's our sales representative; just a moment.' He passed the receiver to R.C. who at once sprang into action.

'R.C. Buckley here,' he intoned. 'Uh, yes, Tony; your source of info is accurate; we do have the Anarch Peak in our inventory; he's currently recovering from rebirth pains at the finest hospital we could locate for him. Naturally I can't tell you its name; you understand that.' He winked at Sebastian. 'May I ask, sir, what your source of information is? We've kept this matter somewhat private . . . because of various conflicting interests

58

involved; as an instance Ray Roberts, whom I believe you mentioned.' He paused, waiting.

Sebastian thought, *How could anybody know?* Only the six of us here, our organization, know. Lotta, he thought, then. She knows, too. Could she have told anyone? Well, it had to come to light eventually, if they expected to sell the Anarch. But this soon, before they had actual physical custody – this made it imperative, he realized, to get the Anarch out of the ground with no delay, law or no law. I'll bet it was Lotta, he thought. Damn her.

Leading Bob Lindy off to the workshop area of the store, he said to him, 'Now we're forced to go ahead. As soon as R.C. is off the phone get on it and round up Dr Sign; you and he and Father Faine meet me at Forest Knolls Cemetery; I'm taking off right now.' He felt the urgency of it. 'I'll see you there. And make it quick; explain the situation to Sign.' He slapped Lindy on the back, then strode up the stairs to the roof field parking area, where his aircar reposed.

In a moment he was airborne and on his way to the small, nearly abandoned cemetery where the Anarch Peak lay.

Chapter 6

Only in a perfect flight from nothingness is Being to be found
in all its purity.   – St Bonaventura

Forest Knolls, Sebastian thought. The cemetery abandoned by everyone, obviously picked with great care by
those who had buried the Anarch. They must have
believed Alex Hobart and his theorum that time was
about to reverse itself; they – those who loved the Anarch
– must have anticipated this exact situation.

He wondered how long and how hard Ray Roberts'
crack corps had hunted for the grave. Not long nor hard
enough, evidently.

The cemetery, a brief, flickering quad of green, sped
by below; Sebastian reversed the flight of his aircar,
coasted back down and came to rest in what had once
been a gravel parking area of the cemetery but which
now had become overgrown, like the graves, with rank
and frightening weeds.

Even in daytime, it was a forbidding place. Despite the
nascent life beneath the ground potentially crying out for
aid. Then shall the eyes of the blind be opened, he
thought in quotation from some vaguely remembered
portion of the Bible. And the tongues of the dead
unstopped. A lovely passage; and now so factually,
accurately true. Who would have thought? All those
centuries, regarded as a pretty and comforting fable by
the world's intellectuals, something to lull people into

accepting their fate. The understanding that, as predicted, it would one day be literally true, that it was not a myth –

Making his way past the less impressive gravestones he came at last to the ornate granite monument for Thomas Peak, 1921–1971.

The grave – thank god – remained as he had last seen it. Untouched. No one in sight, no one to witness this illegal act.

Just to be sure, however, he knelt at the grave, clicked on the bullhorn which he used on such occasions, and said into it, 'Can you hear me, sir? If so, make a sound.' His voice boomed and echoed; he hoped it would not attract persons passing by the cemetery. Getting out the phones he clamped them to his head, placed the sound-sensitive cup against the earth. Listened.

No response from below. A dismal wind stirred the wild, irregular tufts of grass, the wilderness of this little peripheral cemetery . . . He moved the listening cup about, here and there over the grave, straining to pick up something, some response. None.

From several yards off, from a different grave entirely, he heard a weak voice issuing from beneath the sod. 'I can hear you, mister: I'm alive and I'm shut up down here; it's all dark. Where am I?' Panic in the dim, lonely voice. Sebastian sighed; he had awakened, by use of the bullhorn, some other deader. Well, that would have to be attended to, too; he owed it to the trapped old-born person suffocating in the coffin. He walked over to the active grave, knelt there, placed the listening cup to the ground, although really it was unnecessary.

'Don't be frightened, sir,' Sebastian said into the bullhorn. 'I am up here and aware of your plight. We'll get you out, soon.'

61

'But – ' the voice quavered, ebbing and fading. 'Where am I? What is this place?'

'You have been buried,' Sebastian explained; he was accustomed to this: each job his firm handled called for this odd little interval between the time the deader awakened and the time they had him up and out . . . and yet he had never gotten used to it. 'You died,' he explained, 'and were buried, and now time has reversed itself, and you're alive again.'

'Time?' the voice echoed. 'Pardon? I – don't understand; time for what? Can't I get out of here? I don't like it here; I want to go back to my bed, in my room at La Honda General.'

The last memories. Of hospitalization, which had proved terminal. Sebastian said into the bullhorn, 'Listen to me, sir. Very shortly we will have equipment and men here to get you out; try to breathe as little of the air as possible; try not to use it up. Can you relax? Try.'

'My name,' the voice called up quaveringly, 'is Harold Newkom, and I'm a war vet; I get preference. I don't think you ought to treat a war vet like this.'

'Believe me,' Sebastian said, 'it's not my fault.' I had to undergo it, too, he thought somberly; I remember how it felt. Waking up in darkness, in the Tiny Place, as it's called. And some of them, he reflected, bleating without getting a response . . . because the system is all tied up by the goddam bureaucratic laws passed in Sacramento, laws that bind and hamper us, obsolete laws, damn them.

He rose stiffly to his feet – he was not becoming young fast enough – and made his way back to the Anarch's tomb.

When Bob Lindy and Dr Sign and Father Faine arrived, he said to them, 'We've got a live one we have to handle

62

first.' He showed them the grave, and Bob Lindy at once sent his drill driving furiously into the hard-packed soil, bringing down essential air. So that was that; the rest would be routine.

Standing beside him, Dr Sign said sardonically, 'This is lucky. You now have an excuse for being here if the cops come by. You were visiting the cemeteries in your usual rounds and you heard this man . . . correct?' He returned to the grave; now dirt was flying in all directions as Lindy operated the autonomic diggers. Turning again toward Sebastian Hermes he called, over the noise of the diggers, 'I think you're making a big mistake, from a medical standpoint, digging Peak up now while he's still dead. It's risky; it interferes with the natural process of reconstitution of the biochemical entity. We've been told all about that; if the body comes up too soon he ceases to mend; it's got to be *down there*, in the dark, cold, away from the light.'

'Like yoghurt,' Bob Lindy said.

Dr Sign continued, 'And in addition it's bad luck.'

'Bad luck,' Sebastian echoed, amused.

'He's right,' Bob Lindy said. 'There's supposed to be a release of the forces of death, when you dig up a deader prematurely. The forces get loose in the world when they shouldn't, and they always come to rest on one person.'

'Who?' Sebastian said. But he knew the superstition; he had heard this all before. The curse fell on the person who had dug the deader up.

'It'll be on you,' Bob Lindy said; he grimaced and grinned.

'We'll bury him again,' Sebastian said. The diggers had stopped now; Lindy hung over the shallow pit, groping for the rim of the coffin. 'In the basement. Under the Flask of Hermes Vitarium.' He came over; he and Dr

63

Sign and Father Faine helped Lindy to drag up the damp, moldering coffin.

'From a religious standpoint,' Father Faine said to Sebastian as Lindy expertly unscrewed the lid of the coffin, 'it's a violation of God's moral law. Rebirth must come in its own time; you, of all of us, ought to know that – since you underwent this yourself.' He opened his prayer book, to begin his recitation over Mr Harold Newkom. 'My text for today,' he declared, 'is from *Ecclesiastes*. "Cast thy bread upon the waters: for thou shalt find it after many days."' He gave Sebastian a severe look and then continued.

Leaving the others at their various subdivisions of the job, Sebastian Hermes wandered about the graveyard, in his usual fashion, yearning, reaching out, listening . . . but this time as before he found himself drawn toward one grave, to the one place which mattered. Back to the ornate granite monument of Anarch Thomas Peak; he could not keep away from it.

They're right, he thought. Doc Sign and Father Faine; it's a hell of a medical risk and an outright breaking of the law: not just God's law but the civil code. I know all that, he thought; they don't have to tell me. My own crew, he thought gloomily, and they're not backing me up.

Lotta will, he realized. That, he could always count on: her support. She would understand; he couldn't risk *not* digging the Anarch up. To leave him here was to invite Ray Roberts' Offspring of Might in for a murder. A good excuse, he thought wryly. I can rationalize it: it's for the Anarch's safety.

Just how dangerous, he wondered once more, is Ray Roberts? We still don't know; we're still going on 'pape articles.

Returning to his parked aircar he dialed his home phone number.

'Hello,' Lotta's small-girl voice sounded, intimidated by the phone; then she saw him and smiled. 'Another job?' She could see the graveyard behind him. 'I hope this is a valuable one.'

Sebastian said, 'Listen honey – I hate to do this to you, but I don't have the time to do it myself; we're all tied up here with this job, and after him – ' He hesitated. 'Then we've got another waiting,' he said, not telling her who it would be.

'What would you like?' She listened attentively.

'Another research assignment to the Library.'

'Oh.' She managed – nearly – not to show her dismay. 'Yes, I'd be glad to.'

'This time we want to know the story on Ray Roberts.'

'I'll do it,' Lotta said, 'if I can.'

'How do you mean, if you can?'

Lotta said, 'I get – an anxiety attack there.'

'I know,' he said, and felt the fullness of his injury to her.

'But I guess I can do it one more time.' She nodded, drably.

'Remember, absolutely remember,' he said, 'to stay away from that monster Mavis McGuire.' If you can, he thought.

All at once Lotta brightened. 'Joe Tinbane just now did a research of Ray Roberts. Maybe I can get it from him.' Her face showed utter, blissful relief. 'I won't have to go there, then.'

'Agreed,' Sebastian said. Why not? It made sense, the Los Angeles police researching Roberts; after all, the man was about to show up in their jurisdictional area. Tinbane probably had everything there was; to be harsh

65

about it, he had probably done – God forbid, but it was undoubtedly true – he had done a better job at the Library than Lotta could ever do.

As he rang off he thought, I hope to hell she can get hold of Joe Tinbane. But he doubted it; the police were undoubtedly extremely busy right now; Tinbane was probably tied up for the rest of the day.

He had a feeling that Lotta was in for bad luck; very soon and in large measure. And, thinking that, he flinched; he felt it for her.

And felt even more guilty.

Walking back to his crew of employees at the open grave he said, 'Let's try to get this one wrapped up fast. So we can get on to the important one.' He had definitely made up his mind; they would exhume the body of the Anarch, now, on this trip.

He hoped he would not live to regret it. But he had a deep and abiding hunch that he would.

And yet still – to him, at least – it seemed like the best thing to do. He could not shake that conviction.

Chapter 7

You and I, when we argue, are made in each other. For when I understand what you understand, I become your understanding, and am made in you, in a certain ineffable way.   – Erigena

Out cruising his beat in his roving prowl car, Officer Joseph Tinbane got the call over the police radio. 'A Mrs Lotta Hermes asks you to get in touch with her. Is this police business?'

'Yes,' he said, lying; what else could he say. 'Okay,' he said, 'I'll phone her. I have the number; thanks.'

He waited until four o'clock, the end of his shift, and then, out of uniform, called her from a pay vidphone booth.

'I'm so relieved to hear from you,' Lotta said. 'You know what? We have to get all the info we can on that Ray Roberts who heads that Udi cult. You were just at the Library looking him up, and I thought I could get it from you and not have to go back to the Library.' She gazed at him entreatingly. 'I've already gone there once today; I just can't go back, it's so awful, everybody looking at you, and you have to be quiet.'

Tinbane said, 'I'll meet you for a tube of sogum. At Sam's Sogum Palace; do you know where that is, and can you get there?'

'And then you'll tell me all about Ray Roberts? It's getting late in the day; I'm afraid the Library will be closing. And then I won't be able to – '

'I can tell you all you need to know,' Tinbane said. And a great deal more besides, he thought.

He hung up, then buzzed over to Sam's Sogum Palace on Vine. As yet, Lotta had not arrived; he took a booth in the rear where he could watch the door. And presently she appeared, wearing a much too large wintery coat, eyes dark with concern; glancing about, she made her way hesitantly into the palace, not seeing him, afraid he wasn't really there, etc. So he rose, waved to her.

'I brought a pen and paper to write it down.' She seated herself breathlessly across from him, so pleased to find him . . . as if it was a miracle, some special dispensation of fate, that they had contrived to appear at the same place at roughly the same time.

'Do you know why I wanted to meet you here?' he said. 'And be with you? Because,' he said, 'I'm falling in love with you.'

'Oh God,' she said. 'Then I have to go to the Library after all.' She leaped up, picked up her pen and paper and purse.

Also standing, he assured her, 'That doesn't mean I don't have the info on Ray Roberts or won't give it to you. Sit down. Be calm; it's all right. I just thought I should tell you.'

'How can you be in love with me?' she said, reseating herself. 'I'm so awful. And anyhow I'm married.'

'You're not awful,' he said. 'And marriages are made *and* broken; they're a civil contract, like a partnership. They begin; they end. I'm married, too.'

'I know,' Lotta said. 'Whenever we run across you you're always talking about how mean she is. But I love Seb; he's my whole life. He's so responsible.' She gazed at him attentively. 'Are you really in love with me? Honestly? That's sort of flattering.' It seemed, somehow, to make her more at ease; plainly it reassured her. 'Well, let's have all the data on that creepy Ray Roberts. Is he really as bad as the 'papes say? You know why Sebastian wants the info on him, don't you? I guess it won't hurt to tell you; you already know the one secret thing I wasn't supposed to say. He wants the info on Roberts because – '

'I know why,' Tinbane said, reaching out and touching her hand; she drew it away instantly. 'I mean,' he said, 'we all want to know Roberts' reaction to Peak's rebirth. But it's a police matter; as soon as Peak is old-born it's automatically our responsibility to protect him. If my superiors knew your vitarium had located Peak's body they'd send in their own team to dig him right up.' He paused. 'If that happened, your husband would take a great loss. I haven't told Gore. George Gore is my superior in this. I probably should.' He waited, studying her.

'Thank you,' Lotta said. 'For not telling Mr Gore.'

He said, 'But I may have to.'

'At the Library you said it was as if I hadn't told you; you said, "Don't even tell me," meaning that officially as a policeman you hadn't heard me. If you tell Mr Gore – ' She blinked rapidly. 'Sebastian will figure out how you found out; he knows how dumb I am; I'm always the one; it's always me.'

'Don't say that. You're just not constituted for deceit; you say what's on your mind, which is normal and natural. You're an admirable person and very lovely. I admire your honesty. But it is true. Your husband would be sore as hell.'

'He'll probably divorce me. Then you can divorce your wife and marry me.'

He started; was she joking? He couldn't tell. Lotta Hermes was a deep river, unfathomable. 'Stranger things,' he said cautiously, 'have happened.'

'Than what?'

'What you said! Our eventually getting married!'

'But,' Lotta said earnestly, 'if you don't tell Mr Gore then we won't have to get married.'

Baffled, he said, 'True.' In a sense it was logical.

'Don't tell him, please.' Her tone was imploring, but with overtones of exasperation; after all, as she pointed out, he had made it clear that he hadn't – officially – heard. 'I don't think,' she went on, 'that you and I are suited; I need someone older who I can cling to; I'm very clinging. I'm not really grown up any more, and that damn Hobart Phase is making it more true every day.' She made assorted scratches on the pad of paper with her pen. 'What a thing to look forward to: childhood. Being a baby again, being helpless, waited-on. Every day I try to be more grown up; I fight all the time against it, the way ladies used to fight being old, getting middle-aged, fat, with wrinkles. Well, I don't have to worry about that. But see, Sebastian will be an adult still when I'm a child, and that's good; he can be my father and protect me. But you're the same age as I; we'd just be children together, and what's in that?'

'Not much,' he agreed. 'But listen to me. I'll make a deal with you. I'll give you the info on Ray Roberts and I won't tell Gore about Anarch Peak's body being in your vitarium's possession. Sebastian won't know that you told me.'

'Told both of you,' Lotta amended. 'That librarian, too.'

He continued, 'My deal. Do you want to hear it?'

'Yes.' She listened obediently.

Plunging into it, he said hoarsely, 'Could you spread any of your love in my direction?'

She laughed. With malice-free delight. And that *really*

70

mystified him; now he hadn't the foggiest idea of where he stood or what – if anything – he had achieved. He felt depressed; somehow, despite her girlishness, her inexperience, she was controlling the conversation.

'What does *that* mean?' she asked.

It means, he thought, going to bed with me. But he said, 'We could meet like this from time to time. See each other; you know. Go out, maybe during the day. I can get my shift changed.'

'You mean while Sebastian is down at the store.'

'Yes.' He nodded.

To his incredulity, she began to cry; tears ran down her cheeks and she made no effort to stifle them; she cried like a child.

'What's the matter?' he demanded, reflexively getting out a handkerchief and dabbing at her eyes.

Lotta said chokingly, 'I was right; I do have to go back to the Library. Food.' She stood up, gathered her pen and paper and purse, moved away from the table. 'You don't know,' she said, more calmly, 'what you've done to me. Between you and Seb; both of you. Making me go back there for a second time today. I know what's going to happen; I know this time I'll meet that Mrs McGuire; I would have before if you hadn't helped me to find Mr Appleford.'

'You can find him again. You know where his office is; go there, where we were before, where I took you.'

'No.' She shook her head drearily. 'It won't work out that way; he'll be out to sogum or finished for the day.'

He watched her depart, unable to think of anything to say, feeling totally futile. He thought, she's right; I am sending her off to face that. Something and someone she can't face. Between us, between Sebastian Hermes and me, we did it; he could have gone; I could have given her

71

the info. But he didn't go and I wouldn't tell her without something in return. God, he thought; and hated himself. What have I done?

And I say I love her, he thought. And so does Sebastian; he 'loves' her, too.

He stood watching until she was out of sight, and then he went quickly to the payphone on the far side of the sogum palace; he looked up the Library's number and dialed it.

'People's Topical Library.'

'Let me talk to Doug Appleford.'

'I'm sorry,' the switchboard girl said. 'Mr Appleford has left for the day. Shall I connect you with Mrs McGuire?'

He hung up.

Glancing up from the manuscript she had been reading, Mrs Mavis McGuire saw a frightened-looking young woman with long dark hair standing in front of her desk. Irritated by the interruption, she said, 'Yes? What do you want?'

'I'd like what info you have on Mr Ray Roberts.' The girl's face was waxen, without color, and she spoke mechanically.

'"The info we have on Mr Ray Roberts,"' Mrs McGuire said mockingly. 'I see. And it's now – ' She glanced at her wristwatch. 'Five-thirty. Half an hour before closing. And you want me to gather all the sources together for you. Just hand them to you, all assembled and in order. So all you have to do is sit down and read them over.'

'Yes,' the girl said faintly, her lips barely moving.

'Miss,' Mrs McGuire said, 'do you know who I am and what my job is? I'm Chief Librarian of the Library; I

72

have a staff of almost one hundred employees, any one of whom could help you – *if* you had come here earlier in the day.'

The girl whispered, 'They said to ask you. The people at the main desk. I asked for Mr Appleford but he's gone. He helped me before.'

'Are you from the City of Los Angeles? From any civic body?'

'No. I'm from the Flask of Hermes Vitarium.'

Mrs McGuire said harshly, 'Is Mr Roberts dead?'

'I – don't think so. Maybe I better go.' The girl turned away from the desk, hunching her shoulders together, drawing herself together like a sick, crippled bird. 'I'm sorry . . .' Her voice trailed off.

'Just a minute,' Mavis McGuire beckoned her back. 'Turn about and face me. *Somebody* sent you; your vitarium sent you. Legally, you have the right to use the Library as a reference source. You have a perfect right to search for info here. Come into the inner office; follow me.' She stood up, briskly led the way through two outer offices, to her most private quarters. At her own desk she pressed one of the many buttons on her intercom system and said, 'I'd appreciate it if one of the Erads who's free could come down here for a few minutes. Thank you.' She turned, then, to confront the girl. I am not letting this person out of here, Mavis McGuire said to herself, until I find out why she's been sent by her vitarium to get info on Ray Roberts.

And if I can't get the information from her, the Erad can.

Chapter 8

Matter itself (apart from the forms it receives) is likewise invisible and even indefinable.
                                                                    – Erigena

In the work area of the Flask of Hermes Vitarium, Dr Sign listened intently with a stethoscope placed on the unimpressive dark chest of the body of the Anarch Thomas Peak.

'Anything?' Sebastian asked. He felt extremely tense.

'Not so far. But at this stage it frequently comes and goes; this is critical, this period. All the components have migrated back into place and resumed the capacity to function, but the – ' Sign gestured. 'Wait. Maybe I've got it.' He glanced at the instruments which mechanically registered pulse, respiration and cephalic activity; all traced and blipped unwavering lines.

'A body's a body,' Bob Lindy said dispassionately; he showed by his expression the dim view he took of all this. 'A deader is dead, whether he's the Anarch or not, and whether he's five minutes or five centuries from rebirth.'

Reading from a slip of paper, Sebastian said aloud, '"Sic igitur magni quoque circum moenia mundi. Expugnata dabunt labem putresque ruinas." Those last are the key words: "putresque ruinas."'

'What's that from?' Dr Sign asked.

'The monument. I copied it off. The epitaph for him.' He gestured at the body.

'My Latin isn't much good outside medical terminology,' Dr Sign said, 'but I can pick up on the terms putrify

74

and ruin. But he doesn't look it, does he?' He, Lindy and Sebastian viewed the body for a short time in silence. Small as it was it looked complete, ready for life. What's keeping it, Sebastian wondered, from resuming life?

Father Faine said, '"No single thing abides; but all things flow. Fragment to fragment clings – the things thus grow until we know and name them. By degrees they melt, and are no more the things we know."'

'What's that?' Sebastian asked him; he had yet to hear rhymed couplets from the Bible.

'A translation of the first quatrain of the Anarch's epitaph. It's a poem of Titus Lucretius Carus – Lucretius who wrote *De Rerum Natura*. Didn't you recognize it, Seb?'

'No,' he admitted.

'Maybe,' Lindy said caustically, 'if you recite it backward, he'll return to life; maybe that's how you're supposed to handle this.' He turned his hostility directly on Sebastian. 'I don't like trying to bring a corpse back to life; it's completely different from hearing a live person who's trapped underground in the box, and hauling him up.'

'A difference,' Sebastian said, 'only in time. A matter of days or hours, maybe minutes. You just don't like to think about it.'

Lindy said brutally, 'Do you spend much of your time, Seb, remembering the days when you were a corpse? Do you think about that?'

'There's nothing to think about,' he answered. 'I had no awareness after death; I went from the hospital to the coffin and I woke up in the coffin.' He added, 'I remember that; I think about that.' After all he still had claustrophobia because of that. Many old-borners did; it constituted their shared psychological ailment.

75

'I guess,' Cheryl Vale, watching from a distance, said, 'this disproves God and the Afterlife. What you said, Seb; about not having any awareness after you died.'

'No more so,' Sebastian said, 'than the absence of pre-uterine memories disproves Buddhism.'

'Sure,' R.C. Buckley put in. 'Just because the old-borners can't remember doesn't mean nothing happened; like a lot of times in the morning I know I've dreamed like hell all night but I can't remember a damn thing about them, not anything at all.'

'Sometimes,' Sebastian said, 'I have dreams.'

'About what?' Bob Lindy asked.

'A sort of forest.'

'And that's all?' Lindy demanded.

'One other.' He hesitated, then said it. 'A pulsating black presence, beating like a huge heart. Enormous and loud, going thump, thump, rising and falling, in and out. And very angry. Burning out everything in me it disapproves of . . . and that seemed to be most of me.'

'Dies Irae,' Father Faine said. 'The Day of Wrath.' He did not seem surprised. Sebastian had talked with him about it before.

Sebastian said, 'And a sense on my part of it being so alive. It was absolutely living. By comparison – we're a spark of life in a lump that isn't alive, that the spark makes move around and talk and act. But this was totally aware; not out of eyes and ears, just aware.'

'Paranoia,' Dr Sign murmured. 'The sense of being watched.'

'What was it angry at you about?' Cheryl asked.

He pondered, then said, 'I wasn't small enough.'

'"Small enough,"' Bob Lindy echoed in disgust. 'Feood.'

'It was right,' Sebastian said. 'I was in reality much

smaller than I realized. Or admitted; I liked to think I was larger, with large ambitions.' Like seizing the Anarch's corpse, he thought wryly. And trying to cash in big; that was an example, a perfect one. He hadn't learned.

'Why,' Cheryl persisted, 'did it want you to be small?'

'Because it was true. A fact. I had to face the fact.'

'Why?' Lindy demanded.

'That's what happens on the Day of Judgment,' R.C. Buckley said philosophically. 'That's the day you have to face all the reality you've been avoiding. I mean, we all lie to ourselves; we tell our own selves more lies than we ever do other people.'

'Yes,' Sebastian said; that expressed it. 'It's hard to explain,' he said. It would be interesting, if they could bring back the Anarch Peak, to talk to him about it; he might know a good deal. 'He – God – can't help you until you understand that everything you do depends on Him.'

'Religious victuals,' Lindy said contemptuously.

'But think about it,' Sebastian said. 'Literally. I raise my hand.' He raised his hand. 'I think I do it, can do it. But it's done by a complex biochemical, physiological apparatus that I inherited, that I entered; I didn't construct it. A blood clot on one side of the brain, a clot no bigger than a pencil eraser, and I couldn't lift my hand again or move my leg or anything on that side for the rest of my life.'

'So you grovel,' Bob Lindy said, 'before His majesty?'

Sebastian said, 'He can help you if you face it. It's just so damn hard to face. Because when you do you – cease to exist, almost. You shrink down almost to nothing.' But not quite; something real remained.

'"God is angry with the wicked every day,"' Father Faine quoted.

'I wasn't wicked,' Sebastian said. 'Just ignorant. It was necessary for me to be confronted, finally, with the truth. That way – ' He hesitated. 'I could go back to Him,' he said finally, 'where I belonged. And understand that nine-tenths of everything I did in my life was really Him doing it; I was a bystander while He acted through me.'

'You did all that good?' Lindy demanded.

'Everything. Good *and* bad.'

'A heresy,' Father Faine said.

'So?' Sebastian said. 'It was true. Remember, Father; *I've been there*. I'm not spouting my beliefs, my faith; I'm saying what is.'

Dr Sign said, 'I am getting a cardiac fibrillation now. An arrhythmia. Auricular fibrillation; probably what finally killed him. He's successfully passed back to that stage. Normal cardiac rhythm will probably supervene, if we're lucky; if the process continues normally.'

Still continuing the theological discussion, Cheryl Vale said, 'I still don't see why God would want us to feel insignificant. Doesn't He *like* us?'

'Be quiet,' Dr Sign said swiftly.

'We have to be little,' Sebastian said, 'so there can be so many of us. So billions upon billions of separate creatures can live; if one of us were big, the same size as God, then how many would there be? I see it as the only way by which every potential soul can – '

'He's alive,' Dr Sign said. And sagged visibly. 'It worked out; it didn't kill him.' He glanced at Sebastian, smiled slightly. 'Your gamble paid off; we've got a live one, and the live one is the Anarch Thomas Peak.'

'So now what?' Lindy said.

'So now,' R.C. Buckley said, exulting, 'we're rich. We've got an item in our catalog that'll bring prices we've

78

never even heard of before.' He grinned excitedly, his salesman's eyes darting and busy. 'Okay,' he said. 'Here I go. That lead from Italy; that's just one, but they're bidding; that's what counts. And they'll keep bidding, up and up.'

'Wow,' Cheryl Vale said. 'We ought to have a token pipeful of sogum together. To celebrate.' This, she could understand; the theological discussion had baffled her, but not this. Like R.C., she had a good common-sense, seasoned reasonability.

'Get out the sogum,' Sebastian said. 'It's sogum time.'

'So now you've got him,' Lindy said. 'All you have to do is decide who to peddle him to.' He grimaced mirthlessly.

'Maybe,' Sebastian said, 'we'll let him decide.' It was an approach they had not discussed; the Anarch, while still a corpse, had seemed just that: an object, a commodity. But he was, now, appearing among them as a human being, although still technically the property of the vitarium . . . a commercial entity. 'He was – is – a shrewd man,' he pointed out. 'He probably can tell us more about Ray Roberts than the Library can.' And Lotta had not returned; this he noted, and sensed that something had gone wrong. He wondered what . . . and how seriously . . . and kept the thought alive, in the back of his mind. Despite the more pressing problem of the Anarch.

'Are we going to turn him over to a hospital?' R.C. asked.

'No,' Sebastian decided. It was too risky; Dr Sign, here on the premises, would have to provide the medical care.

Dr Sign said, 'Evidently he's going to become conscious. He seems to be passing through the rebirth process unusually rapidly; that indicates his death was originally rapid.'

Bending over the Anarch, Sebastian studied him, studied the tiny, dark, wrinkled face. It was certainly a living face, now; the change struck him as enormous. To see what had been inert organic matter become active . . . this is the real miracle, he said to himself; the greatest of them all. Resurrection.

The eyes opened. The Anarch gazed up at Sebastian, his chest rising and falling regularly; his expression was tranquil, and Sebastian decided that in this state the man had died. Worthy of his calling, he reflected; the Anarch had died like Socrates: hating no one, fearing nothing. He found himself impressed. But always he and his crew at the Flask of Hermes Vitarium missed this moment: this took place before the digging up, the recovery; this took place in the dismal vacuity of the tomb.

'Maybe he'll say something profound,' Lindy offered.

The pupils of his eyes moved; the inert man now living again was seeing each of them here in the room. The eyes roved but the expression in them and on the other features stayed constant. As if, Sebastian thought, we have resurrected a watching-machine. I wonder what he remembers, he asked himself. More than I? I hope so, and it would be reasonable. He, because of his calling, would be more alert.

The dry, cracked, darkened mouth stirred. The Anarch said in a rustling, wind-like whisper, 'I saw God. Do you doubt it?'

There was a moment of silence and then, shockingly, R.C. Buckley said, 'Do you dare to doubt it?'

The Anarch said, 'I saw the Almighty Man.'

'His hand,' Buckley said, 'was resting on a mountain.' He paused, strained to remember; the others in the room watched him. The Anarch watched him, listening for him to go on. 'And he looked upon the world,' Buckley said finally. 'And all about it.'

'I saw him plainer than you see me now,' the Anarch whispered. 'You mustn't doubt it.'

'What's that?' Bob Lindy said.

'An old Irish poem,' Buckley said. 'I'm Irish. It's by James Stephens, I think. As I remember.'

The Anarch said, in a stronger voice, 'He was not satisfied; his look was all dissatisfied.' He shut his eyes then, rested; Dr Sign listened to his heart, checked the registering gauges of body functions. 'He lifted up his hand,' the Anarch said, dimly. As if once more fading back into death. 'I'm in the way, I said. And I will never move from where I stand.'

'He said,' Buckley said, 'dear child, I feared that you were dead. And stayed his hand.'

'Yes,' the Anarch said, and nodded; his expression was peaceful. 'I don't want to forget. He stayed his hand. Because of me.'

Lindy said, 'Were you something special?'

'No,' the Anarch said. 'I was something small.'

'"Small,"' Sebastian echoed, nodding. How well he remembered that. Terribly, completely small, the most meager iota in the universe of things. Now he, too, remembered this: the dissatisfied look; the raising of the hand . . . and then the staying of the hand, because he had said something. The Anarch's words, and Buckley's, had brought it back, the rest of his recollection. That terrifying, angry, lifted hand.

'He said,' the Anarch said, 'that he feared I was dead.'

'Well, you were,' Lindy said practically. 'That's why you were there; right?' He glanced at Sebastian, clearly not impressed. 'What about you, R.C.,' he said to

81

Buckley. 'You were along? How come you know so much?'

'A poem!' Buckley said hotly. 'I remember it from my childhood. For chrissake; forget it.' He looked ill at ease. 'It made a big impression on me when I was a kid. I don't remember it all, but what he said – ' He gestured at the Anarch, 'brought most of it back.'

Sebastian said to the Anarch, 'That's how it was; I remember now.' And more; he remembered more, a great deal. It would take him a long time to sift it and digest it. To Dr Sign he said, 'Can you provide him adequate medical attention? Can we keep him out of a hospital?'

'We can try,' Dr Sign said noncommittally. He continued taking readings, testing the pulse; he seemed particularly concerned about the pulse. 'Adrenalin,' he said, and dived into his medical bag; in a moment he was preparing an injection.

'So R.C. Buckley,' Bob Lindy said, 'the hot-shot salesman, is a poet.' His reaction was a fusion of contempt and disbelief.

'Lay off,' Cheryl Vale said to him sharply.

Again bending over the Anarch, Sebastian said, 'Do you know where you are, sir?'

Faintly, the Anarch said, 'In a medical ward, I think. I don't seem to be in the hospital.' Again his eyes roved, with the curiosity of a child, simple and naïve. Wondering. Accepting, without resistance, what he saw. 'Are you my friends?'

'Yes,' Sebastian said.

Bob Lindy, traditionally, had a down-to-earth fashion of speaking to the old-born; he trotted it forth now. 'You were dead,' he said to the Anarch. 'You died around

82

twenty years ago. While you were dead something happened to time; it reversed itself. So you're back. How do you like it?' He leaned down, speaking louder, as if to a foreigner. 'What's your reaction to that?' He waited, but no response came. 'Now you're going to have to live your entire life over again, back to childhood and finally to babyhood and then back into a womb.' He added, as if by way of consolation, 'It's true of the rest of us, whether we died or not.' He indicated Sebastian. 'This guy here died. Same as you.'

'Then Alex Hobart was right,' the Anarch said. 'I had people who thought so; they expected me back.' He smiled, an innocent, enthusiastic smile. 'I thought it was grandiose, on their parts. I wonder if they're still alive.'

'Sure,' Lindy said. 'Or about to be alive again. Don't you understand? If you think your coming back signifies something, you're wrong; I mean, it has no religious significance; it's just a natural event, now.'

'Even so,' the Anarch said, 'they will be pleased. Have you been approached by any of them? I'd be glad to give you their names.' He shut his eyes again, then, and for a time seemed to have difficulty breathing.

'When you're stronger,' Dr Sign said.

'We should let him get in touch with his people,' Father Faine said.

'Of course,' Sebastian said, irritated. 'It's standard; we always do that; you know.' But this was special. And they all knew it, except of course the Anarch himself. He seemed blissfully glad to be alive again, already thinking of those who had been close to him, those whom he had depended on and those who had leaned on him. The joyful reunion, he thought. Not in the next life, but back here. Ironic . . . this is the meeting place of souls, the

83

Flask of Hermes Vitarium of Greater Los Angeles, California.

Father Faine was speaking to the Anarch, now; two brethren of the cloth, deep in their mutual concern.

'The epitaph on your monument,' Father Faine was saying. 'I know the poem; it's interested me, because I suppose of its complete repudiation of everything in Christianity, the idea of an imperishable soul, an afterlife, redemption. Did you choose it?'

'They chose it for me,' the Anarch murmured. 'My friends. I tended to agree with Lucretius; I suppose that's why.'

'Do you still?' Father Faine asked. 'Now that you've experienced death, the afterlife and rebirth?' He listened intently.

The Anarch whispered, '"This bowl of milk, the pitch on yonder jar, are strange and far-bound travelers come from far. This is a snowflake that was once a flame – the flame was once the fragment of a star."' He nodded, staring up now at the ceiling of the work area. 'I still believe that. I always will.'

'But this,' Father Faine said. '"The seeds that once were we take flight and fly, winnowed to earth, or whirled along the sky, not lost but disunited. Life lives on."'

The Anarch finished: '"It is the lives, the lives, the lives, that die."' His voice was almost inaudible, strange and dim and lonely. 'I don't know. I'll have to think . . . it's too soon.'

'Let him rest,' Dr Sign said.

'Yeah, leave him alone,' Bob Lindy agreed. 'You're always like this, Father; every time we bring a deader back – you always hope it'll come carrying the answers to your theological questions. And they never do; they're like Seb, they just remember a little.'

'This is no ordinary man,' Father Faine said. 'The Anarch was a great religious force and person.' He added, 'And will be again.'

And valuable, Sebastian said to himself. For just that reason. Let's keep first things first; the theology and the poetry come in second. Compared to what's really at stake.

At home in his conapt, following the end of his work day, Douglas Appleford made a person-to-person vidphone call to Rome, Italy.

'I want to talk to Signor Anthony Giacometti,' he told the operator.

Presently he had Giacometti on the line.

'What luck did you have?' Appleford asked. 'With the vitarium.'

Giacometti, in his dressing gown, his hair lavish and long, his powerful eyes intense, said, 'Listen, are you sure they have him? Really sure? They fritted and fratted around; I think if they actually have him like they say they'd have finalized on a price. After all, they're in business; they want a sale.'

'They have him,' Appleford said, with absolute assurance; he had assessed the Hermes woman with what he knew to be complete certitude. 'They're afraid of the Udi people,' he explained. 'They're afraid you represent Ray Roberts; that's why they won't say. But just keep your bid in; hang in there and you'll get title to him.'

'Okay, Mr Appleford,' Giacometti said sullenly. 'I'll take your word for it; you've helped us in the past, we rely on you.'

'And you can,' he declared. 'If I get any more information I'll pass it on to you . . . for the usual fee. She didn't say they'd dug him up, that he was alive; she just said they know where he's buried. That might explain their reluctance – they can't legally sell him until he's been reborn.' He added, 'I'll give her a call and try to get more from her. She doesn't seem able to conceal anything; she's one of those.'

Giacometti, sourly, broke the connection.

As he started away from the vidphone, Appleford heard it ring; he bent, picked up the receiver, expecting to see Giacometti once again, with an afterthought. Instead he found himself facing the reduced but real image of his superior, Mavis McGuire.

'I'm once again involved,' Mavis said, her mouth twisting in aversion, 'with questions regarding Ray Roberts and the Uditi. A young woman, a Mrs Lotta Hermes, is here at the Library wanting to know what we have on Roberts; I'm holding her in my office while I get an Erad in. It should be fairly soon, now.'

Appleford said, 'Did you check with the Council of Erads regarding the burial site of the Anarch Peak?'

'I did. We don't have that information.' Mavis regarded him with the glazed, light-splintered eyes of suspicion. 'This Mrs Hermes says she talked to you previously today. About the Anarch.'

'Yes,' Appleford said. 'She came in with an LA police officer just after I talked to you. They – the vitarium her husband owns – know where the Anarch is buried, so if you want that information you can with a little effort get it from her.'

'I had a feeling she knew,' Mavis said. 'I've been conversing with her; she skirts the topic of the Anarch each time. Afraid of saying too much, I suppose. Tell me the work status of that apologia pro sua vita of Peak's, that *God In a Box*; is there still a typescript manuscript of it, or did you already turn it over to the Erad Council?

86

I know that it never passed through my hands; I'd remember such fulsome platitudes as he used to cast before the swine.'

'I have four printed copies left,' Appleford said, calculating and remembering. 'So it hasn't reached the typescript stage, yet. And I've been told by one of my staff that several more book-forms of it are somewhere in circulation, probably in private libraries.'

'So to some extent it still circulates. It's still theoretically possible for someone to come across it.'

'If they were lucky, yes. But four copies is not much, considering that at one time more than fifty thousand hardbound and three hundred thousand softbound copies were in circulation.'

Mavis said, 'Have you read it?'

'I – glanced through it, briefly. It's powerful, I think. And original. I don't agree with you about "fulsome platitudes."'

'When the Anarch is reborn,' Mavis said, 'he will probably attempt to resume his religious career. If he can avoid assassination. And I have a feeling that he's shrewd; there was a worldly, practical underpinning to his *God In a Box* – he didn't have his head in the clouds. And he will have the benefit of his experience beyond the grave. I think he'll remember it, compared with most old-borns; or anyhow he'll *claim* he remembers it.' Her tone was scathingly cynical. 'The Council is not too pleased at the idea of the Anarch resuming his career of religion-mongering; they're quite skeptical. Just as we manage to erad the last copies of *God In a Box* he shows up again to write some more . . . and we have a feeling that his future work will be worse, more radical, more destructive.'

'Yes, I see,' Appleford said thoughtfully. 'Having been

dead he'll be in a position to claim authentic visions of the hereafter; that he talked with God, saw the Day of Judgment – the usual material the old-born bring back . . . but his will have authority; people will listen.' He contemplated Ray Roberts, then, in that connection. 'I know that you and the Council dislike Roberts,' he said. 'But if you're worried about the doctrines the Anarch will bring back – '

'Your logic is clear,' Mavis McGuire said. She pondered. 'All right, then; we'll keep after the Hermes woman until we have the name of the cemetery, and if we can get it we'll turn it over to Roberts. At least – ' She hesitated. 'I'll recommend that to the Council; the decision will be theirs, of course. And if his body has been taken from the cemetery we'll concentrate on her husband's vitarium.'

'It could be done legally,' Appleford said; he always took a stand in favor of moderation. 'The Anarch can be bought, aboveboard, from the vitarium, by a bid.' He did not, of course, mention his connection with Anthony Giacometti; that was not the Library's affair. Tony is going to have to work fast, he said to himself; once the Council of Erads moves in, things will progress rapidly. He wondered if the principal whom Giacometti represented could – or would – outbid the Library. An interesting thought: a showdown between the Erads and the most powerful religious syndicate in Europe.

Mavis McGuire rang off, and Appleford seated himself with the evening 'pape . . . to read, he discovered, about Ray Roberts' pilg; that seemed to be all there was. Elaborate police precautions, all the rest; he felt bored, and he went into the kitchen to imbile a trifle of sogum.

While he busied himself the vidphone rang again. He gave up on the sogum, plodded back to answer the ring.

It proved to be Mavis McGuire again. 'An Erad is now with Mrs Hermes,' Mavis said. 'They'll question her; it's taken care of. It's their theory that the vitarium probably took a calculated risk and dug up the Anarch, to avoid any chance of losing him; he's too valuable commercially to lose. So it's their assumption that we don't have to locate the cemetery; all we need to do is approach the vitarium now; they want to move in before it closes up shop for tonight.' She added, 'It's my daughter they're sending.'

'Ann?' Appleford said, surprised. 'Why not an Erad?'

Mavis said, 'Annie works well with men, and this will be with a Mr Sebastian Hermes, an old-born, now in his mid-forties. We feel that that kind of approach will be more successful than an out-and-out raid; it's conceivable that they brought the Anarch's body from the cemetery to the vitarium, revived it, and then moved it to another location, a private nursing home that we'd never track down.'

'I see,' Appleford said, impressed. Ann McGuire impressed him, too; he had seen her at work before. Especially with men, as her mother said; she was generally effective whenever the matter of sex became involved.

It had always been his hope, his masochistic plea, that Mavis and the Council would dispatch Ann to do a hatchet job on *him*.

In this situation, with Sebastian Hermes married, Ann would be especially efficient; her specialty was entering a man–woman relationship as a third party, eventually driving out the wife – or mistress; whatever – and reducing the number of players to two: herself and the man.

Lots of luck, Mr Hermes, he thought wryly. And then he

89

thought of timid little Mrs Hermes subjected to the explorations of an Erad, and that made him uncomfortable.

After the interrogation, Lotta Hermes would be different. He wondered which way: for the good or for the worse. The interrogation would either make her or destroy her; it could go in either direction.

He hoped for the former; he had liked the girl.

But his hands were tied.

Chapter 9

God does not know things because they are: they are because
He knows them, and His knowledge of them is their essence.
— Erigena

Officer Joe Tinbane ruminated, I certainly made a horse's
mouth of myself. I've ruined my friendship with the
Hermeses, and because of me she had to go back to the
Library. It's my moral burden, whatever happens to her;
it's on my conscience, until birth.

A lot of times, he reflected, when a person has a
phobia about a particular place or situation, there's a
valid reason. It's a form of precognition. If Lotta's that
afraid of going there, then she probably has reason to be.
Those Erads, he said to himself. Mysterious; who and
what are they? The Los Angeles Police Department
doesn't know; I don't know.

He was home, now, with Bethel. And, as usual, she
was giving him a hard time.

'You're not taking any interest in your sogum,' Bethel
said fiercely.

'I'm going off,' he announced, 'and disgorge. Where I
can be alone and think.'

'Oh? I interfere with your thoughts? Who are they
about?'

He said, stung by her tone, 'Okay; if you want to
know, I'll tell you.'

'Another woman.'

'Right.' He nodded. 'One whom I could love.'

91

'You once said you could never love anyone in the way you loved me; that every other relationship – '

'That was then.' Too many years had passed; talk could not revive a moribund marriage. Why should I be married – stay married – to someone who doesn't basically respect me or like me? he asked himself. The dreary years, passing . . . the accusations. Rising to his feet, he detached himself from his sogum pipe. 'I may have killed her,' he said. 'I take responsibility.' I have to get her out of the Library, he said to himself.

'You're off to visit her now,' Bethel said. 'Without even trying to conceal this – illicit relationship from me, your wife. I took our marriage vows seriously, but you've never tried; if we can't work things out it's because you haven't tried or been responsible. And now you're openly, blatantly, running off to her. Go ahead.'

'Hello,' he said; the conapt door shut after him and he was out in the hall, hurrying toward his parked, unmarked prowl car. Should I go this way? he wondered. Out of uniform? No. He ran back to the door of their conapt – and found it locked.

'Don't try to come back,' Bethel said. 'I'm getting a divorce.' Even through the heavy servofome door her voice was clear. 'As far as I'm concerned you don't live here.'

'I want,' he grated, 'my uniform.'

There was no response. The door stayed shut.

In his prowl car on the roof parking lot he kept a spare doorkey; once more he raced toward the ascent runnel. She can't come between me and my uniform, he declared to himself. That's illegal. Reaching his car he fumbled in the glove compartment. Aw, the hell with it; he got in behind the wheel, started up the engine. As long as I have my gun, he said to himself; he tugged it from his

92

shoulder holster, checked to be sure all twelve chambers were loaded – except the one against which the half-cocked firing pin potentially rested – and then zoomed off into the early evening Los Angeles sky.

Five minutes later he landed on the deserted – or rather almost deserted – roof parking lot of the People's Topical Library. Expertly, he flashed his light into each of the parked aircars. All belonged to Erads, except one registered to Mavis McGuire. So he knew who he could expect to find in the Library besides Lotta Hermes: a gang of at least three Erads and the Chief Librarian.

He quickly reached the roof entrance of the Library, and found it locked. Well, he thought, naturally; it's after hours. But I know she's in there, he thought, even if her car isn't parked up here; she probably came by taxi. Probably she was afraid to drive.

From the trunk of his prowl car he got a lock-analyzer, carried it by its worn leather strap – it had seen a good deal of service – to the Library door. Set in motion, the analyzer probed the lock, listened, then developed a proper tumbler-lift pattern; the door swung open, unlocked, with no damage done to it, no proof that it had been forced.

He returned the lock-analyzer to the car's trunk; then, pausing, inspected the mass of gear which he habitually carted about; what else might help him? Riot gas? Its use could be reported to his superiors in the department; he'd be in trouble. Cephalic-wave detection apparatus, he decided; it'll tell me how many people are in the vicinity and it'll plot their paths; I'll know who's converging on me and from where. So he took the cephalic-wave detector, snapped it on and set it for minimum range; at once the sweep of its scope-screen displayed five distinct dots, five human brains at work within yards from him,

93

probably on the top floor of the Library. He then set the detector for maximum range, and now made out seven dots; so in all, he had six Library officials to cope with, plus Lotta Hermes, whom he assumed to be one of the dots.

He assumed she was still alive, as well as still in the Library.

However, before he entered the Library by its now unlocked roof door, he seated himself in the front of his prowl car, picked up the vidphone receiver and dialed the number of the Flask of Hermes Vitarium; he had that number clear in his mind, now.

'Flask of Hermes Vitarium,' R.C. Buckley said, appearing in cameo on the vidphone screen.

'I'd like to talk to Lotta,' Tinbane said.

'Let me check.' Buckley disappeared briefly, then returned. 'Seb says she hasn't come back from the Library. He sent her there to do some research for him – just a second; here's Seb.'

Now the somber, intelligent features of Sebastian Hermes appeared on the screen. 'No, she hasn't come back, and I'm really worried. I'm beginning to regret that I sent her; maybe I ought to call the Library and ask about her.'

'You'd be wasting your time,' Tinbane said. 'I'm at the Library now, parked on the roof. I know she's in there. The Library is locked up, but that's no problem; I have my prowl car and gear with me; in fact I've already retired the lock. I'm just wondering if I ought to give them a chance to voluntarily release her.'

'*Release* her,' Seb echoed, and blanched. 'It sounds like you think they're holding her.'

'I know,' he said, 'that at closing time they didn't throw her out.' He had an absolute intuition about that; his near-psionic faculty in that direction made him the good police officer that he was. 'She's still in there, and being held; she wouldn't stay unless they detained her.'

'I'll vidphone them,' Sebastian said hollowly.

'And say what?'

'And say I want my wife back!'

'Okay,' Tinbane said, 'you do that.' He gave Sebastian the extension number of his prowl car's phone. 'And then you call me back and tell me what they said.' He continued fixedly to watch the screen of the cephalic-wave detector; it continued to indicate seven brains in the vicinity, moving about slightly; the location of the dots on the screen underwent continual minute relocations. They'll tell you that she was here, he said to himself, and that she left. She never got there at all; maybe they'll say that. And they know nothing. Noli me tangere, he thought; that's what the Library says about itself. Warning: don't meddle with me. Touch me not. The bastards, he said to himself.

Five minutes later his car vidphone light flashed on; he lifted the receiver. 'I got the janitor,' Sebastian said miserably.

'And he said what?'

'That he was alone in the building; everyone else, the staff, everybody, had gone home.'

Tinbane said, 'There are seven living people below me. Okay, I'll go down and take a look. I'll call you back as soon as I have anything definite.'

'Should I call the police?' Sebastian asked.

'I am the police,' Tinbane said, and rang off.

He set the warning circuit of the cephalic-wave detector to activate itself when someone was within five feet of himself, and then, lugging the detector in one hand, his service revolver in the other, he hurried awkwardly to the unlocked entrance door of the Library.

A moment later, by the stairs, he reached the top floor.

Closed doors. Darkness and silence; he fumbled with his infrared flashlight, switched it on. A study of the screen of the cephalic-wave detector showed the seven dots arranged on a horizontal plane vertically distant from him by over five feet; the warning circuit had not triggered. The next floor down, he decided. He tried, as he again descended the stairs, to recall on which floor Mavis McGuire maintained her private suite of offices. On floor three, as I recall, he said to himself.

The warning circuit lit up, blinked on and off at the vertical side of the two-filament bulb. He was on the right floor, distant now only horizontally. Floor six, he noted. The level which the Erad Council is said to occupy. And the overhead lights, on this floor, had not been shut off; bathed in yellow, the corridor of closed doors lay ahead of him.

He walked slowly, glancing intermittently up and then back at the cephalic-wave detector's screen. The seven dots advanced toward him on the horizontal axis. All in one spot, more or less; grouped together in one suite of offices.

I wonder what I'll get out of this, Tinbane asked himself. Probably Library pressure will cost me my job; they reach pretty far up in city government. So the hell with it, he said to himself; it wasn't much of a job anyhow. And, if he could prove that the Erads had forcibly detained Lotta Hermes – anyhow a semblance of a case could be made, if she was willing to back him up. But, he reflected, that might mean Lotta would have to appear in court, or at least sign a complaint, and she would shrink from that; to her it might appear as terrible as the Library. Well, too late to worry about that; he could only hope that, if it came to it, Lotta would vindicate what he – out of uniform but with police equipment – was doing.

The horizontal side of the bulb lit, now, and stayed lit. He was less than five feet from someone. Ahead, a closed office door; he sensed the persons on the far side, the seven of them, but, listening, he could hear nothing. Rats, he said to himself.

Muttering, he hurried all the way back up to the roof, to his prowl car, and, from the trunk, got a monitoring tool, which he laboriously lugged along with the other equipment: his gun, flashlight, cephalic-wave detector, back to floor six and the inhabited, closed office door.

There, working with speed and deft precision, he set the monitoring tool into motion; programmed, it stretched its plastic self thin enough to pass under the door, and then, on the far side, it – presumably – reformed in some neutral shape, and set its aud and vid receptors going.

In his hand he held the vid receiver of the monitoring tool; in his ear he had, squeezed tightly in, the aud outlet.

The aud outlet squeaked into his ear a man's voice. An Erad, he decided. And the vid portion; he peered at the postage-stamp-sized tube surface, gray and vaguely illuminated. The monitoring machinery had not focused; it was still sweeping out a random scan.

' – also,' the Erad was saying in his gloomy, sententious Erad voice, 'we are concerned as to the matter of public safety. It is an axiom of this Library that public safety ranks foremost in value; our eradication of dangerous, disturbing written material – ' It pontificated on. Tinbane inspected the tube surface. Three figures grouped together, a man and two women; he screwed the pan-lens

97

knob clockwise, and the face of one woman grew until it filled the meager screen. It appeared to be Lotta Hermes, but the image was distorted and indistinct, and he could not be sure. He operated the sweep-scanner until it came to rest on the other woman's features. This, he decided, was certainly Mavis McGuire. His identification of her was certain.

And now, in his ear plug, he heard her voice.

'Can't you see how harmful this man is?' Mavis was ranting. 'How pandering to the proles, as he'll try to do, will bring about more riots, more civil disobedience; not only in the Free Negro Municipality, but here among Negroes and white pro-Negroes on the West Coast. Don't forget Watts and Oakland and Detroit; don't forget what you learned in school.'

A harsh, penetrating Erad voice said, 'We might as well all become part of the Free Negro Municipality, when that happens.'

'We've virtually done a complete erad job on *God In a Box*,' Mavis McGuire said. 'His major tract, or whatever you want to call it, is almost gone. Forever. It was *God In a Box* which, thirty years ago, before you were born, helped inflame mass sentiment which brought about the creation of the FNM. The Anarch was personally responsible; if he hadn't made speeches and sermons and written tracts, the FNM would never have been formed, and a whole United States, undivided, would still exist; our country wouldn't have been chopped into three pieces. Four, if you count Hawaii and Alaska; they wouldn't have become separate nations.'

The other woman, presumably Lotta Hermes, cried quietly, her hand over her face, a huddled shape overshadowed by Mavis McGuire and the Erad. And, Tinbane reflected, four more Erads loitered somewhere in

98

the vicinity, probably in the next chamber of the office. Waiting to take turns at her, he thought; he knew the procedure of interrogation, the shifts which spelled each other at regular intervals; the police department worked in this fashion also.

'Now, as to Ray Roberts,' the Erad said. 'He probably knows more about the Anarch than does anyone else alive. What do you suppose his sentiments toward the Anarch's rebirth are? Would you say Roberts is probably profoundly disturbed? Or would you say that he's overjoyed?'

'Do the Council member the courtesy of answering,' Mrs McGuire said to the huddled girl. 'He asked you a reasonable question. You know that Roberts is out here, making his pilg here to the West Coast, because he's distressed. He doesn't want to see this happen. And Roberts is a Negro. And from the FNM. And head of Udi.'

The Erad said, 'Don't you think that tells us what to expect from the old-born Anarch? If Roberts, a fellow Negro and head of Udi and – '

Tinbane removed the aud plug from his ear, set down the visual portion of the gear, freed himself from all his equipment except for his service revolver. I wonder if Erads go about armed, he asked himself. In the light of the overhead hallway fixtures he carefully set the instruction-complex of his service revolver. He calculated distance, how many of them there were to take out, how best to protect Lotta Hermes. And how finally, after the havoc cleared, to make sure that he and Lotta got out of the Library and up to the roof and in his prowl car.

I have about one chance in ten, he decided, of making this work. What will probably happen will be that both

Lotta and I will have disappeared into the Library and never re-emerged. Never seen again.

But just maybe, he thought, I owe this to her.

Once more he adjusted the controls of his weapon. Not kill any of them, he realized; I can't conceivably get away with that – even if Lotta and I did get out, they'd hunt us, hound us, for the rest of our lives. Until we were back in the womb. And, he thought, I don't think they'll go for killing either of us . . . at least not now, not without some Council discussion; a formal decision, if what I know about the Erads is accurate, will have to be arrived at.

Okay, he said to himself. Here goes.

He opened the door and said, 'Mrs Hermes? You're coming home.'

Soundlessly, without moving, the three of them, Lotta and Mavis McGuire and the tall, straw-like Erad with his ugly elongated face, stared at him.

The far door of the office had been left open, and from within four more Erads also peered. Everything had come to a stop. He had frozen the seven of them, suspended them and their activities out of time, just by his presence. By the big gray gun he held; the regulation police-issue mammoth revolver. He was a man with a gun, not a police officer, but he knew how to talk from behind his gun; he knew how to use it without using it.

Beckoning to the hunched-up little shape of Lotta Hermes he said, 'Come over here.' She continued to stare blankly. 'Come over here,' he repeated in exactly the same tone; he made it unvarying. 'I want you,' he told her, 'to come and stand over by me.'

He waited and then, all at once, she rose and made her way over to him, to stand by him. No one interfered; no one even spoke.

The knowledge of wrong-doing – and the recognition of being caught at it – had on most people a paralyzing effect. As long, he thought, as I can keep about me the archetype of authority. Even Erads, he thought, are not exempt. Maybe.

'I've seen you before,' Mavis McGuire said. 'You're a police officer.'

'No,' he said. 'You've never seen me before.' He took hold of Lotta's wrist and said to her, 'Go upstairs to the roof field and wait in my aircar. Make sure you get the right one; it's parked over to the left as you come out of the stairwell.' As she started obediently off he said, 'Feel the hood; the motor's warm. You can tell by that.'

One of the Erads within the inner office fired at him with what he recognized as an illegal pelfrag pistol, very small, with one single fragmenting shot.

The slug, without fragmenting, hit him in the foot. Evidently the ammunition was old, and the pistol probably had never been used; its owner, the Erad, probably did not know how to clean and maintain a gun, and the rim-fire hammer had missed the inner charge.

Tinbane swiftly fired nine random shots, sweeping both offices. He squeezed the trigger of his service revolver until the rooms had become opaque with ricocheting pellets, all of them traveling at a velocity which would stun or inflict a minor injury or blind – he fired once more as he limped into the hall and then, as best he could, he hopped and hobbled up the hall to the stairs, cursing the wound in his foot, feeling the pain and the malfunctioning; he could hardly make any time at all and he felt them behind him, doing something – food, he thought savagely; what a place to be hit. As the stair door swung shut behind him a pelfrag slug detonated in the hall behind him; the glass window of the door shattered and shards slashed at his neck and back and arms. But he continued on, up the stairs. At the top of the stairs, at roof level, he fired his remaining shot back down the stairs, filling the well with rebounding pellets, enough to stop anyone, unless the person was willing to risk blindness, and then he dragged himself and his injured foot to his prowl car.

Beside the car, not inside it, he found Lotta Hermes; she looked up into his face speechlessly, and he opened the car door for her and got her inside. 'Lock your door,' he said, and limped to the driver's side, also getting in, also locking his door. Now a group of Erads had come out onto the roof, but they milled in confusion, some evidently wanting to try one good, planned shot at the prowl car, some wanting to follow in their own cars, some possibly willing to give up.

He took off, gained altitude, accelerated as rapidly as the beefed-up engine which the police department used could manage, and then lifted his microphone and said to the dispatching officer at his substation, 'I'm on my way to Peralta General and I'd like another car waiting for me in the parking lot, just in case.'

'Okay, 403,' the dispatcher acknowledged. '301,' he instructed, 'join 403 at Peralta General.' To Tinbane he said, 'Aren't you off duty, 403?'

Tinbane said, 'I ran into some trouble on my way home.' His foot throbbed and he felt fatigue, general and all-embracing. I'll be laid up for a week, he said to himself as he reached gingerly down to unlace the shoe on his injured foot. Well, there goes the assignment regarding being a bodyguard for Ray Roberts.

Seeing him fussing with his shoe, Lotta said, 'Are you hurt?'

'We're lucky,' he said. 'They were armed after all. But they're not used to a showdown.' Handing her the

102

vidphone receiver, he said, 'Dial your husband at the vitarium; I told him I'd let him know when I had you out of there.'

'No,' Lotta said.

'Why not?'

Lotta said, 'He sent me there.'

Shrugging, Tinbane said, 'I guess that's true enough.' He felt too foolish from his injury to argue; anyhow it was so. 'But I could have given you the info,' he said. 'That's what's rotten about me, about what I did. You might as well blame me as him.'

'But you got me out,' Lotta said.

That, too, was true; he had to agree.

Reaching, Lotta hesitantly touched his cheek, his ear; she examined his face with her fingers, as if she were blind.

'What's that mean?' he said.

Lotta said, 'I'm grateful. I always will be. I don't think they would ever have let me go. It was as if they enjoyed it, as if my knowing about the Anarch was just a – pretext.'

'Very probably,' he murmured.

'I love you,' Lotta said.

Startled, he turned to look at her; the girl's expression was calm, almost peaceful. As if she had resolved some major indecision.

He thought he knew what it was. And his gladness knew no bounds; he was thoroughly elated – more so than in his whole life.

As they drove on toward Peralta General she continued to touch him, as if never intending to let go. He at last took hold of her hand, squeezed. 'Cheer up,' he said. 'You won't have to go back there.'

'Maybe I will,' she said. 'Maybe Seb will tell me to.'

'Tell him to go to hell,' Tinbane said.

Lotta said, 'I want you to tell him for me; I want you to talk for me. You talked to those Erads and Mrs McGuire, you made them do what you ordered them to do. Nobody else has ever stood up for me. Not in my whole life. Not like that, the way you did it.'

Putting his arm around her he held her against him. She seemed, now, very happy. And relieved. My god, he thought, this is a big thing she's done, bigger than what *I* did; she's transferred her dependency from Sebastian Hermes to me. Because of a single incident.

I've got her, he realized. Entirely away from him; *I swung it!*

Chapter 10

Thus God, considered not in Himself but as the cause of all things, has three aspects: He is, He is wise, and He lives.
– Erigena

The vidphone at the Flask of Hermes Vitarium rang; expecting the call-back from Officer Joe Tinbane, Sebastian answered it.

On the screen Lotta's, not Tinbane's, face appeared. 'How are you?' she asked wanly, with a peculiar mechanical listlessness which he had never heard in her voice before.

'I'm fine,' he said, violently relieved to see her. 'But that's not important; how are you? Did he get you away from the Library? I guess he did. Were they actually trying to keep you there?'

'They were,' she said, listlessly. 'How's the Anarch?' she asked. 'Did he come back to life yet?'

Sebastian started to say, We dug him up. We revived him. But instead he took pause; he remembered the call from Italy. 'Whom, specifically, did you tell about the Anarch?' he asked. 'I want you to remember everyone you told.'

'I'm sorry you're mad at me,' Lotta said, still listlessly, as if reading the words from a piece of paper held in front of her. 'I told Joe Tinbane and I told Mr Appleford at the Library and that's all I told. What I called for is to tell you that I'm okay; I got out of the Library . . . Joe Tinbane got me out. We're at the hospital; they're

105

removing a bullet from his foot. It isn't serious but he says it hurts. And he'll undoubtedly be laid up for a few weeks. Sebastian?'

'Yes?' He wondered if she, like Tinbane, had been hurt; he felt his heart speed up in agitation; he felt, now, as concerned as before – actually more so. There was a subtle, unverbalized ominousness in her voice. 'Tell me!' he said urgently.

Lotta said, 'Sebastian, you didn't come and get me out of there. Even after I didn't meet you at the store as we planned. You must have been too busy; I guess you have the Anarch to think of.' Tears, abruptly, filled her eyes; as usual, she made no effort to wipe them away; she cried soundlessly, like a child. Without hiding her face.

'Goddam it,' he said, in a frenzy. 'What is it?'

'I can't,' she wept.

'Can't what? Can't tell me? I'll get over to the hospital; which hospital is it? Where are you, Lotta? Goddam it; stop crying and say.'

'Do you love me?'

'Yes!'

Lotta said, 'I still love you, Seb. But I have to leave you. For a while at least. Until I feel better.'

'Leave me and go where?' he demanded.

Her crying had ceased; her swimming eyes confronted him with unusual defiance. 'I'm not going to say. I'll write to you; I'll figure out exactly how to tell you and I'll put it all in a letter.' She added, 'I can't talk over the phone; I feel so conspicuous. Hello.'

'Oh my god,' he said, unbelievingly.

'Hello, Sebastian,' Lotta said, and hung up; the image of her pinched small face vanished.

Beside Sebastian, R.C. Buckley appeared, apologetically. 'Sorry to bother you at a time like this,' he

106

mumbled, 'but there's someone asking for you. At the front door.'

'We're closed!' Sebastian said savagely.

'She's a buyer. You said never to turn away a buyer, even after six P.M. That's your philosophy.'

Sebastian grated, 'If she's a customer, take care of her; you're our salesman.'

'She asked for you; she won't talk to anyone else.'

'I feel like killing myself,' Sebastian said to him. 'Something terrible must have happened in the Library; I'll probably never find out what it was – she'll never be able to put it into words.' Lotta was so bad with words, he thought. Too many, too few, the wrong ones or to the wrong person; always miscommunicating in one way or another. 'If I had a gun,' he said, 'I would kill myself.' He got out his handkerchief and blew his nose. 'You heard what Lotta said. I let her so badly down she left me. Who's this customer?'

'She says her name – ' R.C. Buckley examined his jotting. 'Miss Ann Fisher. Know her?'

'No.' Sebastian walked toward the front of the store, out of the work area and into the reception lounge with its moderately modern chairs, carpet, and magazines. In one of the chairs sat a well-dressed young woman with smartly clipped, fashionable short black hair. He paused, collecting his wits and considering her. The girl had lovely slim legs; he could not help noticing that. Class, he thought. This girl really has it; even in her earrings. And in the very slight make-up; all tints of her eyes and lashes and lips seemed her own very intense natural coloration. Her eyes, he saw, were blue, unusual for a girl with black hair.

'Goodbye,' she said, and smiled a warm, crinkly smile; her face was extraordinarily mobile; when she smiled her eyes danced with light, and she showed perfect, regular teeth, with mischievous little incisors; he found himself fascinated by her rows of teeth.

'I'm Sebastian Hermes,' he said.

Rising, putting aside her magazine, Miss Fisher said, 'You have a Mrs Tilly M. Benton in your catalog. In the most recent daily supplement.' She fumbled with her smart shiny purse, brought out the addenda ad which the Flask of Hermes Vitarium had placed in that day's evening 'papes. She seemed to be a determined, pert young woman . . . a titanic contrast, he could not help noticing, from Lotta's indecisiveness, which he had over a long period of time been forced to accustom himself to.

'Technically,' he said, 'we're closed for the day. Mrs Benton is of course not here; we have her in a hospital bed, recuperating. We'll be glad to take you over there tomorrow. Are you a relative?'

'She's my great-aunt,' Ann Fisher said, with a kind of philosophical exasperation, as if one had regularly to be ready to cope with reborn elderly relatives. 'Oh, I'm so damn glad you heard her calling,' she went on. 'We kept visiting the cemetery, hoping we'd hear her voice, but it *always* – ' She made a wry face. 'Always seems to happen at weird hours.'

'True,' he agreed. That was indeed part of the problem. He looked at his watch; it was, roughly, sogum time; normally he would want to be at home with Lotta. But Lotta wasn't there. And anyhow he wanted more or less to keep in the vicinity of the store, pending these new, critical hours of life for the Anarch. 'I guess I could take you briefly to the hospital tonight,' he began, but Miss Fisher interrupted him.

'Oh no; thanks, but *forget* it. I'm tired. I've been working all day long and so have you.' Astonishingly, she

108

reached out her smooth, tapered hand and patted his, meanwhile beaming sunlike, radiant understanding, as if she knew him intimately. 'I just want to make sure that the State of California doesn't make her its ward, and turn her over to one of those awful public rest homes for the old-born. We can take her; we have the money, my brother Jim and I.' Miss Fisher examined her wristwatch; he saw that her wrist was lightly, enticingly freckled; more coloration. 'I've just got to get some sogum into me,' she said. 'I'm about to faint. Is there a good sogum palace near here?'

'Down the street,' he said. And once again he thought of Lotta, of the emptiness at home, so bewildering and abrupt; who was she with? Tinbane, evidently; Joe Tinbane had rescued her and – well, it probably was Tinbane; that made sense. In a way he hoped so. Tinbane was a good man. Thinking of Lotta and Tinbane, both of them young, both nearly the same age, he felt fatherly; perversely, he wished her luck, but primarily he wished her back. Meanwhile . . .

'I'll treat you,' Miss Fisher said. 'I just got paid today; if I don't spend these inflation bills they won't be worth anything tomorrow anyhow, And you look tired.' She scrutinized him, and it was a different sort of scrutiny; Lotta had always searched to discern whether he was pleased with her, mad at her, in love with her, not in love with her; Miss Fisher seemed to be judging what he was, not how he felt. As if, he thought, she has the power – or anyhow the ability – to determine whether I'm a man. Or just playing at being a man.

'Okay,' he said, surprising himself. 'But first I have to close up in the back.' He indicated one of the store's reasonably modern chairs. 'You wait here; I'll be back.'

'And we can talk about Mrs Tilly M. Benton,' Miss Fisher said, emitting her approving smile.

He made his way back to the work area of the store, carefully closing the door so that Miss Fisher could not see; having brought the Anarch here they had been forced to become adept at this, on short notice.

'How is he?' he asked Dr Sign. A bed had been fashioned, pro tem. In it lay the Anarch, small, dry, everything about him gray or black, his eyes fixed apparently on nothing; he seemed content, and Dr Sign still looked pleased.

'Healing rapidly,' Dr Sign said. He led Sebastian over to one side, then, out of the Anarch's hearing. 'He asked for a 'pape and I gave him one, the evening edition with our ad in it. He's been reading about Ray Roberts.'

'What's he say about Roberts?' Sebastian asked, chewing his lip. 'Is he afraid of him? Or does he consider Roberts one of those "friends" he mentioned?'

Dr Sign said, 'The Anarch has never heard of Ray Roberts. According to all the public relations material released by Roberts, he was handpicked by the Anarch to succeed him. This appears not to be true. Not unless – ' His voice dimmed to a whisper. 'There may be brain damage, you realize. I've run an EEG now for some time, and find nothing out of order. But – let's call it amnesia. From the rebirth shock. Anyhow, he's puzzled about Udi; not what it is – he remembers founding it – but what it's up to.'

Going over to the bed, Sebastian said, 'What can I tell you? That you'd like to know?'

The old brown eyes, with so much hidden wisdom in them, so much experience, fastened on him. 'I see that, like all other religions, mine has become a hallowed institution. Do you approve of it?'

110

Taken aback, Sebastian said, 'I – don't think I'm in a position to judge. It has its followers. It's still a vital force.'

'And Mr Roberts?' The old eyes were keen.

Sebastian said, 'Opinions differ.'

'Does he believe Udi is for both whites and colored?'

'He – tends to restrict it to colored.'

The eyebrows knitted; the Anarch said nothing, but he no longer looked tranquil. 'If I ask you an embarrassing question,' the Anarch said, 'will you kindly give me a truthful answer? No matter how unpleasant it might be?'

'Yes,' Sebastian said, preparing himself.

The Anarch said, 'Has Udi become a circus?'

'Some people think so.'

'Has Mr Roberts made efforts to locate me?'

'Possibly.' His answer was guarded; this was explosive.

'Have you notified him of my – rebirth?'

'No,' Sebastian said. After a pause he said, 'Generally, an old-born is kept in a hospital for a time, and the vitarium solicits bids on him from relatives and friends. Or, if he's a public figure – '

'If he has no relatives or friends,' the Anarch said, 'and he is *not* a public figure, is he put to death again?'

'He's made a ward of the state. But in your case, obviously you – '

'I would like you to ask Mr Roberts to come here,' the Anarch said in his hoarse, dry voice. 'Since he will be in California on a pilg it won't be much trouble for him.'

Sebastian pondered. And then he said, 'I would prefer that you let us handle your sale. We're experts, Your Mightiness. We do nothing but this. I would prefer not to bring Ray Roberts here, or in fact give him any information about you. He's not the buyer we have in mind.'

111

'Do you want to give me the reason?' The wise eyes again fastened on him. 'Won't the Uditi care to put up the money?'

'It's not a matter of that,' Sebastian said. He made a covert signal to Dr Sign, who immediately came over.

'I think you should rest, Anarch,' Dr Sign said.

'I'll talk to you again later,' Sebastian said to the Anarch. 'I'm going out for a pipeful of sogum, but I'll be back again this evening.' He left the work area and the Anarch, carefully maneuvered the door open and shut; however, Miss Fisher sat reading, engrossed.

'Sorry to keep you waiting,' Sebastian said.

She glanced up, smiled, slid gracefully to her feet, stood facing him; she was relatively tall and very slender with extremely meager breasts; her figure, in fact, was that of a supple adolescent. But her face was sharp-etched and mature, with strong features. And again he thought, This is one of the best-dressed women I have ever seen. And clothes had never impressed him before.

After they had imbibed sogum they wandered along the evening street, looking in store windows, saying very little, glancing cautiously at each other every now and then. Sebastian Hermes had a problem. He still intended to return to his vitarium, to talk further with the Anarch, but he could not very well do it until he had parted company with Miss Fisher.

Miss Fisher, however, did not seem inclined toward the normal, customary moment of saying hello. He wondered why; as time passed it seemed more and more strange.

All at once, as they stood studying a window display of furniture made from Martian wobwood, Miss Fisher said, 'What day is this? The eighth?'

112

'The ninth,' Sebastian said.

'Are you married?'

He thought briefly; one had to calculate carefully in answer to this question. 'Technically,' he said. 'Lotta and I are separated.' It was true. Technically.

'The reason I ask,' Miss Fisher said, starting on, 'is that I have a problem.' She sighed.

It was emerging, now. Her reason for sticking so close to him. He glanced sidelong at her, once again noted her attractiveness, marveled at the amount of communication already achieved between them, and said, 'Tell me. Maybe I can help.'

'Well, see . . . just about nine months ago, there was this lovely little baby, named Arnold Oxnard Ford. You get the situation?'

'Yes,' he said.

'He was so darling.' Her lips pursed, babytalk-wise, motherly. 'And he was there in that children's ward, in the hospital, and he was searching for a womb, and I was doing volunteer work of various kinds for the city of San Bernardino, and I was getting really terribly sick of it, the volunteer work, and I thought, Gee wouldn't it be wonderful to have a sweet little creature like Arnold Oxnard Ford inside my tummy.' She patted her flat stomach as they walked aimlessly along. 'So I went to the nurse in charge of the ward and I said, Could I apply for Arnold Oxnard Ford? And she said, Yes, you look healthy, and I said I was, and she said, It's just about time for him; he'll have to go into a womb – he was in an incubator already – and I signed the papers, and – ' She smiled at Sebastian. 'I got him. Nine months of having him day by day becoming more and more a part of me; it's a marvelous feeling – you have no idea – how it feels to sense another creature, one whom you love, merging

113

molecule by molecule with your own molecules. Every month I had an examination and an x-ray, and it was working out fine. Now, of course, it's really over.'

'I wouldn't know to look,' he agreed; there was no bulge.

Miss Fisher sighed. 'So now Arnold Oxnard Ford is a part of me and always will be, as long as I live. I like to think – a lot of mothers think – that the baby's spirit is still here.' She tapped her black bangs, her forehead. 'I think it is; I think his soul migrated there. But – ' Again she made a face, wistfully. 'You know what?'

'I know,' he said.

'That's right. By the eleventh – the doctor says no later – I have to give up the final physical bit of him. To a *man*.' She made a mocking, but not hostile, face. 'Whether I like it or not, I have to go to bed with some man; as a medical necessity. Otherwise the process won't be complete and I won't ever be able to offer my womb for any other babies again. And – it's strange; for the last two weeks, even longer, I've been experiencing it as a drive, a biological urge. To sleep with some man; any man.' She glanced at him perceptively. 'Or does that offend you? It wasn't meant to.'

Sebastian said, 'Then Arnold Oxnard Ford will be a part of me, too.'

'Does the idea appeal to you? I had pictures of him, but of course the Erads got them. Ideally, you should have seen him; if we had been married you would. But I've been told I'm very good in bed, so maybe you could enjoy just that part alone; would that be enough?'

He pondered. Again astute calculation was required. How would Lotta feel if she knew? Would she know? *Should* she know? And it seemed strange, Miss Fisher selecting him this way, virtually at random. But what she

114

said was true; mothers, nine months after a baby had entered their womb, became – in need. As Miss Fisher said, it was a biological necessity; the zygote had to separate into sperm and egg.

'Where could we go?' he asked artfully.

'My place,' she offered. 'It's nice and you could stay all night; you wouldn't get tossed out after it was over.'

Again he thought, I have to get back to the store. But – this was, at this time, fortuitous. He needed the psychological lift; one woman – probably quite rightly – had abandoned him, and now another had fixed her attention on him. He could not manage to be anything else but flattered.

'Okay,' he said.

Ann Fisher hailed a passing cab and in a moment they were en route to her conapt.

It struck him as beautifully decorated; he roamed about the living room, inspecting a vase here, a wall-hanging there, books, a small jade statue of Li Po. 'Nice,' he said. However, he found himself alone; Miss Fisher had slipped off into the other room to, ahem, disgorge.

Presently she returned, her beaming, warm smile manifesting itself cheerfully in his direction. 'I have some very fine, aged, imported Siddon's sogum,' she said, holding up the flask. 'Care for some?'

'Guess not.' He picked up an LP record of Beethoven cello and piano sonatas. Just think, he thought. Someday, a couple of centuries from now, these will be erased; the Library in Vienna will receive back the original blotchy, tormented note-pages which Beethoven with murderous labor and pain copied from the last printed edition of the score. But, he reflected, Beethoven will also live again; one day he would call up anxiously from within his coffin.

115

But for what? To erad some of the finest music ever written. What a dreadful destiny.

'Want me to put those on the phonograph?' Ann Fisher asked.

'Fine,' he said.

'These are so lovely.' She put the earliest one on, Opus Five Number One; they both listened but after a moment she became restive; obviously attentive listening was not her style. 'Do you think,' she asked him, strolling about the living room, 'that the Hobart Phase will peter out eventually? And normal time will restore itself?'

'I hope so,' he said.

'But you gain. You were dead once. Weren't you?'

'Can you tell?' he said, nettled.

'I don't mean to offend you. But you are about fifty, aren't you? So you have a longer life, this way; in fact you have two complete lives. Are you enjoying this one more than the first?'

'My problem,' he said candidly, 'is with my wife.'

'She's much younger than you?'

He was silent; he inspected a Venusian snoffle-fur-bound copy of English poetry of the seventeenth century. 'Do you like Henry Vaughan?' he asked her.

'Didn't he write the poem about seeing eternity? "I saw eternity the other night"?'

Opening the volume, Sebastian said, 'Andrew Marvell. *To His Coy Mistress.* "But at my back I always hear time's wingèd chariot hurrying near, and yonder all before us lie deserts of vast eternity."' He shut the volume, convulsively. 'I saw it, that eternity; outside of time and space, wandering among things so big – ' He ceased; he still found it pointless to discuss his afterlife experience.

116

'I think you're just trying to hurry me into bed,' Ann Fisher said. 'The title of the poem – I get the message.'

He quoted, ' "The worms shall try that long-preserved virginity." ' Smiling, he turned toward her; perhaps she was right. But the poem kept him from anticipation; he knew it too well – knew it and the experience it envisioned. ' "The grave's a fine and private place," ' he half-snarled, feeling it all return, the smell of the grave, the chill, the cramped, evil darkness. ' "But none, I think, do there embrace." '

'Then let's hop into bed,' Miss Fisher said practically. And led the way to her bedroom.

Afterward they lay naked, with only the sheet over them; Ann Fisher smoked in silence, the red glow identifying her presence. He found it peaceful, now; his grim tension had departed.

'But it wasn't eternity for you,' Ann Fisher said distantly, as if deep down in her own meditations. 'You were dead only a finite time. What, fifteen years?'

'It feels the same,' he said brusquely. 'I try to make this point, and no one who hasn't gone through it understands. When you're outside of the categories of perception, time and space, then it's endless; *no time passes*, no matter how long you wait. And it can be infinite bliss or infinite torment, according to your relationship with it.'

'With what? God?'

'The Anarch Peak called it God,' he said pondering, 'when he came back.' And then, paralyzed, he realized – absolutely and utterly – what he had said.

After a time Ann Fisher said, 'I remember him. Years ago. He founded Udi, this big group-mind cult. I didn't know he was alive again.'

117

What could he say? Words, he thought in terror, that could not be explained. They meant only one thing; they told it all, that Peak had been reborn, that he, Sebastian Hermes had been present. So the Anarch was at the Flask of Hermes Vitarium. In which case, having said this, he might as well discuss it openly.

'We revived him today,' he said, and wondered what this would mean to her; he did not know her, not really at all, and it could mean nothing, just an idle topic, or something of theological interest, or on the other hand – he would have to take the chance. Mathematically, it was unlikely that Ann Fisher had any connections with anyone materially interested in the Anarch; he would be playing the odds with her, from now on. 'He's back at the vitarium; that's why I can't stay here with you – I told him I'd be talking to him again tonight.'

'Could I come along?' Ann Fisher asked. 'I've never seen an old-born in his first hours back . . . I understand they have a certain, special expression on their faces. From what they've seen. They're still watching something else, something vast. And they sometimes say epigrammatic, enigmatic things, like, I am you. Or, it isn't. Sort of Zen-satori cryptic utterances that mean everything to them, but to us – ' In the dim nocturnal light she gestured vigorously, obviously intrigued by the subject. 'To us it conveys nothing . . . yes, I agree; you have to go through it yourself.' She hopped from the bed, padded barefoot to the closet, got out a bra and underpants, began rapidly to dress.

Gradually, feeling old and weary, he, too, began to dress.

I've made a mistake, he realized. I'll never get rid of her, now; something about her is lethal in its persistence. If I could reverse just that one segment of time, my

118

saying those few words . . . he watched her put on an angora sweater and tight, tapered pants, then again resumed his own dressing. She's smart; she's attractive; and she knows she's on to something, he reflected. Below the verbal level I've managed to convey to her that this is *different*.

God knows, he thought, how far she'll go before her interest is satisfied.

Chapter 11

Nothing can be predicated of God literally or affirmatively. Literally God is *not*, because He transcends being.
– Erigena

By cab they flew across Burbank, to the Flask of Hermes Vitarium.

From the outside the store looked empty and closed and dark, and totally deserted for the night. Seeing it, he had trouble believing that the Anarch Peak lay on a makeshift bed inside, presumably with at least Dr Sign in attendance.

'This is exciting,' Ann Fisher said, pressing her lean body close against him and shivering. 'It's cold; let's hurry and get inside. I'm dying to see him; you have no idea how much I really appreciate this.'

'We can't stay long,' Sebastian said, as he unlocked the door.

The door swung open. And there, pointing a pistol at him, stood Bob Lindy, blinking like an owl and at least as watchful.

'It's me,' Sebastian said; he was startled, but it gratified him that his staff was so prepared. 'And a friend.' He shut and locked the door after them.

'That gun scares me,' Ann Fisher said nervously.

Sebastian said, 'Put it away, Lindy. That wouldn't stop anybody anyhow.'

'It might,' Lindy said. He led the way back to the work area; the inner door opened and all at once light shone out. 'He's much stronger; he's been dictating to Cheryl.' He surveyed Ann Fisher critically, and with cynical caution. 'Who's she?'

'A customer,' Sebastian said. 'Negotiating for Mrs Tilly M. Benton.' He walked over to the bed; Ann Fisher followed, breathlessly. 'Your Mightiness,' he said formally. 'You're coming along okay, I hear.'

The Anarch, his voice much stronger now, said, 'I have so much I want to get down; why don't you own a tape recorder? Anyhow, I can't tell you how much I appreciate Miss Vale's facility as an amanuensis. In fact, all the hospitality and attention you've afforded me.'

'Are you actually the Anarch Peak?' Ann Fisher asked, in an awed voice. 'It was so long ago . . . do you feel that way, too?'

'I only know,' the Anarch said dreamily, 'that I've had a priceless opportunity. God has provided me – and others, too – with more than he allowed Paul to witness. I *must* get it all down.' He appealed to Sebastian. 'Don't you suppose you could get me a tape recorder, Mr Hermes? I feel myself forgetting . . . it's vanishing from within my grasp, melting away.' He clenched his fists spasmodically.

To Bob Lindy, Sebastian said, 'It ought to be possible to round up a tape recorder. We used to have one; what happened to it?'

'The lifters jammed,' Lindy said. 'It's back where we got it, being serviced.'

'That was months ago,' Cheryl Vale said severely.

'Well,' Lindy said, 'nobody's had the time to pick it up. We can get it tomorrow morning.'

'But it's departing,' the Anarch wailed. 'Please help me.'

121

Ann Fisher said, 'I own a tape recorder. Back at my conapt. Not a very good one – '

'For voice recording,' Sebastian said, 'fidelity doesn't matter.' He made a quick decision. 'Could you be prevailed on to go get it? And bring it back here?'

'Don't forget tape,' Lindy said. 'Around twelve seven-inch reels.'

'I'd love to,' Ann Fisher said, her eyes intense. 'To be able to help in something as wonderful as this – ' She squeezed Sebastian's arm briefly, then started at a trot toward the front of the store. 'You will let me in when I get back here with it, won't you?'

'We need it,' Bob Lindy said. To Sebastian he said, 'The old guy's talking so fast Cheryl can't really get it down; it's coming out a mile a minute.' He added, mystified, 'None of the others rattled away like this. They usually just sort of sputter a while and then give up.'

Sebastian said, 'He wants to be understood.' He wants to do, he realized, what I wanted to do – and what I, like the others, gave up trying for. He'll wheedle and pester us until we *can* get it down. To him it was impressive. And as he let Ann Fisher out onto the sidewalk he could see by her feverish, illuminated expression that it impressed her, too.

'Half an hour,' she told him. And departed; her sharp heels clicked across the pavement; he saw her waving down an aircab and then he shut and locked the door once again.

Dr Sign, seated in a corner, taking a brief rest, said to him, 'I'm surprised, you bringing that girl here.'

'She's a girl,' Sebastian said, 'who incorporated a baby nine months ago and got me to go to bed with her tonight. She'll bring her tape recorder here, leave it off, and we'll probably never see her again.'

The vidphone rang.

Lifting an eyebrow, Sebastian reached for the receiver. Perhaps it was Lotta. 'Goodbye,' he said, hopefully.

On the screen an unknown man's face formed. 'Mr Hermes?' His voice was slow, extremely methodical. 'I'm not going to identify myself because it isn't necessary. My companion and I have this stake-out across the street from your vitarium.'

'Oh?' Sebastian said; he made his own voice casual. 'So?'

'We photographed the girl when you entered the building with her,' the man continued. 'The one who just now left by cab. We transmitted the photo to Rome and ran an ident-scan through our archives on it. I have here the info, back from Rome.' The man studied a sheet of paper; it obscured his face as he read from it. 'Her name's Ann McGuire; she's the daughter of the Chief Librarian at the People's Tropical Library. The Erads use her from time to time in this area.'

'I see,' Sebastian said mechanically.

'So they've got to you,' the man finished. 'You'll have to get the Anarch right out and somewhere else. Before they make a flying-wedge raid on you. The Erads, I mean. Okay, Mr Hermes?'

'Okay,' he said, and hung up.

Presently Dr Sign said, 'Maybe my house.'

'Maybe it's hopeless,' Sebastian said.

Bob Lindy, who had also listened in on the vidcall, said, 'Get the old man into an aircar; we've got three on the roof. *Get him out of here* – move!' His voice rose to a shout.

'You do it,' Sebastian said thickly.

Both Dr Sign and Bob Lindy disappeared into the back; standing inert, Sebastian heard them getting the

123

Anarch out of bed; he heard the Anarch protesting – he wanted to keep dictating – and then he heard them making their way up the stairs to the roof field.

The noise of an aircar motor. Then silence.

Cheryl Vale approached him. 'They're gone. The three of them. Do you think – '

'I think,' Sebastian said, 'that I'm a mouth-hole.'

'And with you married,' Cheryl said. 'To that sweet little girl.'

Ignoring her, Sebastian said, 'That buyer in Italy. Giacometti. I think he's going to be our customer.'

'Yes, you owe them something.'

And I was just in bed with her, he thought. An hour ago. How can anybody do that? Use themselves like that? 'You can see,' he said, 'why Lotta left me.' He felt totally futile. And defeated, in a way new to him. Not a conventional defeat, but something intimate and personal; something which reached deep within him, as a man and as a human being.

I will sometime see that woman again, he said to himself. And I will do something to her. In return.

'Go home,' he said to Cheryl.

'I intend to.' She gathered up her coat and purse, unlocked the door and disappeared out into the night darkness. He was alone.

In one day, he thought, they got to both of us; they got Lotta and then they got me.

He hunted around the store until he found Lindy's gun, left behind, and then he seated himself by the front counter where he could watch the door. Time passed. For this I returned from death, he thought. To do infinite harm in a finite world. He continued to wait.

Twenty minutes later a tap-tap sounded on the front

door. He rose, put the gun in his coat pocket, and went stiffly to answer it.

"Bye,' Ann Fisher said, gasping for breath as he opened the door and she squeezed into the store carrying her tape recorder, plus a box of tapes. 'Shall I take it in the back?' she asked. 'Where he is?'

'Fine,' he said; again he seated himself at the counter. Ann Fisher passed on by him, lugging her load; he made no move to help her. He merely sat waiting, as he had been doing.

After a moment she returned; he sensed her standing by him, tall and lithe, not saying anything.

'He's gone,' Ann said at last.

'He never was here. It was faked. For your benefit.' He had to play it by ear. Strangely, he felt frightened. Weak and scared.

'I don't get it,' Ann said.

'We received a tip,' he said. 'About you.'

'Oh?' Her voice sharpened; it underwent a fundamental, almost metabolic change. 'Just what did they have to say about me?' He did not answer. 'I'd appreciate knowing,' Ann said. 'Anonymous information – I have a right to know.' He still said nothing. 'Well,' she said, then, 'I guess you don't need my tape recorder. Or me. If you don't trust me.'

He said, without looking up, 'What did your mother do to my wife at the Library today?'

'Nothing,' she said, matter-of-factly; she seated herself in one of the customers' chairs, her legs crossed. Presently she fished out a package of cigarette butts and lit one, inhaling, breathing out, inhaling.

'It was enough,' he said, 'to cause her to leave me.'

'Oh, they got frightened, she and her cop-friend. She didn't leave you because of what mother did; that cop's

125

been trying to get her into bed for months. We know where they are; they're holed up in a motel somewhere in San Fernando.'

'As you and I were,' he said. 'A little while ago.'

She had no comment about that; she merely continued smoking: the cigarette grew longer and longer. 'So now what?' Ann asked finally. 'You moved him; we find him. There're only a finite number of places he can be. And we have a tail on that aircar that left here; I presume you have him in that.'

'There was no Arnold Oxnard Ford,' he said. 'Was there?'

'In a sense, yes. That was the name of my first husband. He left me last year.' She sounded noncommittal, as if nothing of importance were taking place. And perhaps, he thought, she's right. He rose to his feet, walked toward her. Glancing up, she said, 'And now?'

'Get out of my store,' he said.

'Look,' Ann said, 'be intelligent. We're a buyer. We want to be in a position to erad everything he says; that's all we want . . . we're not going to injure him. We don't need to do that; it's your cop-friend who uses a gun, and that technician of yours. Where is that gun now?'

'I have it,' he said. 'So get out.' He held the door to the street open. Waiting.

Ann sighed. 'I see no barrier to our relationship. Lotta is shacking up with someone else; you're alone. I'm alone. What's the problem? We've done nothing illegal; your wife is a phobic child, scared by everything – you're making a mistake, taking her neurotic fears seriously; you ought to tell her, swim or drown. I would.' She lit another cigarette. 'It's that cop-friend of yours, that Joe Tinbane, you ought to be after; doesn't it make you sore, him sleeping with your wife? That's what they're doing

126

right now, and you're mad at me.' Her tone was brittle and accusing, but without heat or even color. A neutral stating of facts. Devastating, he thought. I can't stand much more of it; this isn't the same woman I slept with; nobody can change that much. 'I think,' Ann said, 'you and I ought to forget this quarrel – it isn't doing either of us any good, and then – ' She shrugged. 'Pick up where we left off. We could have a very rewarding relationship, very wholesome and complete. Despite your age.'

He gave her a brutal, violent smack across the mouth.

Unruffled, she bent to retrieve her cigarette; she was, however, shaking. 'Your marriage,' she continued, 'is finished, whether you like it or not. Your old life is over and a new one – '

'With you?' he said.

'It could be. I find you attractive – after a fashion. If we can get this matter regarding the Anarch out of the way, then – ' She gestured. 'I don't see what would obstruct a gainful and quite mutually satisfying relationship between us. Except for this one problem, that of the Anarch, about which you have so much hostility and distrust, I still think we were off to a quite good beginning. Despite your hitting me. I can even overlook that; I don't think you're really like that; that's not you.'

The vidphone rang.

'Aren't you going to answer it?' Ann Fisher inquired.

'No,' he said.

Going over to the vidphone, Ann lifted the receiver. 'Flask of Hermes Vitarium,' she said, with professional resonance. 'We're closed, now; could you call back in the morning?'

A male voice, unfamiliar to Sebastian, said, 'Mrrrrr.' He caught the sound but not the words; he sat impassively, weighed down, his mind drifting. Not Lotta, he

127

thought. The thing is, Ann Fisher is right; my marriage is over because she can *make* it be over. All she has to do is find Lotta and tell her about our going to bed together. And she will paint it as she has just now: as the beginning of something enduring.

In one evening, he thought, this girl has imperiled both my business and my life as I lead it. A day ago I couldn't have believed this.

To him, Ann Fisher said, 'It's a Mr Carl Gantrix.'

'I don't know him,' he said.

She put her hand over the receiver. 'He knows you have the Anarch Peak; it's about that. I think he's a customer.' She held the receiver of the vidphone toward him.

There was no choice. He got up, came over, accepted the receiver. 'Goodbye,' he said. Listlessly.

'Mr Hermes,' Mr Gantrix said. 'Nice to have known you.'

'Likewise.'

'I am contacting you,' Gantrix said, 'officially, for His Mightiness, Ray Roberts, who, at this moment, I am happy to say, is aboard a jet on his pilg to the WUS; he will arrive in Los Angeles ten minutes from now.'

Sebastian said nothing. He merely heard.

'Mr Hermes,' Gantrix said, 'I've called at this unusual hour on the offchance hope that you'd be on your premises. I would in fact speculate that you are busily at work, reviving and caring for the Anarch; am I right in this regard?'

'Who told you,' Sebastian said, 'that we have the Anarch?'

'Ah . . . that would be telling.' Gantrix's face on the vidscreen was sly.

'Your informant was wrong,' Sebastian said.

128

'No, I don't think so.' Again the almost bantering, teasing slyness, as if Gantrix was playing with him. As if Gantrix held all the cards and knew it. 'I, myself,' Gantrix said, 'am already here in the WUS, in Los Angeles, where I will shortly again join Mr Roberts. I do have time, however, to conduct this business matter with you; His Mightiness, Mr Roberts, has instructed me to negotiate for the purchase of the Anarch, and I am so doing. What is he listed at in your catalog?'

'Forty billion poscreds,' Sebastian said.

'That's rather high.'

'Forty-five billion,' Sebastian said, 'with the salesman's commission.'

Standing behind him, Ann Fisher leaned down and said, 'You made a mistake, naming a price.'

'It's a preposterous price,' Sebastian said. 'Nobody could pay it. Not even the Uditi.'

'Not really,' Ann said. 'Not for them. Not for what they're getting.'

'I'll be by your place shortly,' Gantrix said, 'and we can perhaps shave the price a trifle.' He did not seem fazed. Ann was right. 'Hello, then, Mr Hermes, for the time being.'

'Hello,' Sebastian said, and hung up.

'You feel so guilty for hitting me,' Ann said, 'that you're now punishing yourself. By giving up.'

'Maybe so,' he said. But that price; he could hardly believe the Uditi could meet it. 'I'll raise the price,' he said, 'when Gantrix gets here.'

'No you won't,' Ann said. 'You'll capitulate. Anyhow, you don't know if you still have possession of the Anarch. I think you better let me handle this, Sebastian; you've had it.'

'You want,' he said, 'to handle everything.'

'Why not? I'm intelligent; I'm highly educated; I've had a good deal of training in business procedure. You're worn out. Go in the back of the shop and lie down; I'll wake you when Gantrix gets here, and you can act as an adviser to me. You need someone who can take charge when you get dispirited like this. I don't think Lotta could do that for you. That's why she lost out.'

He got up, left the store, walked across the dark street. Searching for the stake-out. For a time he stood, waving his arms, and then from a building to his right a man emerged, the man who had called him to warn him about Ann. 'I need help,' Sebastian said.

'In what regard?' the dark-haired Italian-looking man said. 'To take care of that McGuire girl?'

'You probably saw our aircar take off from our roof, a little while ago.'

'Yes,' the man said, 'and we saw the Library bus go after it.'

Sebastian said, 'I don't know if we still have the Anarch or not.'

'We're waiting to hear about that,' the man said. 'It looked to us, at the stake-out, as if your aircar had a headstart. And it was really moving. Your driver must be an expert.'

That would be Bob Lindy, Sebastian thought. He drives like a maniac. 'How will you know?' he asked the man. 'I have to find out because a buyer, representing Ray Roberts, is on his way here.'

'Gantrix,' the man said, nodding. 'We monitored the vidcall from Gantrix; we know about that. That's quite a price you set; is that your real price? Or was that just to tie up the Uditi?'

Sebastian said, 'I had no idea they could raise it.'

'They can't. Not in WUS poscreds, anyhow. Gantrix

130

will try to get you to take FNM scrip; as you know, it's virtually worthless.' He added, 'You failed to specify.'

'If we don't still have the Anarch,' Sebastian said, 'it doesn't matter.'

'I can notify you as soon as we hear. We sent one of our own cars after the Library's; we should hear any time, now. Stall Gantrix until we phone you.'

'Okay.' Sebastian nodded. Then, awkwardly, he said, 'I appreciate all your help.'

The man said, 'You've got to get rid of that McGuire girl. Can't you get control of her? She's tough; she's a pro – but you're bigger than *her*.'

'What good would throwing her out on the street do?' It seemed futile to him. Pointless. 'She's already told the Library what she found out; there isn't any more harm she can do.'

'She'll tip your hand to Gantrix; that's what she'll do.' The man's voice rose in indignation. 'She'll take charge of the negotiations, and the first you know, she'll have sold the Anarch and it'll all be over.'

A second dark figure emerged from the building on the right; the two stake-out men from the Rome syndicate conferred.

'She's using your store vidphone to call the Library,' the first man said to Sebastian. 'Telling the Erad Council about Gantrix, his meeting with you at the vitarium.'

The other man, earphones still on his head, added, 'And she's telling the Library that she's planted a bomb – she brought it in as part of her phony tape recorder – somewhere on the premises. Which she can detonate by remote any time she feels like.'

'What's that for?' the first man asked him. 'To blow up who? Herself?'

'She didn't say. The Erad at the Library who took her

call seemed to know. Wait.' He tapped his earphones. 'She's making a second call.' He was silent and then he said, 'This is to her husband.'

'Her husband,' Sebastian said. So even that part wasn't true. He felt real hatred for her, deep and abiding.

'This is very interesting,' the man with the headphones said after a time. 'She has a whole bunch of projects humming away. First, she wants your wife, Mrs Hermes, located and watched. Do you know where your wife is, Mr Hermes?'

'No,' he said.

'Second,' the man continued, 'she wants some man named Joe Tinbane killed. And lastly, if that happens, she wants the Erads to pick up your wife so she can't come back to you. Annie McGuire intends to stick around you until the Library gets possession of the Anarch and then – ' He glanced at Sebastian. 'She says she intends to kill you. For what you did to her. What did you do to her, Mr Hermes?'

'I slapped her,' he said.

'Not hard enough,' the man with the headphones said.

Sebastian turned and made his way back across the street, to the vitarium. When he entered he found Ann seated a good distance from the vidphone; she smiled briskly at him. 'And where did you go?' she asked. 'I looked out but it was too dark; I couldn't see.'

'I walked around and thought,' he said.

'And what did you decide?'

'I'm still trying to decide,' he said.

Ann said, 'There's really nothing for you to decide.'

'Yes there is,' he said. 'What to do about you. That's what I have to decide.'

'I'm helping you,' Ann said ingratiatingly. 'Go lie down and get some rest. I'll tell you when Gantrix gets here.

132

And – ' She rose, put her hand on his arm, patted him. 'Don't worry so. If you've lost the Anarch then the Library has him, and that's not so bad; they'll know what to do. And if you still have him – ' She hesitated, calculating; her intense blue eyes flickered mightily. 'I can handle that very well. The negotiations with Carl Gantrix.'

Going into the rear of the store he lay down on the bed which the Anarch had so recently occupied; he stared up sightlessly at the ceiling. My whole store, he thought. She can destroy it and me, everything; there's nothing about me she can't get into and control. Why can't I stop her? he asked himself. I have a gun now; I could kill her.

But he was trained to bring people back to life, not to kill them; his whole orientation, everything he believed, involved bestowing life. On everyone possible, without distinction; the vitarium never asked for a pedigree on the old-born it dug up; it never inquired into whether they *ought* to live again.

It's not that easy to kill a person, he thought. That's not what people do; there has to be another answer. But hitting her hadn't affected her – except to get him placed on her permanent food-list, to be paid back. I don't think I can physically drive her away, he decided. Not if she intends to hang around; words have no influence on her, nor menace to her physical safety. He wondered, Where is the bomb? Here in this room? God, he thought. I have to do something; I can't lie here; I have to act.

In the front room the vidphone rang.

He sprang up, thinking, I can't let her get that. He sprinted, panting, into the receptionist's area; there she sat, already the receiver against her ear – he grabbed it away from her.

133

'They wouldn't talk to me anyhow,' Ann said philosophically. 'They said they'd talk only to you, whoever they are.' She added, 'I didn't like their tone or their voice; you really have some strange friends, if that's what they are.'

It was Bob Lindy. 'Can she hear me?' Lindy asked.

'No.' He carried the phone and the receiver as far away from her as the cord would allow. 'Go ahead,' he said.

'Can't you get rid of her?' Lindy demanded.

'Just go ahead,' he grated.

Lindy said, 'We ditched them. The car following us. It was a real dogfight, like World War One. I looped back and around, and then they looped; I did an Immelmann a couple of times . . . finally I got them going north, with me going south. By the time they turned around I was out of there. We set down just now; he's still in the car.'

'Don't tell me where you are,' Sebastian said.

'Hell no, not with the screwy dame there. She isn't scared of you a bit, is she? Women are never scared of men they've been to bed with. But she's scared of me; I saw it in her eyes when I had that gun on her. You want me to come back? I can leave Sign with the Anarch and join you at the store, say in about forty minutes.'

Sebastian said, 'I've got to handle it myself. Thanks. Call me back two hours from now. Hello.' He rang off.

Standing by the window with her arms folded, Ann said, 'So you still have possession of the Anarch. Well, well.'

'How do you know that?' he said.

'When you told him "Don't tell me where you are." ' She turned away from the window and toward him. 'What is it you're going to handle yourself?'

'You,' Sebastian said.

134

Chapter 12

We do not know what God is . . . because He is infinite and therefore objectively unknowable. God Himself does not know what He is because He is not anything. – Erigena

They faced each other.

'I have a bomb hidden here in the vitarium,' Ann said. 'So don't try to use that gun on me. And even if you get me out of here, I can still detonate the bomb; I can kill you and Carl Gantrix, and if I do that the Uditi will go after your wife; they'll blame you and they're very vengeful.'

He said thoughtfully, 'You won't detonate the bomb while you're still here. Because that would kill you, too, and you're too vital, too active, to deliberately die.'

'Thank you.' She smiled her crinkly smile. 'That's flattering.'

A tap sounded at the front door.

'It's Mr Gantrix,' Ann said; she moved toward the door. 'Shall I let him in?' In answer to her own question she said, 'Yes, I think it would clear the air to have a third party here. Then you wouldn't be making all sorts of violent threats.' She opened the door.

'Wait,' he said.

She glanced up questioningly.

'Don't do anything to Lotta,' he said, 'and I'll let you have the Anarch.'

Her eyes ignited, flared violently, triumphantly.

'But I want her back first,' he said. 'Physically back in

135

my possession, before I give you the Anarch. I don't want your word.' To her, words meant nothing.

Pushing the half-open door aside, a sloppily dressed, rather gaunt and tall Negro said tentatively, 'Mr Hermes? Sebastian Hermes?' He peered into the front room of the vitarium. 'Good to finally meet you, sir, face to face. Goodbye, Mr Hermes.' He walked toward Sebastian, his hand extended.

'Just a moment, Mr Gantrix,' Sebastian said, ignoring the proffered hand. To Ann he said, 'You understand the agreement?' He fixed his gaze on her, trying to read her face; it was impossible to guess what was going on in her mind: he couldn't gauge her response.

'I can see I'm interrupting,' Gantrix said, jovially. 'I'll go take a seat – ' He strode toward one of the chairs. ' – and read, until you're finished.' He glanced at his wristwatch. 'But I do have to meet His Mightiness, Ray Roberts, in an hour.'

Ann said, 'No one has "physical possession" of anyone else.'

'Words,' Sebastian said. 'You use them sadistically; you know what I mean. I just want her back, here, not somewhere else like a motel or the Library, but here in the vitarium.'

'Is the Anarch Peak on the premises?' Gantrix spoke up. 'Could I tiptoe in and have a look at him while you good people carry on your discussion?'

'He's not on the premises,' Sebastian said. 'We were forced to move him. For purposes of safety.'

'But you do have actual and legal custody,' Gantrix said.

'Yes,' Sebastian said. 'I guarantee it.'

Ann said, 'What makes you think I can deliver Lotta

136

back to you? She left of her own free will. I have no idea where she is, except that somewhere in San – '

'But you will find the motel,' he said. 'Eventually. You phoned the Library and told the Erads to keep working until they located her.'

The girl's face blanched.

'I know the content of both calls,' Sebastian said. 'To the Library and to your husband.'

'Those were strictly private,' Ann said sulkily and with indignation – but also, he noticed, with fear. For the first time she had lost control; she was afraid of him. And with reason. Having knowledge of the calls, of her real intentions, had changed him; he felt the newness in him, and Ann evidently could see it. 'I was just griped,' she said. 'Nobody's going to kill Joe Tinbane; that was just talk. You upset me terribly when you hit me; no man has ever hit me in my entire life. And what I said about sticking with you – ' She chose her words scrupulously. He could sense her sorting among the possibilities. 'Frankly, I want to stay with you because I'm attracted to you. I had to give my husband an excuse; I had to tell him *something*.'

'Get the bomb,' he said.

'Hmmm,' she said reflectively, again folding her arms. 'I wonder if I ought to do that.' She seemed less frightened, now.

His attention captured, Carl Gantrix again spoke up. 'Bomb? What bomb?' He stood up nervously.

'Turn the Anarch over to us,' Ann said, 'and I'll defuse the bomb.'

Impasse.

To Carl Gantrix, Ann said, 'I brought the bomb in here when the Anarch was here. To kill him.'

Staring at her, with horror, Gantrix said, 'W-why?'

137

'I'm from the Library,' Ann said. Puzzled by his reaction, she said, 'Doesn't Ray Roberts want the Anarch killed?'

'*Oh my god no!*' Gantrix said.

Both Sebastian and Ann Fisher stared at him, now.

'We revere the Anarch,' Gantrix said, stammering in his vehemence, his disclaim. 'He's our *saint* – the only one we've got. We've waited decades for his return; the Anarch will have all the ultimate wisdom of the afterlife; that's the entire purpose of Roberts' pilg: this is a holy journey, for the purpose of sitting at the feet of the Anarch and hearing his good news.' He walked toward Ann Fisher, now, his fingers clutching; she ducked away, avoiding him. 'The *news*,' Gantrix said. 'The glorious news of the fusion in eternity of all souls. *Nothing else matters but this news.*'

Ann said faintly, 'The Library – '

'You Erads,' Gantrix said; his voice was harsh, bleak with disdain. 'Tyrants. Petty rulers of this earth. What business is it of yours? You intend to eradicate the news which he has brought back?' He turned to Sebastian. 'The Anarch, you say, is physically safe, now?'

'Yes,' Sebastian said. 'They tried to get him; in fact they almost did.' Had he been wrong about Roberts? Was this true? He had a strange, eerie feeling of unreality, as if Carl Gantrix was not actually here, not genuinely saying anything; it was like a dream, Gantrix's words, his dismay and outrage, his avowed dislike of the Library. But if it were true, he thought, then we can do business; we can go ahead and purvey the Anarch to him. Everything is changed.

To Sebastian, Carl Gantrix said, 'Does she have the detonator of the bomb on her?'

'The Library can detonate the bomb,' Ann said huskily.

138

'No,' Sebastian said. 'It's on her.' To Ann he said, 'That's what you said in your vidcall to the Library.'

'Do you think she would let herself be killed by it?' Gantrix asked him.

'No,' Sebastian said. 'I'm positive; she meant to get out of here first.'

Gantrix said, 'Then we can proceed this way: I'll hold her arms while you search for the detonator.' He gripped the girl, then, in an iron-rigid hold. Too rigid, Sebastian thought; he noted that. And then he understood his sense of unreality about Gantrix; it was a robot, operating on remote.

No wonder 'Gantrix' was not frightened by the bomb, now that he – or rather his operator – knew that the Anarch was away and safe. It's only me, Sebastian realized, who'll be killed; me and Ann Fisher McGuire.

'I suggest,' the roby said, 'that you search her as quickly as you can.' Its voice was firm with authority.

Sebastian said, 'Annie, don't detonate it. For your own sake. It won't accomplish anything; this isn't a man – it's only a robot. The Uditi won't seek blood because of the destruction of a robot.'

'Is that true?' she asked 'Gantrix.'

'Yes,' it said. 'I am Carl Junior. Please, Mr Hermes; get the triggering device away from her. We have business to conduct and I have less than an hour.'

He found the mechanism in her purse. After a fifteen-minute search. Thanks to the robot's tight grip on the girl she had no chance of reaching it; they had never genuinely been in danger.

'You have that, now,' Ann said, with tilted composure, 'but my instructions to the Library will stand. About Joe Tinbane and about your wife.' She faced him defiantly, now, as the robot released her.

139

'And about me, too?' Sebastian asked. 'Sticking to me, staying with me, to – '

'Yes, yes, yes,' she said, massaging her arms. She brushed her hair back, smoothed it, shook her head vigorously. 'I think he's lying,' she said, making a quick, furtive gesture at Carl Junior. 'If you turn the Anarch over to him you'll get nothing but worthless FNM poscreds and then they'll announce in a few weeks that the Anarch is ailing and then he'll disappear. He'll be dead. A little while ago, before *it* came, you offered me a quid pro quo. I'll now accept; you'll get Lotta back – as you specified, physically here at the vitarium. And we receive the Anarch.' She studied him, waiting for his answer.

He said, 'But if Udi gets the Anarch – '

'Oh, you conceivably might see Lotta again anyhow. I'm not threatening you; I'm offering you an absolute guarantee.' Once again Ann seemed poised, in control of herself. 'We'll put the resources of the Library behind persuading her to leave Joe Tinbane and returning to you; it won't be coercion; it'll be nothing more than making her appreciate how much you care for her. How much you've given up for her sake. You gave up forty-five billion poscreds to get her back; she'll understand that . . . some of the Erads are very good at making intricate issues clear.'

'I'll take you elsewhere,' Sebastian said to the robot Carl Junior. 'Where we can work the sale out.' He seized Ann Fisher by the arm, led her in one swift motion from the store and out onto the sidewalk. The robot Carl Junior silently followed.

As he locked up the vitarium, Ann said, 'You stupid foodhead. You stupid, stupid foodhead.' Her voice rang sharply, as he and Carl Junior started toward the rickety outside stairs which led to the roof and his parked car.

'We have always pitted ourselves against the Library,' Carl Junior said as they ascended the unpainted wooden stairs. 'They want to erad the new teachings of the Anarch; they want to expunge every trace of the transcendental doctrine which he has brought back. Which I *presume* he has brought back. Is that so, Mr Hermes? Has his discourse so far indicated a religious experience of the magnitude and depth?'

'Very much so,' Sebastian said. 'He's been dictating and talking from the moment we revived him, to everyone in sight.'

They reached his parked car; he unlocked the door and the robot got inside.

'What power does the Library have over your wife?' Carl Junior asked as the car shot up into the night. 'As much as that girl alleged?'

'I don't know,' Sebastian said. He wondered how well Joe Tinbane could protect Lotta, while she remained with him. Probably fairly well, he decided. Joe Tinbane had gotten her out of the Library in the first place . . . he could therefore be expected, reasonably, to keep her from being hauled back. How persistent, really, would the Library be? After all, this was a side issue, a vendetta on the part of Ann Fisher, not a fundamental aspect of Library policy.

And it appeared to be the Erad Council which dictated policy, not Ann.

'A threat,' he said aloud to the robot. 'Intimidation. A power-oriented woman always hints at violence unless you do what she says.' He thought about Lotta, and how different she was; how impossible it would be for her to utilize the intimidation of hinted-at force to get what she wanted.

141

I'm lucky, he thought, to have a wife like that. Or *was* lucky. Whichever it turns out to be. With the help of God.

'If the Library injures your wife,' the robot seated beside him said, 'you will probably retaliate. Against that girl personally. Am I wrong or am I right? Choose one.'

Sebastian said tightly, 'You're right.'

'That girl must realize that. It will probably deter her.'

'Probably,' he agreed. A bluff, he thought, that's what it is; Ann Fisher must know what I'd do to her. 'Let's talk about other topics,' he said to the robot; he was afraid to think further in that direction. 'I'm taking you to my conapt,' he said. 'The Anarch is not there, but we can work out price and the method of custody-transfer. We have a standard operating procedure; I see no reason why it can't be applied in this case.'

'We trust you,' the robot said warmly. 'But of course we'll need to see the Anarch before we pay over the money. To certify that you do in fact have possession of him and that he's alive. And we'd like to talk briefly with him.'

'No,' Sebastian said. 'You can see him but not talk to him.'

'Why not?' The robot regarded him curiously.

'What the Anarch has to say,' Sebastian said, 'isn't a factor in this sale. It never is; the business of a vitarium isn't conducted on that basis.'

After a pause the robot said, 'So we must take your word for it that the Anarch brought something of value back.'

'That's correct,' he agreed.

'At the price you're asking – '

'It makes no nevermind,' Sebastian said. He always

had a canny sense about this aspect of his business; he never budged.

The robot said, 'Payment will be made to you in our own currency. In banknotes of the Free Negro Municipality.'

As Ann Fisher warned me, Sebastian thought with a chill. In this instance she told the truth. And the Rome party – they warned me, too. 'In WUS notes,' he said.

'We deal only in our own specie.' The robot's voice was flat. Final. 'I have no power to negotiate on any other basis. If you insist on WUS notes, then let me off. I'll have to report to His Mightiness Mr Roberts that we couldn't reach an agreement.'

'Then he goes to the People's Topical Library,' Sebastian said. And, he thought, I get my wife back.

'The Anarch would not want that,' Carl Junior said.

True, Sebastian realized. However, he said, 'We're required to make the decision; we possess the legal right, in these cases.'

'There has never been a case like this before,' the robot said, 'in the history of the world. Except,' he hastily amended, 'once. But that happened long ago.'

'Can't you help me get my wife back?' Sebastian demanded. 'Don't the Uditi have a corps of commandos for operations like this?'

'The Offspring exist only for vengeance,' the robot said dispassionately. 'And anyhow we are not strong in the WUS. Back home it would be different.'

Lotta, he thought. Did I lose you? To the Library?

And then, strangely, he found himself contemplating – not his wife – but Ann Fisher. The earlier hours, when they had walked the evening streets window-shopping. When they had fiercely besported themselves in bed. I

143

shouldn't remember that, he realized. That was faked; she had been given a job to do.

But it had proved good, for a time. Before the power-play manifested itself, and the chic, soft exterior ebbed away to reveal the iron.

'An attractive girl, that Library agent,' the robot said, acutely.

'Misleading,' he said gruffly.

'Isn't it always? You buy the wrappings. It's always a surprise. I personally found her typical of Library people, attractive and otherwise. Have you decided to let me off, or will you accept FNM currency?'

'I'll accept it,' he said. It didn't really matter; the ritual of business, which he had maneuvered through for so many years, meant nothing, now. Considering the greater context.

Maybe I can reach Joe Tinbane by way of the police radio system, he conjectured. *Warn him*. That would be enough; if Joe Tinbane knew that the Library was seeking him he'd do the rest . . . for himself and Lotta. And isn't that what matters? Not whether I get her back?

He lifted the receiver of his car's vidphone and dialed the number of Joe Tinbane's precinct station. 'I want to get hold of an Officer Tinbane,' he informed the police switchboard operator, when he had her. 'He's off duty, but this constitutes an emergency; his personal safety is involved.'

'Your name, sir.' The police operator waited.

Food, Sebastian thought. Joe'll think I'm trying to track him down to retrieve Lotta; he won't acknowledge my call. So there's no way I can get through, at least not via the police. 'Tell him,' he said to the operator, 'that Library agents are out after him. He'll understand.' He rang off. And wondered bleakly if the message would be conveyed.

'Is he your wife's paramour?' the robot inquired.

Sebastian, soundlessly, nodded.

'Your concern for him is most Christian,' the robot acknowledged. 'You are to be commended.'

Sebastian said curtly, 'This is the second calculated risk I've taken in less than two days.' Digging up the Anarch in advance of his rebirth had been risky enough; now he gambled that the Library wouldn't reach out and squash Tinbane and Lotta. It made him ill: he did not possess the mental constitution for such ventures, one right after the other. 'He'd do the same for me,' he said.

'Does he have a wife?' the robot asked. 'If so, perhaps you could arrange to make her your mistress, while he has Mrs Hermes.'

'I'm not interested in anyone else. Only Lotta.'

'You found that Library girl exciting. Even though she threatened you.' The robot's tone was all-knowing. *We want the Anarch before you run into her again.* I, at remote, have conferred by phone with His Mightiness Ray Roberts; I am instructed to obtain custody tonight. I am to stay with you rather than meeting His Mightiness.'

Sebastian said, 'You think I'm that vulnerable to Ann Fisher?'

'His Mightiness thinks so.'

I wouldn't be surprised, Sebastian thought unhappily, if His Mightiness were right.

At his conapt he switched on the phone relay; Bob Lindy's call-back to the vitarium would be switched here. All he had to do was wait. Meanwhile he prepared a quantity of prime sogum from his reserve, extra-special stock, imbibed it in an effort to raise both his physical energy-level and his morale.

'A weird custom,' the robot said, observing him. 'Before the Hobart Phase you would never have performed such an act before the eyes of another.'

'You're only a robot,' he said.

'But a human operator perceives through my sensory apparatus.'

The vidphone rang. So soon? he thought, glancing at his watch. 'Goodbye,' he said tensely into the receiver.

On the screen the image formed. It was not Bob Lindy; he faced the negotiator for the interested Rome party, Tony Giacometti. 'We followed you to your conapt,' Giacometti said. 'Hermes, you are deeply in spiritual debt to us; if it hadn't been for our stake-out, Miss Fisher would have blown up the Anarch with her bomb.'

'I realize that,' he said.

'In addition,' Giacometti continued, 'you would not have known the contents of the two phone calls she made from your vitarium. So we may have saved your wife's life and possibly yours.'

He repeated, 'I realize that.' The Rome buyer had him. 'What do you want me to do?' he said.

'We want the Anarch. We know he's with your technician, Bob Lindy. When Lindy got in touch with you we put a trace on the call; we know where he and the Anarch are. If we wanted to take the Anarch forcibly we could do that, but that's not the approach we traditionally favor. This purchase must be accomplished on an above-board ethical basis; Rome is not the People's Topical Library nor the Uditi – we do not, under any circumstances, operate as they do. You understand?'

'Yes.' He nodded.

Giacometti said, 'Morally, therefore, you are obliged

146

to make your sale to us, rather than to Carl Gantrix. May we send our buyer to your conapt to negotiate the transfer? We can be there in ten minutes.'

'Your method of operation,' he conceded, 'is effective.' What else could he do? Giacometti was right. 'Send your buyer over,' he said, and hung up.

The robot Carl Junior had observed the conversation and had heard his end. But, oddly, it did not appear perturbed.

'Your Anarch,' Sebastian said to it, 'would be dead, now. If they hadn't – '

'What you're forgetting,' the robot said patiently, as if explaining to a naïve child, 'is that the disposition of the Anarch depends on his own preference. *That* is the binding moral obligation. Your solution will be this: suspend the negotiations until your technician phones in, and then inquire of the Anarch as to whom he wishes to be sold.' It concluded confidently, 'We are certain that it will be ourselves.'

'Giacometti may not agree,' Sebastian said.

The robot said, 'The decision is not his. All right; the Rome people have placed this on an ethical basis; we are delighted. However, our ethical basis is superior to theirs.' It beamed.

Religion, Sebastian thought wearily. More ins and outs, more angles, than ordinary commerce. The casuistry had already gone beyond him; he gave up. 'I'll let you explain it to Giacometti when his buyer arrives,' he said. And imbibed, to fortify himself, an additional ten ounces of sogum.

'The Rome party,' the robot said, 'has had centuries more experience than we. Their buyer will be clever. I entreat you to avoid various diverse pitfalls which he may dig for you, as the expression goes.'

147

'You talk to him,' Sebastian said wearily. 'When he gets here. Explain to him what you spelled out to me.'

'Gladly.'

'You feel capable of out-arguing him?'

The robot said, 'God is on our side.'

'Is that what you're going to tell him?'

Pondering, the robot decided, 'He would cite apostolic succession. Free will, I believe, is the best argument. Civil law regards an old-born individual as the chattel of the vitarium which revives it. This however is not in accord with theological considerations; a human being cannot be owned, old-born or otherwise, since both possess a soul. I will therefore first establish the fact that the old-born Anarch has a soul, which the Rome buyer will admit, and then deduce from that premise that only the Anarch can dispose of himself, which is our position.' Again it pondered. For quite some time. 'His Mightiness, Mr Roberts,' it declared at last, 'agrees with this line of reasoning. I am in touch with him. If the Rome buyer can counter it – which is unlikely – then Mr Roberts himself, rather than I, Carl Gantrix, will operate Carl Junior; it will become Ray Junior. You can now see that we were prepared for this development from the beginning; for this, His Mightiness, Mr Roberts, has traveled to the West Coast. He will not return to the FNM empty-handed.'

'I wonder what Ann Fisher is doing,' Sebastian said, brooding.

'The Library is no longer a factor. The conflict as to who is the proper buyer has been reduced to two principals: ourselves and Rome.'

'She won't give up.' For her it would be impossible. He walked to the window of his living room, gazed out on the dark street below. Often, he and Lotta had done this;

148

every object in the conapt reminded him of her, every object and every spot.

A knock sounded at the living room door.

'Let him in,' Sebastian said to the robot. He seated himself, picked up a cigarette butt from the ashtray, lit it, and prepared to endure the imminent debate.

'Goodbye, Mr Hermes,' Anthony Giacometti said, entering; he had come himself . . . for the same reasons which had prompted Carl Gantrix to bring *his* principal. 'Goodbye, Gantrix,' he said sourly to the robot.

'Mr Hermes,' the robot declared, 'has asked me to inform you of the position he takes. He is tired and very worried about his wife – so he would rather not attempt to discuss this matter himself.'

To Sebastian, and not to the robot, Giacometti said, 'What does it mean? We came to an agreement on the phone.'

'Since then,' the robot said, 'I have informed him that only the Anarch can promise delivery.'

'Scott versus Tuler,' Giacometti said. 'Two years ago, the Superior Court of Contra Costa County. Judge Winslow presiding. The option of disposal of an old-born belongs to the owner of the reviving vitarium, not to his salesman, not to the old-born himself, not to – '

'We have here, however,' the robot interrupted, 'a spiritual matter. Not a juridical one. The civil law regarding old-borns is two hundred years out of date. Rome – yourselves – recognizes an old-born as possessing a soul; this is proved by the rite of Supreme Unction conferred when an old-born is severely injured or – '

'The vitarium does not dispose of a soul; it disposes of the soul's possessor: its body.'

'Negative,' the robot disagreed. 'A deader, before the soul re-enters it and reanimates it, cannot be dug up by a

149

vitarium. When it is only a body, a corpse of flesh, the vitarium cannot sell or – '

'The Anarch,' Giacometti said, 'was illegally dug up before returning to life. The Flask of Hermes Vitarium committed a crime. Under civil law, the Flask of Hermes Vitarium does not in fact own the Anarch. Johnson versus Scruggs, the California Supreme Court, last year.'

'Then who does own the Anarch?' the robot asked, puzzled.

'You claimed,' Giacometti said, and his eyes kindled, 'that this is not a juridical matter but a spiritual one.'

'Of course it's juridical! We need to establish legal ownership before either of us can buy.'

'Then you concede,' Giacometti said quietly, 'that Scott versus Tyler is the precedent for this transaction.'

The robot was silent. And then, when it resumed, there was a subtle but real difference in its voice. A deepening into greater power. His Mightiness Mr Roberts, Sebastian decided, was now operating it; Carl Gantrix had been snared by the argument of the Rome party and hence had been retired. 'If the Flask of Hermes Vitarium does not own the old-born Anarch Peak,' it declared, 'then according to law the Anarch is ownerless, and holds the same legal status as an old-born who, as occasionally happens, manages to open his own coffin, claw the dirt aside, and exhume himself without external aid. He is then considered the proprietor of himself, and his own opinion as to his disposition is the sole factor obtaining. So we Uditi still maintain that as an ownerless old-born the Anarch alone can legally sell himself, and we are now waiting for his decision.'

'Are you certain you dug up the Anarch too soon?' Giacometti asked Sebastian, cautiously. 'Do you actually stipulate that you acted illegally? It would mean a severe

150

fine. I advise you to deny it. If you so stipulate, we'll refer this to the Los Angeles County District Attorney's Office.'

Sebastian said woodenly, 'I – deny we dug up the Anarch prematurely. There's no proof that we did.' He was positive of that; only his own crew had been involved, and they wouldn't testify.

'The real issue,' the robot said, 'is spiritual; we must determine and agree on the precise moment at which the soul enters the corpse in the ground. Is it the moment when it is dug up? When its voice is first heard from below, asking for aid? When the first heart beat is recorded? When all brain tissue has formed? In the opinion of Udi the soul enters the corpse when there has been total tissue regeneration, which would be just prior to the first heart action.' To Sebastian he said, 'Before you dug the Anarch up, sir, did you detect heart action?'

'Yes,' Sebastian said. 'Irregular. But it was there.'

'Then when the Anarch was dug up,' the robot said triumphantly, 'he was a person, having a soul; hence – '

The vidphone rang.

'Goodbye,' Sebastian said into the receiver.

This time Bob Lindy's leathery, tense features formed. 'They got him,' he said. He ran his fingers shakily through his hair. 'Library agents. So that's that.'

'You can end your theological argument,' Sebastian said to the robot and Giacometti.

It was unnecessary; the argument had already ended.

The living room of his conapt, for the first time in quite a while, was silent.

Chapter 13

Man is an animal, that is his genus, but man is a species, reasoning, that is the difference, capable of laughter, that is his property.
                                                                      – Boethius

In the small hotel room, Officer Joe Tinbane lounged in such a fashion that he could see outside. In case anyone showed up. His wife Bethel, Sebastian Hermes, Library commandos – he had to be ready for any and all of them. No combination would have surprised him.

Meanwhile, he read the latest edition of the most lurid 'pape in North America, the Chicago *Monday-Herald*.

DRUNKEN FATHER EATS OWN BABY

'You never know how life is going to work out for you,' he said to Lotta. 'When you're either new-born or old-born – I'll bet this guy never expected he'd wind up this way, a headline in the *Monday-Herald*.'

'I don't see how you can read that,' Lotta said nervously; she sat combing her long dark hair, on a chair on the far side of the room.

'Well, as a peace officer I see a lot of this. Not exactly this bad – this one, where this father eats his own baby, is rare.' He turned the page, inspected the headline on page two.

CALIFORNIA LIBRARY KILLS AND KIDNAPS: A LAW UNTO ITSELF, SAFE FROM REPRISAL

'My god,' Tinbane said. 'This could be about us; here's an article on the People's Topical Library. About it doing what they tried with you – holding you hostage.' He read the article, interested.

How many Los Angeles citizens have disappeared behind the grim gray walls of this forbidding structure? Public authorities make no official estimate, but privately, guesses are running as high as three unexplained disappearances each month. The motives of the Library are not well-understood and are believed to be complex. A desire to erad in advance writings which . . .

'I don't believe it,' Tinbane said. 'They couldn't get away with it. Take my case, for instance; if anything happened to me my boss George Gore would spring me. Or, if I was dead, he'd pay them back.' Thinking about Gore he remembered that Ray Roberts was due any minute now; Gore was probably trying to get hold of him for the special bodyguard detail. 'I better call in,' he said to Lotta. 'I forgot about all that.'

Using the motel apartment's vidphone he called Gore.

'A message came in for you,' the police switchboard operator told him, when he identified himself. 'Anonymous Library agents are out after you, he states. Does this mean anything to you?'

'Hell yes,' Tinbane said. To Lotta he said, 'Library agents are searching for us.' To the police operator he said, 'Let me talk to Mr Gore.'

'Mr Gore is at the Los Angeles airport, supervising security precautions for Ray Roberts,' the operator said.

'Tell Mr Gore when he comes back that if anything happens to me,' Tinbane said, 'it was the Library that did it, and if I'm missing to look for me in the Library. And especially if I'm dead, they did it.' He rang off, feeling depressed.

'Do you think they can find us here?' Lotta asked.

'No,' he said. He pondered awhile, and then he rooted through the drawers of the motel room's dresser until he found the vidphone book; he leafed through it glumly until at last he found Douglas Appleford's home phone number; several times he had called it in the past, and had usually found Appleford in.

He called that number now.

'Goodbye,' Appleford said presently, appearing on the screen.

'Sorry to bother you at home,' Tinbane said, 'but I need your immediate personal help. Can you get hold of your superior, Mrs McGuire?'

'Possibly,' Appleford said. 'In an emergency.'

'I consider this an emergency,' Tinbane said. He explained the situation, as he knew it, to the librarian. 'See?' he said in conclusion. 'I'm really in a difficult spot; they really have reason to be hostile to me. If they do show up here where I am, somebody's going to get killed; probably them. I'm in touch with the LA police department; as soon as I'm in trouble I'll be reinforced. My superior, Gore, knows my situation and he's sympathetic. They have a prowl car – at least one – floating around in the neighborhood, at all times. I just don't want an incident; I have a lady with me, and on her account I'd prefer to see no violence – as far as I personally am concerned, I couldn't care less. After all, it's my job.'

'Where exactly are you?' Appleford asked.

'Oh no,' Tinbane said. 'I'd be nuts to tell you that.'

Appleford acknowledged. 'I suppose you would.' He, too, pondered; his face was vague. 'There's not much I can do, Joe. I don't make Library policy; that's up to the Erads. I can put in a good word for you, tomorrow when I run into Mrs McGuire.'

154

'Tomorrow,' Tinbane said, 'is too late. In my professional opinion, this is going to come to a head tonight.' After all, virtually every LA police officer was tied up guarding Ray Roberts; this would be the ideal time for the Library to pick him off. There most decidedly was *not* a prowl car cruising about overhead, nor would there be one; at least not until he had hold of Gore.

'I can tell them,' Appleford said, 'that you're expecting them. And that of course you're armed.'

'No, they just would send a bigger team. Tell them to forget it; I regret having had to do what I did – going in there at gunpoint to get Mrs Hermes out – but I had no option; they were detaining her.'

'Oh, did the Erads do that?' Appleford said, obviously uncomfortable. 'Are they still – '

'Tell them,' Tinbane interrupted, deciding, 'that I stopped at the police arsenal and picked up a weapon that fires a slug the size of a land mine. And it's rapid-fire, one of those Skoda lightweight monsters. *I* can operate it openly, because I'm a police officer; I can use any weapon available. But they've got to skulk around; they're severely limited, and tell them I know it. Tell them I'm looking forward to seeing them show up. It'll be a pleasure. Hello.' He hung up.

Still combing her hair, Lotta said, 'Do you really have a gun like that?'

'No,' he said. 'I have a pistol.' He whapped his belt holster. 'And in the car,' he said, 'I have a regulation issue rifle. Maybe I better go get it.' He started toward the door.

'Who do you think the anonymous caller was?' Lotta asked.

'Your husband.' He hobbled out of the motel room,

155

across the sidewalk to the on-street parking lot, and got his rifle from the car.

The night seemed cold and empty, with no life, no activities; he sensed the lack of ominousness. Everybody is at the airport, he thought. Where I ought to be. I'll probably get hell from Gore for this, he thought. For not having shown up for the bodyguard detail. But that's the least of my worries, what I've done to my career.

He returned to the motel room, locking the door behind him.

'Did you see anyone?' Lotta asked softly.

'Nothing. So relax.' He checked the magazine of the rifle, made sure it held a full clip.

'Maybe you should call Sebastian.'

'Why?' he said irritably. 'I got his message. No,' he said, 'I don't feel up to talking directly to him. Because of you; I mean, because of our relationship.' He felt embarrassed. This sort of activity came with difficulty to him. In fact he had never done anything such as this – hiding in a motel room with someone else's wife – before in his life. He mulled it over, his attention turned inward.

'You're not ashamed, are you?' Lotta inquired.

'Just – ' He gestured. 'It's delicate. I wouldn't know what to say to him.' He eyed her. 'If you want to, you can call him; I'll listen in.'

'I – still think I'd rather write him.' She had already begun laboriously composing a letter; a paragraph and a half, scrawled across a folded page, lay on the bed, a pen beside it: she had ceased working for the time being. Evidently the task confronting her had been overwhelming.

'Okay,' he said. 'You write to him; he'll get it next week.'

156

She gazed about unhappily. 'Do you have anything to read in your car?' she asked.

'Read this.' He tossed her the *Monday-Herald*.

Shrinking away, Lotta said, 'Oh no. Not ever.'

'Are you already bored with me?' Tinbane asked, still irritable.

'I always read, about this time in the evening.' She wandered around the room, poking here and there. On the table by the bed she found a Gideon Bible. 'I could read this,' she said, reseating herself. 'I'll ask it a question and then open it at random; you can use the Bible that way. I do it all the time.' She concentrated. 'I'll ask it,' she decided, 'if the Library is going to get us.' Opening the book, she put her finger, eyes closed, on the top left-hand page. '"Whither is thy beloved gone, O thou fairest among women?"' she read aloud, studiously. '"Whither is thy beloved turned aside?"' She glanced up, eyes solemn. 'You know what that means? You're going to be taken away from me.'

'Maybe it means Sebastian,' he said, half-jokingly.

'No.' She shook her head. 'I'm in love with you. So it must refer to you.' Once more consulting the book she asked, 'Are we in a safe place, here at the motel, or should we hide somewhere else?' Again she opened at random, blindly found a passage. 'Psalm 91,' she informed him. '"He that dwelleth in the secret place of the most High shall abide under the shadow of the Almighty."' She reflected. 'I guess this is a secret place. So we're as safe here as anywhere . . . but they're going to get us, even so. There's nothing we can do about it.'

'We can shoot our way out,' Tinbane offered.

'Not according to the Book. It's hopeless.'

Amused, but also indignant at her passivity, he said, 'If I had that attitude I'd have been dead years ago.'

157

'It's not my attitude; it's – '

'Sure it's your attitude. You make it mean what you subconsciously want it to mean. In my opinion, a human being, a man, controls his own fate. Maybe it's not true about women.'

'I think in connection with the Library,' Lotta said sadly, 'it doesn't make any difference.'

'There is a fundamental difference in the thinking of men versus that of women,' Tinbane declared. 'In fact there's a fundamental difference between various types of women. Consider yourself in comparison to Bethel my wife. You haven't met her, but the difference between the two of you is enormous; consider just as an example the way in which you give your love. You do it unconditionally – the man, me in this case, doesn't have to do anything or be anything in particular. Now, Bethel, on the other hand, demands certain criteria be upheld. In the matter of how I dress, for example. Or how many times I take her out as for instance to a sogum palace three times a week. Or whether I – '

Lotta said, fearfully, 'I hear something on the roof.'

'Birds,' he said. 'Running across.'

'No. It's larger.'

He listened. And heard it too. Patter on the roof; someone or something scrambling. Children. 'It's kids,' he said.

'Why?' Lotta said. Now she stared fixedly at the window. 'They're looking in,' she said.

He turned swiftly, saw a pinched little face earnestly pressed to the window of the motel room. 'The Library,' he said thickly, 'uses them. From its Children's Department.' He got out his pistol. Going to the door he put his hand on the knob. 'I'll get them,' he said to Lotta. He opened the door.

158

His shot, aimed too high, aimed at an adult, passed over the head of the tiny child standing there. Adult agents who have dwindled, he realized as he took aim again. Can I kill a child? But it's going back into a womb anyhow; its time is short. He started to fire again at the four of them darting about inside the motel . . .

Lotta squalled in a travesty of adult fright, which annoyed him. 'Get down!' he yelled at her. One of the small children was aiming a tube at him, and he recognized the weapon: an old wartime laser beam, not intended for domestic matters; its use was denied even the police departments. 'Put that thing down,' he said to the child, aiming his gun at the child. 'You're under arrest; you're not supposed to have one of those.' He wondered if the child knew how to operate it; he wondered –

The laser beam glowed its adequately ruby red, its old intentional color. The beam reached out.

And Tinbane died.

Cowering behind the big double bed of the motel room, Lotta saw the laser beam kill Joe Tinbane; she saw more and more children, a dozen of them, working silently, their faces transfigured with glee. You horrible little creeps, she thought in terror. 'I give up, please,' she called to them in a wavering voice not her own. 'Okay?' She stood up awkwardly, stumbled against the bed and almost fell. 'I'll come back to the Library; okay?' She waited. And the laser beams did not come on again; the children seemed satisfied: now they were speaking into their intercoms, with their superiors. Telling them what had happened and getting instructions. Oh god, she thought, looking down at Joe Tinbane. I knew they'd do

159

it; he was so sure of himself, and that always means the end. That's when you're destroyed.

'Mrs Hermes?' one of the children piped shrilly.

'Yes,' she said. Why pretend? They knew who she was. They had known who Joe Tinbane was – the man who had attacked the Erads and gotten her out of the Library.

An adult appeared, now. It was the motel man who had rented them the room; he was, she realized, an informer for the Library. The man conferred with the children, then raised his head and beckoned to her.

'How could you shoot him?' she asked, in dazed wonder; she stepped past Joe Tinbane, lingered; maybe she should stay here with him, get shot as he had – maybe that was better than returning to the Library.

The motel man said, 'He attacked us. First at the Library and then here. He boasted to Mr Appleford that he could handle us; it was his declaration.' The man nodded in the direction of a parked VW airbus. 'Would you get in, Mrs Hermes?' On the side of the bus the lettering read: PEOPLE'S TOPICAL LIBRARY. An official, marked bus.

Stumblingly, she got inside; the children, sweaty and breathing excitedly, piled in after her and crowded around her. They did not speak to her, however; they chattered in low, exultant tones, among themselves. They were so pleased, she realized. So glad to still be of use to the Library, even in their dwindled state. She hated them.

160

Chapter 14

But it hath not yet attained tomorrow and hath lost yesterday. And you live no more in this day's life than in that movable and transitory moment.   – Boethius

The TV news announcer said, 'On the local scene it seemed as if all Los Angeles turned out tonight to stare at or cheer for the head of the Faith of Udi, his Mightiness Ray Roberts, who touched down at the Los Angeles airport shortly before seven o'clock this evening. On hand to meet him was Mayor Sam Parks of Los Angeles, and, as a special rep of the Governor's Office in Sacramento, Judd Asman.' The TV screen showed a great, dense-packed throng of people, many of them howling and waving, others carrying banners with hand-lettered slogans ranging from GO HOME to WELCOME. In general, the people appeared good-natured.

A big event in our meager, paltry lives, Sebastian thought acidly.

'His Mightiness,' the announcer continued, 'will be whisked by motorcade to Dodger Stadium, where, under the lights, he will deliver a speech to the packed crowd of spectators, mostly his supporters, but not a few of the curious, the just plain interested; this marks the first time in a decade that a major religious leader has visited Los Angeles, and hearkens back to the good old days when Los Angeles was one of the religious capitals of the world.' To his companion announcer, the announcer said, 'Wouldn't you say, Chic, that the festive, exuberant

161

atmosphere of Dodger Stadium is reminiscent of the days of Festus Crumb and Harold Agee, back in the '80s?'

'Yes I would, Don,' Chic said. 'With one difference. The crowds which greeted Festus Crumb and to a certain extent Harold Agee had a more militant atmosphere about them; these four million people are here at Dodger Stadium and at the airport for a good time and to see someone famous, someone who delivers a dramatic, notable speech. They've watched him on TV, but somehow this is not the same.'

The motorcade had now begun its trip from the airport to Dodger Stadium; all along the way people could be made out. Idiots, Sebastian thought. Watching that galoomf when the real religious figure is again alive and back with us. Even though the Library has him.

'Of course in seeing Ray Roberts,' Chic the announcer said, 'one can't help but be reminded of his predecessor, the Anarch Peak.'

'Isn't there some talk, Chic, about an imminent return of the Anarch to life?' Don asked. 'And a belief current among many that Ray Roberts is here principally to visit with the recently old-born Anarch and perhaps persuade him to return to the Free Negro Municipality?'

'There has been such speculation,' Chic said. 'And also not a little speculation as to whether it would be in the best interests of Udi – or rather would Ray Roberts consider it in the best interests of Udi – for the Anarch to reappear just at this time. Some think Roberts might try to stall the Anarch's return, if such indeed does occur, as many apparently think.' There was temporary silence; the screen still showed the motorcade.

The announcer at the TV station cut back in and said, 'Briefly, while we're waiting for Ray Roberts to reach Dodger Stadium, a review of other local news. A Los

162

Angeles police officer, Joseph Tinbane, has been found slain at the Happy Holiday Motel in San Fernando, and the police are speculating that it might be the work of religious fanatics. Other guests at the motel reported seeing a woman in the company of Officer Tinbane at the nearby sogum palace, earlier this evening, but if she exists she has disappeared. More on this, including an interview with the motel owner, during the eleven o'clock news. Floods in the northern hills near – '

Sebastian shut the TV set off. 'Christ,' he said to the robot, once more Carl Junior. 'They've got Lotta and they killed Tinbane.' His warning hadn't reached him; it had been futile. Hopeless, he thought as he found a place to sit; he crouched with his head in his hands, staring down at the floor. There's nothing I can do. If they could wipe out a professional like Tinbane they'd have no trouble with me.

'It seems almost impossible,' the robot said, 'to penetrate the Library. Our efforts to seed a nest of miniaturized robots in Section B dismally failed. We do not know what else to do. If we had someone sympathetic working there – ' The robot pondered. 'We hoped that Doug Appleford might cooperate; he appeared to be the most reasonable of the librarians. But in that we were disappointed: it was he who expelled our nest.' It added, 'Turn the TV on again, please; I wish to watch the motorcade.'

He gestured. 'You turn it on.' He did not have the energy to get to his feet again.

The robot turned the TV set back on, and once again Chic and Don held forth.

'. . . and a good number of whites, too,' Don was saying. 'So this has turned out to be, as His Mightiness promised, a bi-racial event, although, as we observed shortly ago, Negroes outnumber whites by a ratio of – I'd estimate five to one. What estimate would you give, Chic?'

'I find that about right, Don,' Chic said. 'Yes, five colored to each – '

Giacometti said, 'We must get someone sympathetic into the Library. On its staff.' He plucked, scowling, at his lower lip. 'Otherwise the Anarch will never emerge again.'

'Lotta,' Sebastian said. Her, too.

'That is of considerably lesser importance,' the robot said. 'Although to you subjectively, Mr Hermes, it undoubtedly looms large.' To Giacometti it said, 'Can the Rome party be of any use in forging credentials which would admit one of us to the Library? I understand your people are very good at that.'

Sardonically, Giacometti said, 'Our reputation is undeserved.'

'Given time,' Carl Junior ruminated, 'we could construct a simulacrum robot resembling, for example, Miss Ann Fisher. But that would take weeks. Perhaps, Mr Giacometti, if we pool our resources, we can shoot our way into the Library.'

'My principal does not operate on that basis,' Giacometti said. And that was that. His tone was flat and final.

To the robot, Sebastian said, 'Ask Ray Roberts what I can do. To get into the Library.'

'At this moment His Mightiness – '

'Ask him!'

'All right.' The robot nodded and was silent for several minutes. Sebastian and Giacometti waited. At last the robot spoke up again, its tone now firm. 'You are to go to Section B of the Library,' it said. 'You are to ask to see Mr Douglas Appleford. Would he know you on sight, Mr Hermes?'

'No,' Sebastian said.

'You are to say,' the robot said, 'that a Miss Charise McFadden has sent you. Your name will be Lance Arbuthnot and you have written a demented thesis on the psychogenic origins of death by meteor-strike. You are a crank, originally from the FNM, but expelled because of your peculiar views. Mr Appleford is expecting you; Charise McFadden has already sounded him as regards you and your queer thesis. He will not be glad to see you, but in line with his job he must.'

Sebastian said, 'I don't see that that gets me anywhere.'

'It will provide a cover,' the robot said, 'and a pretext. Your comings and goings, your presence in the Library, will be understandable. It is common for crank inventors to hang around Section B; Appleford is accustomed to their presence. Mr Giacometti.' It turned its attentions toward the advocate of the Rome principal. 'Will you and your people cooperate with Udi in preparing Mr Hermes a survival kit for use within the Library? Our combined resources are required.'

After a thoughtful pause Giacometti nodded. 'I think we can assist. Providing nothing destructive to human life is involved.'

'Mr Hermes will only be operating defensively,' the robot said. 'No aggressive program is envisioned. Offensive action on the part of one man against the Library is vainglorious. It could never succeed.'

Sebastian said, 'What if Lance Arbuthnot actually shows up?'

'There is no "Lance Arbuthnot,"' the robot said succinctly. 'Miss McFadden is one of the Uditi; her request to Mr Appleford was a ploy on our part from the beginning. It stems, in fact, from the teeming, fertile mind of Ray Roberts himself. We even have prepared his

165

hoky thesis on psychosomatic factors in death by meteor-strike; tomorrow it will be delivered, bright and early, to your conapt door. By special Udi messenger.' The robot beamed.

On the TV screen Don was saying, '. . . at least. There has been a very substantial turnout, here at Dodger Stadium, considering the weather. Oh, we understand His Mightiness, Ray Roberts, is expected to put in his appearance any moment.' The crowd noises, muted until now, all at once surged up deafeningly. 'Mr Roberts is emerging from the visitors' dug-out,' Don's voice could be heard saying. 'Let's have a close-up of him; I think we can catch him with our camera.' The camera zoomed in, and on the screen four figures, marching across the infield toward the improvised lectern, could be discerned.

'I want absolute silence in this room,' the robot said, 'while Mr Roberts is speaking.'

'Can you see what he's doing now, Don?' Chic was asking.

'He seems to be blessing those gathered at the lectern,' Don answered. 'He's waving his hand in the direction of their heads, as if shaking holy water at them. Yes, he is blessing them; they're all kneeling, now.' The crowd continued to yell.

Sebastian said to the robot, 'Then there's nothing we can do tonight. Toward getting into the Library.'

'We must wait until it reopens tomorrow morning,' the robot confirmed. Now it raised its finger to its lip in a shushing motion.

Standing before the microphones, Ray Roberts surveyed the crowd.

His Mightiness was a slightly built man, Sebastian observed. Quite delicate, with a bird-cage chest, slender arms – and unusually large hands. His eyes cast a

166

penetrating brilliance; they blazed intensely as he sized up the audience before which he now spoke. Roberts wore a simple dark robe and a skullcap, and, on his right hand, a ring. One ring to rule them all, he thought, remembering his Tolkien. One ring to find them. One ring to – how did it go? – bring them all and in the darkness bind them. In the Land of Mordor where the Shadows lie. The ring of earthly power, he thought. Like that fashioned from the Rheingold, carrying a curse with it, to whoever put it on. Maybe the operation of the curse, he conjectured, is manifest in the Library's seizing the Anarch.

'*Sum tu*,' Ray Roberts said, raising his hands. 'I am you and you are I. Distinctions between and among us are illusory. What doo dat mean?, as the old Negro janitor asks in the ancient joke. It means – ' His voice rose booming and echoing; he stared upward, his gaze fixed on a point in the sky beyond Dodger Stadium. 'The Negro cannot be inferior to the white man because he *is* the white man. When the white man, in former times, did violence to the Negro he destroyed himself. Today, when a citizen of the Free Negro Municipality injures and molests a white, he, too, is injuring and molesting himself. I say to you: strike not the ear of the Roman soldier off; it will fall, like a dead leaf, of its own accord.'

The crowd roared its cheers.

Going into his kitchen, Sebastian lit a cigar butt, puffed some angry smoke into it, rapidly. It grew longer. Maybe Bob Lindy could get me into the Library tonight, he said to himself. Lindy has an ingenious mind; he can do anything mechanical, or electrical. Or R. C. Buckley; he can talk his way in anywhere, any time. My own staff, he thought. I ought to be depending on them, not on Udi.

167

Even if Udi does possess a prearranged plan all ready to go into gear.

'I am reminded,' Roberts was expostulating in the living room, 'of the little old lady who had been recently old-born and whose greatest fear had been that, when they excavated her, they would find her improperly clothed.' The audience chuckled. 'But neurotic fears,' Roberts continued, now somberly, 'can destroy a person and a nation. The neurotic fear by Nazi Germany of a two-front war – ' He droned on; Sebastian ceased listening.

Maybe I'll have to accept the robot's method, he said to himself, and wait until tomorrow. Joe Tinbane shot his way in, got her and shot his way out, and what good did it do? Tinbane is dead and Lotta is once more inside the Library; nothing got accomplished.

The Library, he reflected, *must be dealt with in a certain way* – a way customary and familiar to them. Udi is right; I must be accepted voluntarily into the Library.

But how, when I get in there, he asked himself, can I keep from running amuck? When I actually face them . . . the strain will be overwhelming. Enormous. And I will have to sit there chatting with Appleford, about a deranged pseudo-manuscript –

He returned to the living room. Over the din of Ray Roberts' tirade he yelled at the robot, 'I can't do it!'

The robot, annoyed, cupped its ear.

'I'm getting into the Library tonight,' Sebastian yelled, but the robot paid no attention to him; its head had swiveled back and once more it was drinking up the noise from the TV set.

Giacometti rose, rook him by the arm and led him back to the kitchen. 'In this case the Uditi are right. This must be done slowly, bit by bit; we – especially you

168

yourself – must be patient. You'll simply get yourself killed, like the police officer. It all must be – ' He gestured. 'Indirect. Even – tactfully. You see?' He studied Sebastian's face.

'Tonight,' Sebastian said, 'I'm going there now.'

'You will go, but you won't come back.'

Setting down his completed cigar, Sebastian said, 'Hello. I'll see you later; I'm leaving.'

'Don't try to approach the Library! Don't – ' Giacometti's words blended with the howl of the TV set, and then Sebastian shut the conapt door after him; he was outside, in the hall, in welcome silence.

For what seemed like hours he roamed the dark streets, hands deep in his trouser pockets, passing stores, passing houses that, as time progressed, became increasingly darkened until, at last, he glanced up at a block of residences which showed no light at all. Now no one passed him on the sidewalk; he was entirely alone.

All at once he found himself confronted by three members of Udi, two men and one young woman. Each wore the *sum tu* button; the girl had placed hers at the farthest projection of her right breast, like an enlarged, winking metal nipple.

They greeted him cheerfully. 'Valé, amicus,' they chorused. 'What did you think of His Mightiness' speech tonight?'

'Excellent,' Sebastian said. He tried to remember it; only one phrase came to mind. 'I liked that about the Roman sentry's ear,' he said. 'That gripped me.'

'We have some spirit-sogum,' the taller of the two Uditi men informed him. 'Want to join us? Even if you're not part of the brotherhood, you can celebrate with us.'

He could not turn such an offer down. 'Fine,' he said.

It had been years since he had imbibed any spirit-sogum; roughly, it resembled the old-time alcoholic mixtures sold at liquor stores and in bars – this took him back years, to before the Hobart Phase.

Presently they had all squeezed into a parked aircar and were passing the flask with its long pipe back and forth. The atmosphere became increasingly genial.

'What are you doing out so late?' the Udi girl asked him. 'Hunting for a woman?'

'Yes,' Sebastian said. The spirit-sogum had relaxed his tongue; he felt himself among friends. And probably he was.

'Well, if that's what you want, we can go – '

'No,' Sebastian said, interrupting her. 'It's not what you think. I'm looking for my wife. And I know where she is, only I can't get her out.'

'We'll get her out,' the shorter of the Uditi men said happily. 'Where is she?'

'At the People's Topical Library,' Sebastian said.

'Feood,' all three Uditi said in enthusiastic union, 'let's go.' One of them, at the wheel, started the motor of the car.

'It's closed right now,' Sebastian pointed out.

That – temporarily – dimmed their enthusiasm. The three of them conferred and at last their spokesman presented their joint idea for his inspection. 'The Library has an all-night slot, for books past their erad date. One of those no-questions-asked slots. Couldn't you squeeze in through there?'

'Too small,' Sebastian said.

That, too, dampened their ever-increasing enthusiasm. 'You gotta wait until tomorrow,' the girl informed him. 'Unless you want to call the police. But feood; I understand they have a hands-off policy as regards the Library. A sort of live and let live.'

'Except,' Sebastian said, 'the Library killed a Los Angeles patrolman earlier tonight.' But he couldn't prove it had been the Library; he had already heard the TV blame it on 'religious fanatics.'

'Maybe you could get Ray Roberts to include your wife in one of his prayers,' the Udi girl said at last. Hopefully.

'I still think,' the taller of the two men said, 'the four of us ought to go somewhere and have an orgy.'

He thanked them, got out of the car, and wandered on.

The car, however, followed after him. When it came abreast with him, one of the Uditi rolled down the window, leaned out and yelled to him, 'If you want to bust in, we'll give you a hand. We're not scared of the People's Topical Library.'

'You're goddam right we're not,' the Udi girl chimed in warmly.

'No,' Sebastian decided. He had to do this alone; the three Uditi, good-intentioned as they were, couldn't really help him.

'Go on home, fella,' their spokesman now implored him. 'You can't do nothing tonight; give it another try tomorrow.'

They were right; he nodded. 'Okay,' he said. He felt overwhelming fatigue, now, as soon as he recognized that fact: as soon as his mind gave up, his body readily followed suit. He waved hello – or rather salvé – to the three of them, and roamed on toward a lighted intersection ahead, searching for a cab.

He had never felt as dejected before in all his life.

Chapter 15

God's knowledge also surpassing all motions of time, remaineth in the simplicity of His presence.   – Boethius

When he returned to his conapt, half an hour later, he found it mercifully deserted; Giacometti and the robot Carl Junior had at last departed. Full-length cigarettes filled every ashtray; he wandered about, stuffing them into packages, then gave up in numb despair and got into bed. At least the air in the room smelled clean and fresh; the desmoking of so many cigarettes had accomplished that.

The next he knew, someone was rapping on the door. He rose from the bed groggily, found himself fully dressed, stumbled to the door. No one there; it had taken him too long. But there, at the door, a brilliant blue, carefully wrapped package. The spurious thesis of Lance Arbuthnot.

Jesus, he said to himself in pain; his head ached and he felt ill in every part of his body. Nine o'clock, the clock told him, from its place on the kitchen wall. Morning. The Library was already open.

Shakily, he seated himself in the living room, unwrapped the parcel. Hundreds of typescript pages, with painstaking pen annotations; an utterly convincing job . . . it impressed him, this handiwork of the Uditi. Wherever he dipped into it he found it making a sort of sense; it had its own outré logic – such anyhow as was required by the situation. Clearly it would pass Library inspection.

172

Without having ingested any sogum or put on his morning pat of whiskers, he phoned the Library and asked for Douglas Appleford.

The features of a pompous, dim little functionary formed. 'This is Mr Appleford.' He eyed Sebastian.

'My name,' Sebastian said, 'is Lance Arbuthnot. Miss McFadden talked to you about me.'

'Oh yes.' Appleford nodded distastefully. 'I've been expecting you to call. The meteor-deaths man.'

Holding the typescript manuscript up before the screen Sebastian said, 'May I bring my thesis over sometime this morning?'

'I could squeeze you in – briefly – around ten o'clock.'

'I'll see you then,' Sebastian said, and rang off. I now possess access up through all the sections with the exception of the top-floor A Section, he realized. The Uditi were experienced operators . . . it made a difference, having them on his side.

The vidphone rang; he answered it and found himself confronted by His Mightiness Ray Roberts. 'Goodbye, Mr Hermes,' Roberts said sententiously. 'In view of the importance of your activity vis-à-vis the Library, I believe I should consult directly with you. To be certain there is no misunderstanding. You received the manuscript of Arbuthnot's thesis.'

'Yes,' Sebastian said. 'And it looks good.'

'You will be in the Library, as far as they are concerned, only a matter of minutes; Douglas Appleford will receive the manuscript, thank you and file it away. Ten minutes in all, perhaps. That will not be enough, of course; what you must do is become lost in the confusing maze of offices and reading rooms and stacks for a good part of the day. To do that you will need a pretext.'

173

'I can tell them – ' Sebastian began, but His Mightiness interrupted him.

'Listen, Mr Hermes. Your excuse has been carefully prepared, far, far in advance. This is a long-term plan. While you are sitting in Mr Appleford's office, with the manuscript still in your possession, you will glance through it and inadvertently notice page 173. You will thereon see an error of major magnitude, and you will ask Appleford for use of a restricted-area reading room in which you can make pen-and-ink alterations. After you have corrected the copy, you will tell him, it will be turned over to him; you compute the time required for the changes to lie between fifteen and forty-five minutes.'

'I see,' Sebastian said.

'The restricted-area reading rooms are not patrolled,' Ray Roberts said, 'because there is nothing in them except long hardwood tables. So no one will see you leave the reading room. If they do intercept you, say you got lost trying to find your way back to Mr Appleford's office. It is essential, now, for us to speculate on the probable location of the Anarch. Our analysis of the Library puts his location, tentatively, on the top floor, or in any case the top two floors. So it will be on those higher floors that you will search . . . and those, of course, will be the most difficult to gain entrée to. An armband with a special dye, which gives back correct responses to a minified radar scope, is worn by Library employees on those floors. It is a luminous, spectacular blue – the utility being that a Library guard, at long distance, can tell at a glance who is wearing one and who is not. The paper which the manuscript came wrapped in: it is made from this specially treated blue material. You will cut yourself an armband from the wrapper, following the dotted lines which we made on it; you will carry it in your pocket and after you have left Appleford you will put it around your left arm.'

'Left,' Sebastian echoed. He felt weak and dizzy; he needed sogum and a cold shower and a change of clothes.

'Now, if you will look in your disgorged victuals refrigerator,' Ray Roberts said, 'you will find the survival kit which the robot Carl Junior and Mr Giacometti prepared jointly. It will be essential to you.' He paused. 'One more matter, Mr Hermes. You love your wife and she is precious to you . . . but in terms of history, she does not count – *as does the Anarch*. Try to recognize the distinction, the finiteness of your personal needs, the almost infinite value of Anarch Peak. It will be instinctive for you to seek out your wife . . . so you will have to gain conscious control of this almost biological drive. You understand?'

'I want,' Sebastian said between his rigid teeth, 'to find Lotta.'

'Possibly you will. But that is not your primary purpose in the Library; it is not for finding *her* that we have so equipped you. In my opinion – ' Ray Roberts leaned toward the vidscreen so that his eyes swam up and enlarged hypnotically; Sebastian sat silently and passively, like a chicken, listening. 'They will release your wife unharmed once we have the Anarch back. They are not genuinely interested in her.'

'Oh yes they are,' Sebastian said. 'Vengeance toward me, because of what happened between me and Ann Fisher.' He did not follow – or believe in – Ray Roberts' logic on this point; he sensed it as façade. 'You've never met her. Spite and hate and holding a grudge play a major rôle in her – '

'I have met her several times,' Ray Roberts said. 'As a matter of fact the Council of Erads had her stationed in

175

Kansas City as a sort of emissary sine portfolio to our federal government. She periodically holds power in the council halls of the Library and then abruptly loses it by overreaching herself. She may have done this as regards police officer Tinbane; we have dropped it in the ear of the Los Angeles Police Department that Library agents killed Tinbane, not "religious fanatics."' His face contorted in a rhythm of distilled wrath. 'The Uditi are always blamed for crimes of violence; it is common police and media policy.'

Sebastian said, 'Do you think Lotta also will be found on the top two floors?'

'Most likely.' His Mightiness surveyed Sebastian. 'I can see that despite my exhortation you will spend the majority of your brief time searching for her.' He gestured philosophically; it was an emphatic reaction, one of understanding, not condemnation. 'Well, Hermes; go inspect your survival kit and then get off to the Library for your appointment. It was nice talking to you. I assume we will talk again, perhaps later today. Hello.'

'Hello, sir,' Sebastian said, and hung up the phone.

Eagerly, at the refrigerator filled with various favorite victuals ready to go to the supermarket, he inspected the small white carton which Giacometti and the robot had left him. To his disappointment it contained only three items. LSD, in vapor-under-pressure form, to be set off by grenade. An oral antidote to the LSD – probably a phenothiazine – to be carried in a plastic capsule in his mouth, during his hunt at the Library: those made up two of the three. And the third. He studied it for several minutes, at first not recognizing what he held. An intravenous injection device, containing a small amount of pale, saplike liquid; it came with a removable wrapper of

176

instructions, so he removed the wrapper to read the brochure.

For a limited period an injection of the solution would free him of the Hobart Phase.

He would, he realized, be stationary in time; for all intents and purposes moving neither forward nor backward. It would, paradoxically, be for a finite period: by common time, no more than six minutes. But, from his standpoint, it would be experienced as hours.

This last item, he discovered, came from Rome; in the past, he recalled, it had been used, with limited success, for prolonged spiritual meditation. Now it had been officially banned and could not be obtained. But still, here it was.

The Rome principal overlooked nothing of a practical nature, in conjunction with its perpetual spiritual quest.

A combination of the items, the LSD imposed on the Library guards, and the injection for himself – he would be in motion and they would not; it was as simple as that. And, in accordance with Giacometti's wishes, no one would be injured.

For a subjective period of one to three hours he would probably be free to go anywhere, do anything, on the upper floors of the Library. It struck him as an extremely well-thought-out survival kit, simple as it was.

He took a quick shower, changed to properly soiled clothes, patted dabs of whiskers in place, imbibed sogum, divested himself of various victuals in the ritual dishes, and then, with the manuscript under his arm, left his empty, lonely conapt and made his way out onto the street where he had, the night before, parked his car. His heart hung in his throat, strangling him with fear. My one chance, my *last* chance, he realized. To get Lotta out.

And with her, if possible, the Anarch. If this fails then she's really gone. Slipped away. Forever.

A moment later, in his car, he soared up into the bright morning sky.

Chapter 16

These thoughts I revolved in my miserable heart, overcharged
with most gnawing cares, lest I should die ere I had found the
truth.   – St Augustine

'A Mr Arbuthnot to see you, sir,' Doug Appleford's
secretary said, over the intercom to his office.

He groaned. Well, here it was finally; the burden
wished on him by perpetually enthusiastic Charise
McFadden. 'Send him in,' Appleford said, and tipped his
chair back, folded his hands and waited.

A large, imposing, nattily dressed older man appeared
at the doorway of the office. 'I'm Lance Arbuthnot,' he
mumbled; his eyes roamed in unease, like those of a
trapped animal.

'Let's see it,' Appleford said, with no preamble.

'Of course.' Shakily Arbuthnot seated himself in the
chair before Doug Appleford's desk, handed him a bulky,
dog-eared typescript manuscript. 'The labor of a lifetime,'
he muttered.

'So you maintain,' Doug Appleford said briskly, 'that
if a person is killed by a meteor it's because he hated his
grandmother. Some theory. Anyhow you're realistic
enough to want it eraded.' He leafed cursorily through
the manuscript, reading a line here and there, at random.
Dull phrases, jargon, strained and inverted cliché sen-
tences, claims of a fantastic nature . . . it had familiar
quality. The Library saw ten such trashy manuscripts of
that sort a day. It constituted routine business for
Section B.

'May I have it back a moment?' Arbuthnot asked hoarsely. 'For one last look. Before I consign it to your office permanently.'

Appleford dropped the bulky manuscript on his desk. Lance Arbuthnot picked it up, studied it, then turned pages. After a pause he stopped turning pages, read one particular page, his lips moving.

'What's the matter?' Appleford demanded.

'I – seem to have garbled an important passage on page 173,' Lance Arbuthnot muttered. 'It'll have to be set straight before you erad it.'

Pressing the button of his intercom, Appleford said to his secretary Miss Tomsen, 'Please show Mr Arbuthnot to a reading room up on one of the restricted floors, where he can work without being interrupted.' To Arbuthnot he said, 'How soon will you get it back to me?'

'Fifteen, twenty minutes. Anyhow, under an hour.' Arbuthnot rose, clutching his precious grubby manuscript. 'You will accept it for eradication?'

'You're darn right. You go fix it up and I'll see you later.' He, too, rose; Arbuthnot hesitated, then bumbled his way once more out of Appleford's office, into the outer waiting room.

And Appleford turned to other business; he forgot the crackpot inventor Lance Arbuthnot almost at once.

Alone in the reading room Sebastian Hermes with trembling fingers got out his armband and fastened it on his sleeve. He dug into his coat pocket, got out his survival kit, and placed the capsule of LSD-antidote in his mouth, being careful not to bite down on it. The grenade he held in his left hand, clumsily, thinking, This isn't me. I don't know how to do this. Joe Tinbane could have. He was trained for this.

Virtually unable to make his hand and arm work, he injected himself with the small quantity of pale, saplike fluid. Well, he had begun; he was in it. And would be, for what – to him – would seem hours.

Opening the door of the reading room he glanced down the hall. No one. He began to walk; he saw a sign reading STAIRS and headed for it.

There was no problem in climbing the stairs; still he saw no one. But when he opened the door at what he guessed to be the next to top floor, he found himself facing a cold-eyed uniformed Library guard.

The guard, in slow-motion, began to move toward him.

With no difficulty he eluded the guard; he ducked past him and hurried down the corridor.

Ann Fisher, from a side door, appeared with an armload of papers, moving in hazy slow-motion, like the guard. She saw him, turned gradually over a matter of what seemed to him minutes; her jaw, by retarded degrees, dropped until at last, at agonizing last, she registered amazement.

'What – are – you – doing – ' she began to say. But he could not wait for the enormously prolonged sentence to be completed; he knew everything had gone wrong – he never should have run into her, and certainly not so soon – and he slipped by her and on down the corridor, realizing futilely that despite the time-difference between them he had stood still long enough for her to identify him. I should always have been in motion, he realized. Constant, accelerated motion. But too late now.

An alarm bell would ring; it would take her minutes, by his time-scale. But it would come. Inevitably.

Ahead, two uniformed guards, armed, stood rigidly

before a doorway. He darted toward them, moving as swiftly as possible. The guards seemed to sense him feebly; their heads rotated, as if mechanical – but by then he had slid past them and turned the knob of the door.

The alarm bell rang. Din-din-din, with measurable intervals between each impact. Like a tape recorder, he thought, at the wrong speed. With the slower speed. He opened the office door.

Four Erads – he recognized them by their neo-togas – lounged about the office. On a chair in the center sat the Anarch Peak.

'I don't want you,' Sebastian said, deciding instantly. 'I want my wife; where's Lotta?' None of them understood him; to them it was a blur of noise. He ducked back out of the room, leaving the dry, wizened little figure of the Anarch; in the hall once more he passed two armed sentries, who by now had turned to follow him inside . . . he wiggled between them, tugged free as their arms came gradually up, and hurried toward the next office.

Nothing but an empty desk. File cabinets.

He tried a third office. Someone – unfamiliar – talking on the phone; he hurried on.

In the fourth room he found stored supplies. Dead and inertly cold.

The next floor, he said to himself; ahead he saw the sign STAIRS once more, and ran that way.

On the top floor he encountered a number of men and women in the corridor, and all, like him, wore the luminous blue armband. He darted among them, opened a door at random.

Behind him he heard someone, invisible to him, cock a weapon; he twisted around and saw the barrel of a rifle rise.

Clumsily, he threw the LSD hand grenade. And at the same time bit into the antidote capsule.

The barrel ceased rising. The gun, lugubriously, fell from the guard's hands; the guard settled to a heap on the floor, his hands up, warding off something assailing him. Hallucinations.

The LSD, like smoke, billowed up and spread throughout the corridor. He waded through it, past slow-motion figures, tried door after door. More Library officials at work; he saw, several times, the insignia of the Erad Council – he saw the hierarchy of the Library disintegrating because of his presence and what he had brought with him. But not Lotta.

He cornered at last, alone in her office, one frail, elderly female Erad who regarded him wide-eyed. 'Where,' he said, slowing his speech to her time-phasing, 'is – Mrs – Hermes. On – what – floor.' He moved toward her, menacingly.

However, the LSD had by now reached her; she had begun to fall into a groveling heap, an expression of awe on her face. Bending over her he grabbed her by the shoulder, repeating his question.

'On – the – basement – level,' the reply, with agonizing slowness, came at last. And then the elderly Erad dissolved into a private world of colors; he left her to it and hurried on, once more out into the hall.

The hall resounded with people and noises. But everyone had devolved into a personal realm; there remained no interpersonal action, no coordinated effort. So he had no trouble making his way to the elevator; no one paid any attention to him.

He pressed the button, and after a fantastically long period, the elevator arrived.

183

Fully armed and ready Library guards filled the elevator. They wore gas masks; they eyed him as he – to them – flitted away, and one of them after a moment managed to fire his side arm.

The shot missed. But at least they had been able, at last, to shoot in his general direction. And the LSD gas would not affect these men.

I can't get Lotta, he realized. I can't get on the elevator, not when it's full. *Ray Roberts was right*; I should have lugged the Anarch out of here and forgotten about Lotta. The dead shall live, he thought ironically, the living die. And music shall untune the sky. I am untuned, he said to himself. They have me. I didn't get anyone out, as Joe Tinbane did. Even temporarily. It might have worked out differently if I hadn't run across Ann Fisher, he thought.

He had a strange impression of timelessness, now, from the drug with which he had injected himself. A sense, almost, of immortality. But not of strength, not of majestic power; he felt weak, tired and hopeless. So Ann Fisher gets all she wanted, he thought. Her prophecies are coming true, one by one; I am the last part, and I, like Joe Tinbane and the Anarch and Lotta, have come about.

I messed it up, he realized. In only a few minutes. If Joe Tinbane had been here it would be different; I know it would be.

He could not stop thinking that; his awareness of his own inferiority overwhelmed him. He versus Joe. His defects; Joe's prowess. And yet they got him, he reflected hopelessly. Joe is dead!

And I will be, he thought. Presently.

Maybe we could have done it working together, Joe and I, he reflected. The two of us in unison trying to get

184

Lotta out; we both love her. And one by one, alone, we die. It just didn't work out. If he had gotten my warning; if he had called me from the motel, if –

I'm old and I'm impotent, he thought. I should have been left in my grave; they dug up nothing. An emptiness: only the deadness; the chill, the mold of the tomb still clings to me and infects whatever I try. I feel myself dying again, he thought. Or rather, I never stopped being dead.

He thought: if they kill me it doesn't matter because it doesn't change me. But Lotta is different, just as Tinbane was different.

Maybe, he thought, even if I can't get out of here, can't save anyone, including myself – maybe I can still kill Ann Fisher. That would be worth something. For Joe Tinbane's sake.

Chapter 17

But time present how do we measure, seeing it hath no space?
It is measured while passing, but when it shall have passed, it
is not measured; for there will be nothing to be measured.
                                                    – St Augustine

Seizing a rifle from one of the slowed-down Library
guards Sebastian Hermes scampered toward the stairs.
As he reached them he heard voices below, echoing up.
Maybe they're below the next floor down, he hoped; he
descended rapidly. And found himself unopposed.

. The corridor of the next floor down, like that above,
teemed with halting, heavily weighed armed men. He
saw, as through a glass clearly, Ann Fisher, a great
distance off, standing by herself. So he hurried in that
direction, evading without difficulty those who languidly
tried to intercept him . . . and then, as before, he
confronted her; once again she blanched in recognition.

Slowly, matching his words to her time-sense, he said,
'I – can't – get – out. So – I – will – kill – you.' He raised
the rifle.

'Wait,' she said. 'I'll – make – a – deal – with – you –
right – here – and – now.' She peered at him, trying to
make him out, as if she perceived him only dimly. 'You –
let – me – go,' she said, 'and – you – can – take – Lotta –
and – leave.'

Did she mean it? He doubted it. 'You – have – the –
authority – to – order – that?' he asked.

'Yes,' she nodded.

186

'But I'm taking you along,' he said. 'Until she and I are out of here.'

'Pardon?' She strained, trying to follow his too-rapid discourse. 'Okay,' she said finally, evidently having deciphered what he had said. She seemed fatalistically resigned; surprisingly so.

'You're afraid,' he said.

'Well *of course* I am.' Astonishingly, her speech did not seem slowed, now; evidently the injection had begun to wear off. 'You come bursting in here and running about berserk, lobbing grenades and threatening everyone. I want to get you out of the Library and I don't care how I do it.' She spoke, then, into her lapel microphone. 'Put Lotta Hermes into an aircar on the roof. I'll join her there.'

'You have the authority?' he asked, amazed.

'My father is pro tem Chairman of the Erad Council. And you've met my mother. Shall we go up to the roof?' She seemed calmer now, with a good deal of her old poise. 'I don't want to get killed by some psychotic,' she said patiently. 'I know you, don't forget. I just happened to be very much afraid you'd do this, exactly what you've done. I would have stayed away from the Library entirely, but in the present complex situation – '

'Let's get up to the roof,' he interrupted. 'Come on.' He goaded her, with the rifle, toward the nearby elevator.

'Calm down,' Ann said, frowning reprovingly. 'Nothing's going to happen except for what we agreed on: Lotta will be waiting. If you go mad and fire off that rifle it's she that might be killed, and you don't want that.'

'No,' he agreed. She was right; he had, now, to get control of himself. The elevator arrived and Ann Fisher motioned the armed guards out of it. 'Get lost,' she told them brusquely. 'Guns,' she said disdainfully to Sebastian as he and she ascended. 'And the kind of people who use them. Compensates for a weak ego. Look at you with that thing; all of a sudden you're not afraid of anything, because you can make anyone do anything you want. Vox dei, as the Udi commandos call guns. The voice of God.' She reflected. 'I suppose it was a mistake to seize your wife and detain her for a second time; we were pressing our luck.'

'Killing Officer Tinbane,' Sebastian said, 'was a dreadful act of wanton cruelty. What did he ever do to you?'

'He did what you did,' Ann Fisher said. 'He burst in here with a gun and shot it out with a few harmless old Erads – unarmed Erads.'

'Vengeance for that,' Sebastian said bitterly. 'I assume you're going to go after me, now, for what I've done today. Until you get me, too.'

'We'll see,' Ann Fisher said with tranquility. 'The Council will have to meet and vote on it. Or else they can vote to let me make the decision.' She eyed him.

'The Library,' he said, 'respects violence.'

'Oh yes; we certainly do. In fact we're very much afraid of it; we know what it can accomplish. We employ it ourselves, not gladly, but in admission of its efficacy. Look what *you* accomplished, today.' They had reached the roof; the elevator had stopped and the doors now slid soundlessly open. 'Where did you get that rifle?' she asked curiously. 'It looks like one of ours.'

'It is,' he said. 'I came here unarmed.'

'Well,' Ann said resignedly, 'guns have no loyalty; they're not like dogs.' The two of them stepped out onto the Library's roof field. 'There she is,' Ann said, straining to see. 'They're just leaving her off. Come on.' She strode long-legged ahead of him; he hurried to catch up. The

188

guards who had brought Lotta to the roof field furtively ducked off and disappeared; he paid no attention to them: Ann Fisher and his wife alone concerned him.

As soon as he and Ann reached the parked aircar, Lotta said, 'Did you get the Anarch out, Sebastian? I overheard them talking; they have him down there, too.'

At once Ann Fisher said briskly, 'No deal on that.'

Stoically, Sebastian herded her into the front seat of his car, got in behind the wheel and handed Lotta the rifle. 'Keep this pointed at Miss Fisher,' he instructed her.

Hesitantly, Lotta said, 'I – '

'Your life,' he said, 'depends on it, and so does mine. Remember what they did to Joe Tinbane? It was this woman's decision to do that; she gave the order. Now will you keep the rifle pointed at her?'

'Yes,' Lotta whispered; he saw the barrel of the rifle come up: realization about Joe Tinbane had done it. 'But what about the Anarch?' she asked again.

'I can't get him out,' Sebastian said, his voice rising hoarsely. 'I can't work miracles. I'm incredibly lucky to get you and me out. So will you lay off me?'

Behind him, Lotta nodded in mute obedience.

He turned on the car's motor and in a moment they were in the air above the Library, joining in with the mid-morning shoppers' traffic.

Parking briefly on the roof of a downtown public building Sebastian Hermes let off Ann Fisher – taking her lapel microphone with him. Again he sent the aircar up into the sky; he and Lotta rode in silence for a time and then Lotta said, 'Thanks for coming to get me.'

'I was lucky,' he said shortly. He did not tell her that he had given up, that he intended only to destroy Ann

189

Fisher. That saving his wife had, in effect, been virtually an accident. But one, however, which he rejoiced in; he appreciated it. 'The news about Joe Tinbane flashed on the TV,' he said. 'So that's how we knew. And the TV said he had been with a woman who had disappeared after the crime.'

'I'll never get over his death,' Lotta said wanly.

'I don't expect you to. Not for a long time.'

Lotta said, 'They killed him right in front of me. I saw it happen, all of it. Children from the Library . . . it was grotesque, like a dream. He fired at them but he's used to firing up high, at a full grown adult; so his shots passed right over their heads.' Again she fell silent.

Roughly, wanting to make her feel better, he said, 'Anyhow you're out of the Library. This time it'll be permanent.'

'Will the Uditi be mad at you?' she asked. 'For not getting the Anarch out? That's really a shame . . . he's so important a person, and I'm not; it seems so unfair.'

'You're important to me,' Sebastian pointed out.

'Where did you get all those devices you were using? That speeded you up, and that LSD smoke bomb; I heard them discussing it; it took them completely by surprise. You don't normally have possession of LSD and –'

'Udi gave them to me,' he broke in harshly. 'They outfitted me. Arranged a pretext for getting me in and up to Section B.'

'Then they *will* be sore,' Lotta said, with perception. 'They did it expecting you to haul the Anarch out, didn't they?'

He didn't answer; he concentrated on driving the car and watching to make certain they were not followed.

'You don't have to say,' Lotta said. 'I can tell. Don't the Uditi have those Offspring of Might, those killer

190

commandos? I've read about them . . . do they really exist?'

'They exist,' he admitted. 'To some extent. I suppose.'

Speculatively, Lotta said, 'Maybe Mr Roberts will send them into the Library and not after you. That's what they should have done; it's not your job to get the Anarch out. You're not a commando.'

'I wanted to go,' he said.

'Because of me?' She studied him; he could feel the intensity of her scrutiny. 'Because you didn't get me out the first time? Now you've made up for it, haven't you?'

'I tried to,' Sebastian said. That had been the idea.

'Do you love me?' Lotta asked.

'Yes.' Very much. More than ever before; he realized that as he sat beside her here in the aircar. Just the two of them.

'Are you – resentful? About me visiting Joe Tinbane?'

'About the motel?' he said. 'No.' It had, after all, been his own fault. And there had been his journey with Ann Fisher. 'I'm just sorry Joe got killed,' he said.

'I'll never get over it,' Lotta said. As if promising.

'What did they do to you at the Library?' he asked, and prepared himself.

'Nothing. They had scheduled me to see a psychiatrist they keep; he would have done something to my mind. And that woman, that Miss or Mrs Fisher – she showed up and talked to me awhile.'

'About what?'

'About you.' In her characteristic small voice Lotta continued, 'She claimed that you and she had been intimate. That you – hopped into bed together. She claimed a lot of things like that.' She added, 'But of course I didn't listen to her.'

'Good for you,' he said, and felt the burden of the lies

– *his* lies – weighing upon him. First to his wife and then, shortly, to Ray Roberts; he would have to give them a story, too. Everyone had to be placated . . . that's the style of life, Sebastian realized, that I've begun to lead. As bad as R. C. Buckley, who does it naturally. But for me, he thought, it isn't natural. And yet – here I am.

'It wouldn't have bothered me,' Lotta said, 'even if what she said about you and her turned out to be true. After all, look what I did . . . the motel, I mean. I wouldn't hold it against you; I couldn't.'

'Well, it's not true,' he said laconically.

'She's very attractive with that absolutely black hair and those blue eyes. A lot more attractive than me.'

Sebastian said, 'I detest her.'

'Because of Joe?'

'That, and other reasons.' He did not amplify.

'Where are we going now?' Lotta asked.

'Back to our conapt.'

'Are you going to call Udi? And tell them – '

'They'll call me,' Sebastian said, stoically resigned.

Chapter 18

I will pass then beyond this power of my nature also, rising by degrees unto Him Who made me. And I come to the fields and spacious palaces of my memory.   St Augustine

At their conapt he phoned the vitarium to make sure it was still in business. Cheryl Vale answered. 'Flask of Hermes,' she said merrily.

'I'm not coming in today,' Sebastian said. 'Is everybody else there?'

'Everyone but you,' Cheryl said. 'Oh, Mr Hermes – Bob Lindy wants to talk to you; he wants to give you the details on how the Library got the Anarch away from him. Do you have time – '

'I'll talk to him later,' Sebastian said. 'It can wait. Hello.' He hung up, feeling terrible.

'I've been thinking,' Lotta said, seated on the couch across from him; her face showed agitation. 'If the Library took a vengeful position regarding Joe Tinbane and what he did, then they'll take the same position regarding you.'

'I thought of that,' Sebastian said.

'And then the Offspring of Might,' Lotta said. 'I'm afraid – '

'Yes,' he said brusquely. All of them, he thought. The Rome party, the Library, Udi – because of what he had done he had managed to line all of them – *all of them* – up against him. Even the LA Police Department, he thought; they may think I killed Joe Tinbane because he

193

was ensconced at a motel with my wife; I'd have an alleged motive.

Lotta asked, 'Who can you turn to?'

'No one,' he answered. It was a dreadful, terrifying feeling. 'No one but you,' he corrected himself; he did, after all, have Lotta back, now. And that made up for a great deal.

But it was not enough.

'Maybe,' Lotta continued, 'we should hide, you and I. Go somewhere else. What they did to Joe – it's so vivid in my mind; I can't forget it, seeing it like I did. I remember the pitpat of their feet on the roof, and then one of them, that one particular child, peering in through the window. And Joe had guns and he knew they were coming – but it still did no good. I think we should leave Los Angeles and maybe the Western United States. Maybe even Earth.'

'Migrate to Mars?' he said broodingly.

'The Uditi have no power there,' Lotta said. 'The UN is the only authority, and I understand they run the colony-domes very well. Everything's always under control. And they're always soliciting for volunteers. You see their ad on TV every evening.'

'You can't return from there,' he said. 'Once you've emigrated. You're told that before you sign the legal papers. It's a one-way trip.'

'I know that. But at least we'd be alive. We wouldn't one night hear noises on the roof or outside the door. I guess you really should have gotten the Anarch out, Sebastian; then at least you'd have Udi to help you. But this way – '

'I tried,' he repeated, mechanically. 'You heard Ann Fisher; I couldn't make a deal regarding him. I took what I could get – I took you – and got the hell out. Ray

194

Roberts will have to like it; it's the truth.' But he knew, inside, that he had never at any point really tried to release the Anarch. He had been thinking only of Lotta. As Roberts had said, it constituted a near biological drive. A drive which Roberts had feared, which had, in the end, as Roberts anticipated, won out. Once he entered the Library all talk about the 'transcendental value to history' had evaporated, gone up in the smoke of the LSD grenade.

'I'd really enjoy going to Mars,' Lotta said. 'We've talked about it, remember? It's supposed to be fascinating . . . you get a sort of intangible sense of the cosmic, of the awesomeness of it – man on another planet. It has to be experienced, they say, to be understood.'

'The only work I can do,' Sebastian grated, 'is sniffing.'

'Finding deaders who're about to return to life?'

'You know that's my only talent.' He gestured. 'What good would that be on Mars? On Mars the Hobart Phase tests out weak, almost nil.' And because of that he had another reason. There, he would resume normal aging, and for him that would soon prove lethal: in that direction he lay only a few years from illness and death.

For Lotta, of course, it would be different. She had decades to live in normal time; more in fact than under the Phase.

But what do I care, he thought, if I die again soon? I've gone through it once; it's not all that bad. In some ways I'd welcome it . . . the great endless rest. The absolute relief from all burdens.

'That's right,' Lotta admitted. 'There're no deaders on Mars. I forgot.'

'I'd have to become a manual laborer or a clerk,' he said.

'No, I think your managerial ability would be worth a

lot, your talent for organization. They'd undoubtedly give you aptitude tests; I'm positive they do. So they'd know about all your many abilities. See?'

He said, 'You have the optimism of youth.' And I, he thought, the despair of old age. 'Let's wait,' he decided, 'until I've talked to Ray Roberts. Maybe I can sell him a story he'll believe. I mean,' he amended, 'maybe I can make him understand the situation I was in. And like you say, maybe their commandos can rescue the Anarch. It really is a task for them, not for me. I'll point that out, too.'

'Good luck,' Lotta said wistfully.

Within the hour Ray Roberts' call came.

'I see you're back,' Roberts said, inspecting him tautly – and critically. He seemed extremely tense, very keyed-up and expectant. 'How did you make out?'

'Not well,' Sebastian said, with caution; he had to play this right all the way through, with not the slightest misstep.

'The Anarch,' Roberts said, 'is still being detained in the Library.'

'I reached him,' Sebastian said, 'but I couldn't – '

'What about your wife?'

With frozen, tomb-like care, he said, 'I did get her. By accident. They – the Library authorities – decided to release her. I didn't ask for it; the idea, as I say, was theirs.'

'A détente,' Roberts said. 'You received Lotta in exchange for vacating the Library premises; it turned out in a friendly manner.'

'No,' he said.

'That's what it sounds like.' Roberts continued to scrutinize him, expressionlessly; no affect showed on the

196

dark, alert face. 'They bought you off. And – ' His voice rose into sharpness. 'They wouldn't have done that unless you stood a good chance of getting the Anarch out.'

'Ann Fisher decided it,' Sebastian countered. 'I started to kill her; she bought her way out. I took her with me; I even – '

'Did it occur to you,' Roberts continued, 'that this is the reason why they again took your wife into the Library? To act as a hostage? In order to neutralize you?'

'I had a choice,' Sebastian said doggedly, 'between – '

'They fathomed your psychological makeup,' Roberts said witheringly. 'They have psychiatrists; they knew the deal you'd buy. Ann Fisher isn't afraid of death. That was an act; she didn't "buy her way out." She got *you* out, away from the Anarch. If Ann Fisher had been truly afraid of you she wouldn't have been loitering anywhere in sight.'

Grudgingly, Sebastian said, 'Maybe – you're right.'

'You managed to see the Anarch? He's definitely alive?'

'Yes,' Sebastian said. He felt himself collecting perspiration from the atmosphere; it collected under his arms, down his back. He felt his pores trying to – and failing to – absorb it all. Too much had gathered.

'And the Erads were working him over?'

'There – were Erads with him. Yes.'

'You've changed human history, you know,' Roberts said. 'Or rather *you've failed to change it*. You had your chance and now it's gone. You could have been remembered forever as the vitarium owner who revived and then saved the Anarch; you would never have been forgotten by Udi or by the rest of the planet. *And an entirely new basis for religious belief would have been established*. Certitude would have replaced mere faith,

197

and a totally new body of scriptures would have emerged.' No trace of anger had entered Ray Roberts' voice; he spoke calmly, merely reciting known facts. Facts which Sebastian could not deny.

'Tell him,' Lotta said urgently from behind, 'that you'll try again.' She put her hand on his shoulder, rubbed encouragingly.

Sebastian said, 'I'll go back to the Library. Once more.'

'We sent you,' Roberts said, 'as a compromise with Giacometti; he asked us to avoid violence. Now our arrangement regarding you has died; we are free to send in our zealots. But – ' He paused. 'They will probably find a corpse. The Library will identify the Offspring as being present in the area – immediately, as soon as the first one enters the building. As Giacometti pointed out to me last night. Still, there is nothing else we can do. With them no negotiations are possible; nothing we have or can promise will induce the Library to release the Anarch. It does not resemble the situation with Mrs Hermes.'

'Well,' Sebastian said, 'it's been nice talking to you. I'm glad to learn the situation; thanks for – '

The screen faded. Ray Roberts had rung off. With no salutation.

Sebastian sat holding the receiver for a time and then, by degrees, placed it back on the hook. He felt fifty years older . . . and a hundred years more tired.

'You know,' he said presently to Lotta, 'when you wake up in your coffin you first feel a weird fatigue. Your mind is empty; your body does nothing. Then you have thoughts, things you want to say, acts you want to perform. You want to yell and to struggle, to get out. But still your body doesn't respond; you can't speak and you can't move. It goes on for – ' He estimated. 'About forty-eight hours.'

'Is it very awful?'

'It's the worst experience I've ever had. Much worse than dying.' He thought. *And I feel like that now.*

'Can I bring you something?' Lotta asked perceptively. 'Some warm sogum?'

'No,' he said. 'Thanks.' He got to his feet, walked slowly across the living room to the window overlooking the street. *He's right,* he said to himself. *I have failed to change human history; I made my personal life more important – at the expense of every other living human being, and especially the Uditi. I've destroyed the whole newly forming basis for world theology; Ray Roberts is right!*

'Can I do anything for you?' Lotta asked softly.

'I'll be okay,' he said, gazing down at the street below, the people and sardine-like surface vehicles. 'The thing about lying there in your coffin like that,' he said, 'the part that makes it so bad, is that your mind is alive but your body isn't, and you feel the duality. When you're really dead you don't feel that; you're not related to your body at all. But that – ' He gestured convulsively. 'A living mind tied to a corpse. Lodged inside it. And it doesn't seem as if the body will ever become animated; you seem to wait forever.'

'But you know,' Lotta said, 'that it can never happen to you again. It's over with.'

Sebastian said, 'But I remember it. The experience is still part of me.' He tapped his forehead, knocking it fiercely. 'It's always in here.' *This is what I think of,* he said to himself, *when I'm really terribly frightened; this swims up to confront me. A symptom of my terror.*

'I'll make the arrangements,' Lotta said, somehow

199

reading his mind, somehow managing to understand him. 'For our emigration to Mars. You go in the bedroom and lie down and rest and I'll start making calls.'

'You know you hate to use the vidphone,' he said. 'You dread it. The vidphone is your bête noire.'

'I can do it this time.' She guided him toward the bedroom, her hands gentle.

Chapter 19

But in these things is no place of repose; they abide not, they
flee; and who can follow them with the senses of the flesh?
— St Augustine

In his sleep Sebastian Hermes dreamed of the grave; he
dreamed he once more lay within his tight plastic casket,
in the Tiny Place, in the darkness. He called over and
over again, 'My name is Sebastian Hermes and I want to
get out! Is there anyone up there who can hear me?' In
his dream he listened, and, far off, for the second time in
his life, he felt the weight of footsteps, of someone
moving toward his grave. 'Let me out!' he squeaked, over
and over again; and, against the confining plastic, he
struggled like a damp insect. Hopelessly.

Now someone dug; he felt the impact of the spade.
'Get air down to me!' he tried to yell, but since there was
no longer any air he could not breathe; he was suffocating. 'Hurry!' he called, but his call became soundless in
the absence of air; he lay compressed, crushed, by an
enormous vacuum; the pressure grew until, silently, his
ribs broke. He felt that, too, his bones one by one
snapping.

'If you get me out of here,' he tried to say, wanted to
say, 'I'll go back into the Library and find the Anarch.
Okay?' He listened; the excavation continued: dulled
thumps, methodically. 'I promise,' he said. 'Is it a deal?'

The blade of the spade rasped across his coffin's lid.

I admit it, he thought. I could have gotten him out, but

201

I chose to save my wife instead. *They* didn't stop me; I stopped myself. But I won't do that again; I promise. He listened. Now, with a screwdriver, they had begun removing the lid, the last barrier between him and light, the air. It'll be different next time, he promised. Okay?

The lid, noisily, was dragged aside. Light spilled in and he looked up, saw into a face which peered down at him.

A wizened, dark, little old face. The Anarch's.

'I heard you calling,' the Anarch said. 'So I dropped what I had been doing and came to give aid. What can I do for you? Do you want to know the year? It is 4 B.C.'

'Why?' Sebastian asked. 'What does that signify?' He felt that it portended something vast; he felt awe.

The Anarch said, 'You are the savior of mankind. Through you it will be redeemed. You are the most important person ever born.'

'What do I have to do,' Sebastian said, 'to redeem mankind?'

'You must die again,' the Anarch answered, but now the dream became wraith-like and hazy and he began to wake up; he sensed himself here in bed in his conapt, beside Lotta; he sensed that he had dreamed and so the dream ebbed away from him – leaving a peculiar residue.

Some message, he thought as he turned over, sat up, pushed the covers away from him and rose unsteadily to his feet to stand by the bed, deep in thought. Trying to remember as much of the dream as possible.

I must what? he asked himself. What did the Anarch want to say to me? Die? The dream told him nothing, only that he felt trapped and impotent, that he felt guilty, boundlessly so, for leaving the Anarch in the Library; all things he consciously knew. Big deal, he thought gloomily.

He stumbled into the kitchen – and found three men,

wearing black silk clothes, seated at the table. Three Offspring of Might. The three men looked tired and fretful. Before them, on the table, lay a heap of creased handwritten notes.

'This is the man,' one of them said, indicating Sebastian, 'who left the Anarch in the Library. When he could have gotten him out.'

The three Offspring of Might regarded Sebastian with mixed emotions visible on their weary faces.

To Sebastian the spokesman of the Offspring explained, 'We're going to make our move against the Library tonight. Nothing subtle; we're going to drag a cannon up and fire nuclear shells at it until it falls apart. We may not get the Anarch but at least we'll have taken care of *them*.' His tone indicated contempt and irate hostility.

'You don't think you could get in and get out?' Sebastian asked. It appalled him, the clumsy quality of their plans. The nihilism. Not saving the Anarch but destroying the Library; they had missed the entire point.

'There's a minuscule chance,' the spokesman of the Offspring conceded. 'That's why we stopped off to talk to you; we want to know exactly where you found the Anarch and how they're guarding him . . . how many men with what weapons. Of course, it all will be changed by the time we arrive – it's probably all changed now – but there may be something we can make use of.' He eyed Sebastian, waiting.

Lotta, sleepy-eyed, appeared in the kitchen doorway behind him. 'Are they here to kill us?' she asked, slipping her arm through his.

'Apparently not,' Sebastian told her; he patted her arm, trying to soothe her. 'All I remember is armed

203

Library guards,' he said to the Offspring. 'I don't remember which office I found him in, except that it was on the next to top floor. It seemed to be an ordinary office, like all the others; they probably selected it at random.'

'Have you dreamed about the Anarch since?' the spokesman of the Offspring asked, surprisingly. 'We're told that in his previous life the Anarch occasionally communicated with his followers through their dreams.'

'Yes,' Sebastian said guardedly. 'I did dream about him; he told me something, about myself. That I had to do something. The year, he said, was 4 B.C. and I would be the savior of mankind. By doing this thing.'

'Not very helpful,' the spokesman of the Offspring commented.

'But in a sense true,' another of the Offspring spoke up. 'If he *had* brought the Anarch out he *would* have been the savior of mankind. That's what the Anarch wanted him to do; we don't need to hear the dream to know that.' He jotted notes, scowling.

'You missed your chance, Mr Hermes,' the first Offspring said. 'The biggest chance of your life.'

'I know,' Sebastian said woodenly.

'Maybe we should kill him,' the third Offspring said. 'Kill both of them. Now, instead of after the thrust on the Library.'

Sebastian felt his pulse cease; he felt his body shrink into death. As it had been in the Tiny Place. But he said nothing; he merely hugged Lotta against him.

'Not as long as he may be helpful,' their spokesman said flatly. Again he surveyed Sebastian. 'Did you come across any weapons more formidable than laser beams and automatic rifles?' he inquired.

'No.' Sebastian stiffly shook his head.

'There seemed to be no force-field, nothing modern, protecting the highly sensitive top levels of the structure.'

'All hand weapons,' Sebastian said.

'By what system are the Library guards alerted? Radio?'

'Yes.' Again he nodded.

'They didn't try to stop you with nerve gas?'

Sebastian said, 'I was the only one who used gas. Supplied to me by His Mightiness and the Rome party.'

'Yes, we know what you were supplied with.' The spokesman of the Offspring toyed with his pencil, licking the corner of his mouth and concentrating. 'They had gas masks?'

'Some of them.'

'Then they have gas – one kind or another – available. In case of an out-and-out invasion. And when our first shell hits the building we may see something larger than hand weapons emerge from within there.' He once more contemplated Sebastian. 'I don't believe it. I mean, I believe *you* – but I know they're better defended. They really didn't try to stop you; if it had been a team instead of one man, you'd have gotten the Anarch out.' He turned to consult his two companions. 'The Library is still an enigma,' he told them. 'Twice, within forty-eight hours, a man has gone in there and hauled Lotta Hermes out. Yet, there sits the Anarch, as if available; as if a fast-moving *putsch* could be carried off. In my opinion the Anarch is already dead and what Hermes saw consists of nothing more than a simulacrum-robot, prepared in advance.'

One of his companions said, 'But Hermes' dream. It implies that His Mightiness is still alive. Somewhere. Maybe not in the Library, though.'

205

Lotta detached herself from Sebastian and seated herself at the kitchen table across from the three Offspring of Might. 'Haven't the Uditi ever been able to – ' She gestured, not knowing the word. 'Gotten one of you in – you know. On the staff. A spy.'

'They use quasi-telepathic probes in screening applicants,' the spokesman said. 'We tried several times. They gunned the individual down each time; we got back a corpse.'

'You couldn't say you were the inventor of a book,' Sebastian said.

'*That* you used up,' the spokesman said cuttingly. 'A gambit we prepared months ago. Because of the interference of the Rome party, you got hold of that. That didn't please us . . . the Offspring. Hermes, it may have perplexed Ray Roberts that you failed, but it doesn't perplex us. We have an enormous regard for the resources, the ingenuity of the Library; we will, on orders from Roberts, kill you to avenge the Anarch . . . but in our own separate opinion, you didn't have the foggiest ghost of a chance.'

Sebastian said huskily, 'But I didn't even try.'

'That makes no nevermind. Not if what you saw consisted of a simrobot. Or they had more sophisticated weapons, ready to be lugged out as soon as you showed success. How readily did they agree to the détente? You getting out alive with your wife but without the Anarch?'

'They made the offer,' Sebastian said.

'It's a trap,' the spokesman of the Offspring said. 'To lure us into a kamikaze raid; *all* the Offspring: our entire corps. The Anarch probably has been taken miles from here, to one of the branch Libraries up the Coast toward Oregon. Any one of the more than eighty branches in the WUS.' He brooded. 'Or he could be in one of the private residences of an Erad. Or in a hotel. Do you know

206

anyone high up in the Library hierarchy, Hermes? An Erad? A librarian? I mean personally.'

'I know Ann Fisher,' he said.

'Yes. The daughter of the Chief Librarian and the pro tem Chairman of the Council.' The Offspring nodded. 'How intimately do you know her? Be accurate; this could be vital.'

'Ignore your wife temporarily,' another of the Offspring spoke up. 'This takes precedence.'

Sebastian said, 'I've been to bed with her.'

'Oh,' Lotta gasped, 'then what she told me was true.'

'That makes two of us,' Sebastian said.

'I guess it does,' Lotta said, forlornly. She buried her face in her hands, rubbed her forehead, then lifted her head and gazed up at him. 'Could you tell me why you –'

'You have the balance of your lives to discuss this,' the spokesman of the Offspring broke in. 'Do you think you could lure Ann Fisher out of the Library?' he asked Sebastian. 'On a pretext? So we could put our own telepathic probe on her?'

'I could,' he said.

'What would you tell her?' Lotta said. 'That you wanted to go to bed with her again?'

'I would say,' he said, 'that the Offspring of Might had been instructed to kill us. And I wanted to arrange sanctuary for you and me in the Library.'

The spokesman pointed to the vidphone in the living room. 'Call her,' he said.

Sebastian made his way into the living room. 'She has an apartment,' he said. 'Outside the Library; that's where she took me. It'll probably be there, not here.'

'Any place,' the spokesman said. 'So long as it's where we can get our hands on her and attach a probe.'

Seated at the vidphone he dialed the Library.

'People's Topical Library,' the operator said presently.

He turned the vidphone set around, so that the camera would not pick up the four people in the kitchen of his conapt. 'Let me talk to Miss Ann Fisher,' he said.

'Who is calling, please?'

'Tell her Mr Hermes.' He sat waiting; the screen had now become blank. Then, after a sputter, it relit.

On the screen Ann Fisher's attractive face formed.

'Hello, Sebastian,' she said quietly.

He said, 'I'm marked to be killed.'

'By the Offspring of Might?'

'Yes,' he said.

'Well, Sebastian,' Ann said, in her clear voice, 'I really do think you brought it on yourself. You couldn't resolve your loyalty; you came to the Library, you forced your way in, but instead of trying to bring the Anarch out – and you had equipment supplied by Udi; we recognized it – instead of doing that – '

'Listen,' he said harshly, breaking in. 'I want to meet you.'

'I can't help you.' Her voice was neutral, pert; his situation did not impinge on her savoir-faire. 'After what you did in – '

'We want to arrange sanctuary,' Sebastian said. 'In the Library. Lotta and I.'

'So?' Ann raised her thin eyebrows. 'Well, I can ask the Council; I know it's been done on rare occasions. But don't get your hopes up. I doubt if the answer would be yes, in your case.'

Appearing beside Sebastian, Lotta took the receiver from him and said, 'My husband's a very effective organizer, Miss Fisher. I know you could make use of his ability. We had planned to go to the UN and try to make it to Mars, but the Offspring of Might are too near; we'll be killed before we can get our medical examinations and passports.'

'Has the Offspring of Might contacted you?' Ann asked; she seemed more interested, now.

'Yes,' Sebastian said, retrieving the vidphone receiver.

'Do you know,' Ann said in a cold, hard voice, 'if they have any plans regarding the Anarch?'

'They said one thing,' Sebastian said cautiously.

'Oh? Tell me what it was.'

'I'll tell you,' he said, 'when we meet you. Either here at our conapt or at your apartment.'

Ann Fisher hesitated, calculated, then decided. 'I'll meet you in two hours. At my place. You remember the address?'

'No,' he said; he reached out, and one of the Offspring quickly handed him a pencil and pad.

She gave him the address and then rang off. Sebastian sat for a moment, then rose stiffly. The three Offspring regarded him wordlessly.

'It's arranged,' he said. And it will give me satisfaction, he said to himself. No matter how it works out, whether they get the Anarch or not. 'Here.' He handed the spokesman the slip of paper on which he had written Ann Fisher's address. 'What do I have to do? Am I supposed to go in there armed?'

'Probably she has a standard search-beam system across her doorway,' the spokesman said, examining the address. 'It'll sound you for any weapons. No, just go in there and talk to her. We'll toss a gas grenade through the window, something like that . . . don't worry about that part; that's up to us.' He mused. 'Maybe a thermotropic dart. We'd get both of you, but you'd recover; we'd be bringing you both around.'

To the spokesman Lotta said, 'If my husband helps you this way, will you not kill us?'

'If Hermes makes it possible for us to get back the Anarch,' the spokesman of the Offspring said, 'we'll commute the death sentence which Ray Roberts passed on him.'

Chilled, Sebastian said, 'It's that formal, then.'

'Yes.' The spokesman nodded. 'Done in official session of the Elders of Udi. His Mightiness took time off from his spiritual pilg to participate in that decision.'

'Do you think,' Lotta said to Sebastian, 'that you can really get Miss Fisher out of the Library?'

'She'll come,' he said. But whether the Offspring can grab her – that's something else, he thought. He had a high regard for Ann Fisher's alertness; she probably would be prepared for something just like this. After all, Ann knew how he felt about her.

They won't question her, he realized. Somehow, in some fashion that none of us can envision, she'll kill them. And perhaps me as well. But, he thought, Ann Fisher may die, too. That consoled him; out of all this, that one grim possibility appealed to him. I could never kill her myself, he thought. That's beyond me; I'm not constituted to perform an act like that. But the Offspring: as with Joe Tinbane, killing is their vocation.

He felt immeasurably better. He had steered the assassins of Udi onto Ann Fisher: a great accomplishment.

Onto Ann and away from himself and Lotta!

210

Chapter 20

So then when they rise and tend to be, the more quickly they grow that they may be, so much the more they haste not to be.
– St Augustine

Two hours later he sat in his aircar, parked on the roof of Ann Fisher's apartment building, thinking introspective thoughts about his life and what he had tried to do during it.

Closing his eyes he imagined the Anarch; he tried to revive the truncated dream of a few hours ago. *You must*, the Anarch had said to him. You must do what? he wondered; he tried to induce the dream to continue on past that point. Again he made out the dried, shriveled little face, the dark eyes and wise – both spiritually and earthly wise – mouth. You must die once more, he thought; was that it? Or live? He wondered which. The dream refused to resume and he gave up; he sat upright and opened the car door.

The Anarch, wearing a white cotton robe, stood beside the parked car. Waiting for him to get out.

'My God,' Sebastian said.

Smiling, the Anarch said, 'I am sorry that my earlier talk with you became interrupted. Now we can continue.'

'You – got away from the Library?'

'They still hold me,' the Anarch said. 'What you see is nothing more or less than an hallucination; the antidote capsule to the LSD gas which you carried in your mouth failed the task of neutralizing the gas completely; I am a

211

remnant of that gas operation.' His smile increased. 'Do you believe me, Sebastian?'

Sebastian said, 'I could have been hit by the gas. A little – ' But the Anarch looked substantial. Sebastian reached out to touch him . . .

His groping hand passed through the Anarch's body.

'You see?' the Anarch said. 'I can leave the Library spiritually; I can appear in men's dreams and as drug-induced visions. But physically I am still there *and they can kill me any time they wish.*'

'Do they intend to?' he asked hoarsely.

'Yes.' The Anarch nodded. 'Because I will not give up my views, my specific, certain knowledge; I can't forget what I have learned during death. Any more than you can eradicate the horror of finding yourself buried; some memories remain throughout life.'

Sebastian said, 'What can I do?'

'Very little,' the Anarch said. 'The Offspring of Might are correct when they say that you really had no chance of conveying me from the Library; a splinter-bomb had been rigged and I was the booby trap. If you had lifted me to my feet the bomb would have killed us both.'

'Are you just saying that,' Sebastian said, 'to make me feel better?'

'I am telling you the truth,' the Anarch said.

'And now what?' Sebastian said. 'I'll do anything you want. Anything I can.'

'Your meeting with Miss Fisher.'

'Yes,' he said. 'The Offspring are waiting. I'm like you; I'm a booby trap. For her.'

The Anarch said, 'Let her go.'

'Why?'

'She has a right to live.' The Anarch seemed tranquil, now; once more he smiled. 'I can't be saved,' he said.

'The Offspring can blow up the entire Library and all it will – '

'But,' Sebastian said, 'we can get her too.'

'They possibly might get her,' the Anarch said, 'when they blow up the Library. But, it is all the same.'

'*They* can get her,' Sebastian said. 'But this way *I* can get her.'

The Anarch said, 'You don't actually hate Ann Fisher. In fact it's the opposite; you are deeply, violently in love with her. That's why you're so anxious to see her destroyed: Ann Fisher draws off huge quantities of your emotions; the major share, in fact. Killing her won't bring you closer to Lotta; you must meet Ann Fisher here on the roof when she lands and warn her not to go into her apartment. Do you understand?'

'No,' Sebastian said.

'You must, in fact, warn her not to go back to the Library; you must tell her about the proposed attack. Tell her to arrange for the Library to be evacuated. The attack will come at six this evening; at least that is the present operating schedule of the Offspring. I think they possibly will do it; as you have thought yourself, killing is their vocation.'

Hearing his own thoughts read back to him jarred him; he felt acutely uncomfortable. He said haltingly, 'I don't think Ann Fisher is that important one way or another; I think *you* are important – you and your safety. The Uditi are absolutely right; it's worth blowing the Library to bits if there's any chance – '

'But there isn't,' the Anarch said. 'No chance at all.'

'So your doctrines, your knowledge of the ultimate reality beyond the grave, disappear. Eradicated by the Erads.' He felt futile.

'I am appearing to Mr Roberts in vision-form,' the

213

Anarch said peacefully. 'I am busily communicating with him. To a certain, limited extent inspiring him. Substantial parts of my new understanding will therefore reach the world, through him. And your secretary, Miss Vale, possesses reams of dictation which she took from me.' The Anarch did not seem perturbed; he radiated, in fact, an aura of saintly acceptance.

'Am I really in love with Ann Fisher?' Sebastian asked.

The Anarch did not answer.

'Your Mightiness,' Sebastian said urgently.

Reaching up, the Anarch pointed into the afternoon sky. And, as he pointed, he wavered; cars beyond him became visible, and then, by degrees, he flickered out.

Above the roof an aircar glided down, seeking a landing.

Here she comes, Sebastian realized. It could be no one else.

As the aircar landed he walked toward it. When he reached it he found Ann Fisher industriously wriggling out of her safety belt. 'Goodbye,' he said to her.

''Bye,' she said, preoccupied. 'Goddam this belt; it always gives me trouble.' She glanced up at him, then, her blue eyes penetrating. 'You look odd. As if you want to say something but can't.'

He said, 'Can we talk up here?'

'Why up here?' Her eyebrows knitted. 'Explain.'

'The Anarch,' he said, 'appeared to me in a vision.'

'Oh my mouth he did. Tell me what the Offspring are up to; tell me here, if you want. But start telling!' Her eyes blazed impatiently. 'Something's the matter with you; I can tell. Did he really appear to you? That's a superstition; he's back at the Library, locked up with half a dozen Erads. The Uditi have been getting to you; *they* think he can manifest himself wherever he wants.'

Sebastian said, 'Let him go.'

'He'll undermine the structure of society, a nut like that. A baboon come back from the dead, spouting holy writ. You should be around him, the way I've been; you should hear some of the things he says.'

'What does he say?'

Ann Fisher said, 'I didn't come here to discuss that; you told me you knew what the Udi fanatics are doing.'

Seating himself in the car beside her, he said, 'I consider the Anarch on a par with Gandhi.'

Ann sighed. 'Okay. He says there's no death; it's an illusion. Time is an illusion. Every instant that comes into being never passes away. Anyhow – he says – it doesn't really even come into being; it was always there. The universe consists of concentric rings of reality; the greater the ring the more it partakes of absolute reality. These concentric rings finally wind up as God; he's the source of the things, and they're more real as they get nearer to him. It's the principle of emanation, I guess. Evil is simply a lesser reality, a ring farther from him. It's the lack of absolute reality, not the presence of an evil deity. So there's no dualism, no evil, no satan. Evil is an illusion like decay. And he kept quoting bits of all those old-time medieval philosophers, like St Augustine and Erigena and Boethius and St Thomas Aquinas – he says for the first time he understands them. Okay, is that enough?'

'I'll listen to any more you remember.'

'Why should I pass on his doctrines? Our whole function is to erad them, not tout them.' She got a cigarette butt from the car's ashtray, lit it and began puffing smoke into it rapidly. 'Let's see.' She shut her eyes. 'Eidos is form. Like Plato's category – the absolute

215

reality. It exists; Plato was right. Eidos is imprinted on passive matter; matter isn't evil, it's just inert, like clay. There's an anti-eidos, too, a *form-destroying* factor. This is what people experience as evil, the decay of form. But the anti-eidos is an eidolon, a delusion; once impressed, the form is eternal – it's just that it undergoes a constant evolution, so that we can't perceive the form. The way, for instance, the child disappears into the man, or, like we have now, the man dwindles away into the child. It looks like the man is gone, but actually the universal, the category, the form – it's still there. The problem is one of perception; our perception is limited because we have only partial views. Like Leibnitz's monadology. See?'

'Yes,' he said, nodding.

'Nothing new,' Ann said. 'Just a rehash of Plotinus and Plato and Kant and Leibnitz and Spinoza.'

Sebastian said, 'We weren't necessarily expecting something new. We didn't know what it would be like, when it arrived.'

'You died; didn't you experience all that?'

'It's like during life. Each person experiences different – '

'Yes, like Leibnitz's monads.' She placed the completed cigarette in its paper package, along with others like it. 'Is that enough? At last?' She waited, her body tense with impatience.

'And this doctrine,' he said, 'you want to erad.'

'Well, if the doctrine's true,' Ann said, 'we *can't* destroy it. So there's nothing for you to get your mouth in an uproar about.'

Sebastian said, 'The Offspring of Might will spring a trap on you as soon as you enter your apartment.'

Her eyes flickered. 'This is why you wanted to meet me?'

216

'Yes,' he said.

'You changed your mind?'

He nodded.

Reaching, Ann squeezed him on the knee. 'I appreciate it. All right; I'll duck back to the Library.'

'Evacuate the Library,' he said. 'Totally. Before six tonight.'

'They're going to bombard it with some heavy weaponry from the FNM?'

'They have an atomic cannon. Nuclear shells. They know they can't get the Anarch back. They'll settle for leveling the Library.'

'Vengeance,' Ann said. 'That always animates them. Back to the days of Malcolm X's assassination.'

Again he nodded.

'Well, what do you personally say about this?' she demanded.

'I've given up,' he said, simply.

'They'll be sore as hell at you for stopping me,' Ann said. 'If they were mad at you before – '

'I know.' He had thought of that. While the Anarch was telling him. He had, in fact, been thinking about it ever since.

'Can you get away somewhere? You and Lotta?'

'Maybe Mars,' he said.

Once more she squeezed his knee. 'I appreciate your telling me. Good luck. Now get out; I'm getting terribly nervous – I want to take off while I still can.'

He slid from the car and shut the door. Instantly Ann started up the engine; the car rose swiftly and headed in the direction of mid-afternoon cross-town traffic. Standing there, he watched it go until it had disappeared.

From the elevator extrance two silk-clad Offspring of

Might appeared, gun in hand. 'What happened?' one demanded. 'Why didn't she and you come downstairs?'

I don't know, he started to say. But then, instead, he told them, 'I warned her off.'

One of the Offspring raised his pistol, started to point it in Sebastian's direction. 'Later,' the other said rapidly. 'Maybe we can catch her; let's go.' He raced toward their parked car, and, indecisively, the other forgot about Sebastian and sprinted after him. A moment later they, too, were airborne; he watched them streak off and then he walked to his own car. Inside he sat for a time doing nothing, not even thinking; his mind had become empty.

At last he picked up the car's phone and dialed his own number.

'Goodbye,' Lotta said breathlessly, in answer; her eyes dilated when she recognized him. 'Is it over?' she asked.

'I tipped her off,' he said.

'*Why?*'

Sebastian said, 'I'm in love with her. Evidently. What I did would seem to substantiate that.'

'Are – the Offspring upset?'

'Yes,' he said curtly.

'You really love her? That much?'

'The Anarch told me to do it,' he said. 'He appeared to me in a vision.'

'That's silly.' She had, as always, begun to cry; tears rolled unobstructed down her cheeks. 'I don't believe you; nobody has visions any more.'

'Are you crying because I love Ann Fisher?' he asked. 'Or because the Uditi will be after us again?'

'I – don't know.' She continued to cry. Helplessly.

Sebastian said, 'I'm coming home. I don't mean I don't love you; I love you in a different way. I'm just hung up on her; I shouldn't be but evidently I am. In time I can get rid of it. It's like a neurosis; like obsessive thinking. It's an illness.'

'You bastard,' Lotta said, choking with grief.

'Okay,' he said leadenly. 'You're right. Anyhow, the Anarch told me that, told me how I really feel about her. *Can* I come home? Or should I – '

'Come on home,' Lotta said, wiping at her eyes with her knuckle. 'We'll decide what to do. Hello.' Wanly, she rang off.

He started the engine of his car and ascended into the sky.

When he arrived back at his conapt, Lotta met him on the roof. 'I've been thinking,' she said, as he emerged from the parked car, 'and I realize I have no right to blame you; look what I did with Joe Tinbane.' Hesitantly, she reached her arms out toward him. He hugged her, tightly. 'I think you're right when you regard it like an illness,' she said, against his shoulder. 'We both have to view it that way. And you will get over it. Just like I'm getting over Joe.'

Together, they walked to the elevator.

'Since I talked to you,' Lotta continued, 'I phoned the UN people here in LA and talked to them about our emigrating to Mars. They said they'd mail us the forms and instructions today.'

'Fine,' he said.

'It'll be an exciting trip,' Lotta said, 'if we actually do it. Do you think we will?'

He said, candidly, 'I don't know what else we can do.'

Downstairs, in their apartment, they faced each other across the small expanse of their living room.

219

'I'm tired,' Sebastian said; he massaged his aching eyes.

'At least now,' his wife said, 'we don't have to worry about Library agents. Isn't that so? They're probably grateful to you for saving her hide; wouldn't you imagine?'

'The Library won't do us any more harm,' he agreed.

'Do you find me insipid?' Lotta asked.

'No,' he said. 'Not at all.'

'That Fisher girl is so – dynamic. So aggressively active.'

Sebastian said, 'What we've got to do is hide until all our papers are in order and we're aboard a ship heading to Mars. Can you think of any place?' At the moment he could not. He wondered how much time they had. Possibly only minutes. The Offspring could return at each new tick of the clock.

'At the vitarium?' Lotta offered hopefully.

'No chance. They'll look here first, there second.'

'A hotel room. Picked at random.'

'Maybe,' he said, chewing on it.

'Did the Anarch really appear to you in a vision?'

'It seemed so. Maybe – he said it himself – I inhaled too much of the LSD. And what spoke to me consisted of a part of my own mind.' He would probably never know. Perhaps it didn't matter.

'I'd like that,' Lotta said. 'To have a religious vision. But I thought you had visions of people dead. Not living.'

'Maybe they had already killed him,' Sebastian said. He probably is dead by now, he conjectured. Well, that's that. *Sum tu*, he thought, quoting Ray Roberts. I am you, so when you died I died. And, while I still live, you, too, live on. In me. In all of us.

Chapter 21

Thou calledst, and shoutedst and burstest my deafness. Thou flashedst, shinest and scatteredst my blindness . . . Thou did touch me, and I burned for Thy peace.   – St Augustine

That evening, drably, he and Lotta watched the news on TV.

'All day,' the announcer exclaimed, 'a crowd of Uditi, the followers of His Mightiness Ray Roberts, has been growing in the vicinity of the People's Topical Library; a restless crowd, surging back and forth in a manner suggesting anger. Los Angeles police, who have kept an eye on the crowd without attempting to interfere with it, expressed fear shortly before five P.M. that an attack on the Library would be soon forthcoming. We talked to a number of persons in the crowd, asking them why they had assembled here and what they proposed to do.'

The TV screen showed disjointed scenes of people in motion. Noisy people, mostly men, waving their arms, yelling.

'We talked to Mr Leopold Haskins and asked him why *he* had come to parade in front of the Library, and he had this to say.'

A burly Negro man, probably in his late thirties, appeared on the TV screen, looking sullen. 'Well, I'm here,' he said gruffly, 'because they got the Anarch in there.'

Holding out the portable microphone the TV news announcer said, 'They have the Anarch Thomas Peak in the Library, sir?'

'Yeah, they got him in there,' Leopold Haskins said. 'We heard about ten this morning that not only do they got the Anarch in there but they plan to dispatch him.'

'To murder him, sir?' the TV announcer inquired.

'That right; that what we hear.'

'And what do you propose to do about it, assuming this to be true?'

'Well, we plan on goin' in there. That what we plan.' Leopold Haskins glanced about self-consciously. 'They told us that we going to get him out if at all possible, so that why I'm here; I'm here to keep the Library from doin' that terrible thing they plan on doin'.'

'Will the police try to stop you, do you think?'

'Uh, no,' Leopold Haskins said, taking a deep, shuddering breath. 'The LA police, they hate the Library bad as we do.'

'And why is that, sir?'

'The LA police know,' Haskins said, 'that it was the Library that kilt that policeman yesterday, that Officer Tinbane.'

'We were told – '

'I know what you were told,' Haskins said excitedly, his voice rising to a falsetto, 'but it wasn't any "religious fanatics" like they said. They know who did it and we know who did it.'

The camera switched, then, to focus on an ill-at-ease very thin Negro wearing a white shirt and dark trousers. 'Sir,' the TV announcer said, mike in hand, 'can we have your name, please?'

'Jonah L. Sawyer,' the thin Negro said in a rasping voice.

'And why are you here today, sir?'

'The reason I'm here,' Sawyer said, 'is because that

222

Library won't listen to no reason and won't let the Anarch out.'

'And you're assembled here to get him out.'

'That right, sir; we here to get him out.' Sawyer nodded earnestly.

The TV announcer asked, 'And how, specifically, do you propose to do that, sir? Do the Uditi have definite plans?'

'Well, we got our elite organization, the Offspring of Might, and they in charge; they the ones that ask us to come here today. I of course not know specifically what they plan to do, but – '

'But you think they can do it.'

'Yes, I think they can do it.' Sawyer nodded.

'Thank you very much, Mr Sawyer,' the TV announcer holding the mike said. He then metamorphosed into his later self, seated – live – at his desk, with a stack of news bulletins before him. 'Shortly before six this evening,' he continued, 'the crowd around the People's Topical Library, by then several thousand in number, became extremely tense, as if sensing that something was about to happen. And happen it did. From out of nowhere, or so it seemed, a cannon appeared and began poorly aimed, sporadic firing, lobbing shell after shell on the large gray stone building comprising the People's Topical Library. At this, the crowd went wild.' The TV screen now showed the crowd going wild, milling and shouting, faces ecstatic. 'Earlier in the day I talked with Los Angeles Police Chief Michael Harrington and asked whether or not the Library had requested police assistance. Here is what Chief Harrington had to say.'

The screen now showed a thick-necked white, with pocked skin and codfish eyes, wearing a uniform and glancing about slyly as he wet his lips to speak. 'The

223

People's Topical Library,' he intoned in a loud, assertive voice, as if making a formal speech, 'have made no such request. We have made various attempts to contact them, but our understanding is that at approximately four-thirty this afternoon all Library personnel vacated the building, and that it is now empty, pending the disposition of the matter of this disorderly, illegal crowd and their intentions toward the Library.' He paused, chewed his cud. 'I have also been told – but this has not been confirmed, to my knowledge – that a militant faction of the Udi people has plans to use an atomic warhead cannon against the Library building in an effort to smash it open so that the crowd can then rush in and rescue their former leader, the Anarch Thomas Peak, whom they assume to be there.'

'*Is* the Anarch Peak in there, Chief Harrington?' the TV announcer asked.

'To our knowledge,' the LA police chief answered, 'the Anarch Peak may well be in there. We do not know for sure.' His voice faded off, as if he had his mind somewhere else; continually he glanced at something or someone out of the corner of his eye. 'No, we have no knowledge of that one way or another.'

'If the Anarch were in there,' the announcer said, 'as the Uditi appear to believe, would they, in your opinion, be justified in attempting forced entry? As they seem bent on? Or do you regard – '

'We regard this crowd,' Chief Harrington said, 'as constituting an unlawful assembly, and we have already made several arrests. At the present time we are attempting to persuade them to disband.'

Again the announcer rematerialized at his desk, handsomely attired and unruffled. 'The crowd,' he stated, 'did not disband as Chief Harrington hoped. And now, from

224

later reports directly at the scene, we understand as we said before that the atomic cannon referred to by Chief Harrington has in fact appeared, and we further understand is at this moment doing considerable damage to the Library building. We will interrupt our regular programs during the evening to keep you informed of the progress of this virtually pitched battle between the proponents of the cult of Udi, as represented by the noisy, milling, and quite angry, crowd, and the – '

Sebastian shut the TV set off.

'It's a good thing,' Lotta said thoughtfully. 'The Library disappearing. I'm glad it's gone.'

'It's not gone. They'll rebuild. The whole staff and all the Erads got out; you heard what the TV said. Don't get your hopes up.' He rose from the couch where he had been sitting and began to pace.

'We're probably safe for a little while,' Lotta pointed out. 'The Offspring are tied up trying to get into the Library; they're probably so busy they've forgotten about us.'

'But they'll remember us again,' he said. 'When they're through with the Library.' He thought, I wonder if by some miracle they could possibly reach the Anarch before he's killed. My god, he thought; I wonder . . . it's theoretically possible, at least.

But he knew, in his heart, that it would not work out that way. The Anarch would never be seen again alive; he knew it, the Anarch had known it, and the Uditi knew it. Ray Roberts and the Uditi knew it most of all.

'Turn the news back on,' Lotta requested, restlessly.
He did so.

And saw, on the screen, the face of Mavis McGuire.

'Mrs McGuire,' the TV announcer was saying, 'this attack on your Library – have you made any statement to

225

the crowd to the effect that you are *not* holding their former spiritual leader? Or do you think such a frank announcement would have the desired effect of quieting them?'

Mrs McGuire said in her severe, frigid voice, 'Early today, we called in representatives of the news media and read them a prepared statement. I will read it to you again, if you wish; will somebody – thanks.' She received a sheet of paper, glanced over it, and then began to read in her crisp, no-nonsense Library voice. ' "Because of the presence of Mr Ray Roberts in Los Angeles at this time, religious bigotry has been fanned by a considerable – and deliberate – flame of intended violence. That the People's Topical Library is a prime target earmarked for this violence does not surprise us, inasmuch as the Library stands for the maintenance of the physical and spiritual institutions of present-day society – institutions the overthrow of which the so-called Uditi have a vested interest in. As regards the use of police to protect us, we welcome any assistance which Chief Harrington may render, but incidents of this kind date back to the Watts riot in the 1960s and their constant recurrence – "'

'Oh God,' Lotta said, clapping her hands to her ears and gazing at him with stricken fear. 'That voice; that awful voice, babbling away at me – ' She shuddered.

'We also talked to Miss Ann Fisher,' the TV news announcer said, 'the daughter of Chief Librarian Mavis McGuire. And she had this to say.' The screen now showed Ann, in the living room of her conapt, seated across from the TV camera and announcer; she looked poised and pretty and calm, undisturbed by what was taking place.

' – that it appears to have been planned long ago,' Ann said. 'I think the idea of razing the Library dates back

226

months, and that this explains the visit of Ray Roberts to the West Coast.'

'You think, then,' the announcer said, 'that the attack on your Library – '

' – is and has been the cardinal target-goal of Udi for this year,' Ann continued. 'We're on their timetable; it's as simple as that.'

'So the attack was not spontaneous.'

'Oh no. Certainly not; it has all the hallmarks of being meticulously planned, and long in advance. The presence of their cannon demonstrates that.'

'Has the Library tried to communicate directly with His Mightiness Ray Roberts? To assure him that you are not in fact holding the Anarch?'

Ann said placidly, 'Ray Roberts has managed to make himself totally unavailable at this time.'

'So efforts on your part – '

'We've had no luck. Nor will we have any.'

'You feel, then, that the Uditi will be successful in destroying the Library?'

Ann shrugged. 'The police are making no attempt to stop them. As usual. And *we* aren't armed.'

'Why, Miss Fisher, do you think the police are not attempting to halt the Uditi?'

'The police are afraid. They've been afraid since 1965 when the Watts riots broke out. Howling mobs have controlled Los Angeles – in fact most of the WUS – for decades. I'm surprised this didn't happen to us sooner.'

'But you will rebuild? Afterward?'

Ann Fisher said, 'We will construct, on the site of the old Library building, a much larger, much more modern structure. Blueprints have already been drawn up; we have an extremely fine firm of architects at work right now. Work will begin next week.'

227

'"Next week"?' the announcer queried. 'It sounds as if the Library anticipated this mob violence.'

'As I said, I'm surprised it didn't happen long ago.'

'Miss Fisher, are you personally afraid of the Udi zealots, the so-called Offspring of Might?'

'Not at all. Well, perhaps a little.' She smiled, showing her fine, even teeth.

'Thank you, Miss Fisher.' Once more the announcer appeared at his desk, facing his TV audience with an appropriate worried expression on his face. 'Mob violence in Los Angeles: an evil which has haunted the city since, as Miss Fisher said, the Watts riots of 1965. A venerable building, a landmark, at this moment being blown to pieces . . . and still the mystery of the whereabouts of the Anarch Peak – assuming that it is true that he has returned to life – remains unsolved.' The announcer pawed among his news dispatches, then once more raised his eyes to confront his viewers. 'Is the Anarch in the People's Topical Library?' he inquired rhetorically. 'And if he is – '

'I don't want to hear any more,' Lotta said; getting up, she reached to shut off the TV set.

'They ought to interview you,' Sebastian said. 'You could tell the TV viewers something about the Library's venerable method of operation.'

Frightened, Lotta said, 'I couldn't get in front of a TV camera; I wouldn't be able to say a word.'

'I was joking,' he said, humanely.

'Why don't *you* call the 'papes and the TV stations?' Lotta asked. 'You *saw* the Anarch in there; you could vindicate the Uditi.'

For a time he toyed with the idea. 'Maybe I will,' he said. 'In the next day or so. This will be in the news for some time.' I'll do it, he thought, if I'm still alive. 'I could

228

tell them something about the Offspring of Might while I'm at it,' he said. 'I'm afraid that what I have to say would cancel itself out.' Would indict both parties, he realized. So I probably had better stay entirely out of it.

Lotta said earnestly, 'Let's leave here; let's not stay in the conapt any longer. I – can't *stand* it, just sitting and waiting like this.'

'You want to go to a motel?' he said brusquely. 'That didn't do Joe Tinbane much good.'

'Maybe the Offspring of Might aren't as smart as the Library agents.'

'They're about equal,' he said.

'Do you love me?' Lotta asked timidly. 'Still?'

'Yes,' he said.

'I thought love conquered everything,' Lotta said. 'I guess that isn't true.' She roamed about the room, then started off for the kitchen.

And screamed.

In an instant he had reached her; he gripped the shovel from the fireplace – it happened to be near at hand – and pushed her blindly behind him, the shovel raised.

Small and withered and old, the Anarch Peak stood at the far end of the kitchen, holding together his dingy cotton robe. Grief seemed to hang about him; it had shrunk him, but not defeated him: he managed to lift his right hand in greeting.

They've killed him, Sebastian thought with a thrill of sick sorrow. I can tell; that's why he isn't speaking.

'You see him?' Lotta whispered.

'Yes.' Sebastian nodded, lowered the shovel. Then it hadn't been the LSD; his vision, on the roof of Ann Fisher's building, had been genuine. 'Can you talk to us?' he asked the Anarch. 'I wish you could.'

229

Presently, in a voice like the dry rasping of an abandoned winter leaf, the Anarch said, 'An Offspring of Might has left Ray Roberts, with whom he has been conferring, and now is on his way here. This man they consider their ranking assassin.'

There was silence, and then, by degrees, Lotta – as always – began to cry.

'What can we do, Your Mightiness?' Sebastian asked, helplessly.

'The three Offspring who came here earlier in the day,' the Anarch said, 'placed a device on you, Mr Hermes, which informs them continually of your location. No matter where you go, the device will register with them.'

Sebastian groped at his coat, his sleeves, seeking the device.

'It consists of an electronically active non-eradicable dye,' the Anarch said. 'You can't remove it, because it is on your skin.'

'We wanted to go to Mars,' Lotta managed to say.

'You still will,' the Anarch said. 'I intend to be here when the Offspring of Might arrives. If I can be.' To Sebastian the Anarch said, 'I am very weak, now. It is difficult . . . I don't know.' His face showed pain, acute and terrible.

'They've killed you,' Sebastian said to him.

'They injected me with a toxic agent, organic, to blend with my general deteriorated condition. But it will take several minutes . . . it is slow-acting.'

The bastards, Sebastian thought.

'I am lying on a bed,' the Anarch said. 'In a dark narrow room. At a branch of the Library; I don't know which one. No one is with me any longer. They injected the toxin and now they have left.'

'They didn't want to see,' Sebastian said.

The Anarch said, 'I feel so very tired. I have never felt so tired, in all my life. When I awoke in my coffin I could not move my body, and that frightened me, but this is worse. But it will end in a few more minutes.'

'In view of your own condition,' Sebastian said, 'it's good of you to care what happens to us.'

'You revived me,' the Anarch said faintly. 'I will never forget that. And we talked together, I and you, I and your staff. I remember that; it pleased me very much. Even your salesman; I remember him, too.'

Sebastian said, 'Can't we do anything for you?'

'Keep talking to me,' the Anarch said. 'I don't want to fall asleep. "It is the lives, the lives, the lives, that die."' For a moment he said nothing; he appeared to be thinking. And then he said, '"Tissue by tissue to a soul he grows, as leaf by leaf the rose becomes the rose. Tissue from tissue rots; and, as the sun goes from the bubbles when they burst, he goes."'

'Do you still believe that?' Sebastian asked.

There was no answer. The Anarch, paltry in substance, trembled and drew his cotton robe tighter around him.

'He's dead,' Lotta said quaveringly, shocked.

Not yet, Sebastian thought. Another two minutes. *One* more.

The remnants of the Anarch drifted away. And disappeared.

'Yes, they killed him,' Sebastian said. He's gone, he thought. And this time he won't be back; this finishes it. The last time.

Gazing at him, Lotta whispered, 'Now he can't help us.'

'Maybe it doesn't matter,' Sebastian said. The lives die, he thought. They have to, ours included. His. Even the assassin on his way here; eventually he will dwindle

231

away and be gone, too – slowly, over years, or in an instant: all at once.

A knock sounded on the hall door.

Going to the door, shovel in hand, Sebastian opened it.

The black-silk figure with cold eyes standing there tossed something small into the living room. Sebastian, dropping the shovel, grabbed the Offspring by the neck and dragged him from the hall, into the room.

The room exploded.

The body of the Offspring over him, Sebastian felt himself lifted up, as by a wind; he crashed against the far wall of the room, as in his hands, the assassin writhed. Now smoke filled the room. He – and the assassin – lay against a broken door; shards of wood projected from the assassin's back. The assassin had died.

'Lotta,' Sebastian said, pulling himself free from the lolling, inert mass of body; now fire licked up the walls, consuming the drapes, the furniture. The floor itself burned. 'Lotta,' he said, and groped about for her.

He found her, still in the kitchen. Without picking her up he could see that she was dead. Fragments of the bomb had entered her brain and body. Had killed her more or less immediately.

The fire crackled; the air, consumed by it, became opaque. He lifted his wife up, carried her from the apartment and out into the hall. Already, people filled the hall. Their voices yammered and he felt their hands plucking at him – he shoved them away, still carrying Lotta.

Blood, he discovered, ran in trails down his face. Like tears. He did not wipe it away; instead he made his way toward the elevator. Someone, or several people, got the elevator for him; he found himself inside it.

232

'Let us get her to the hospital,' voices – unfamiliar – said to him, voices accompanying the plucking hands. 'And you're badly hurt too; look at your shoulder.'

With his left hand – his right seemed paralyzed – he found the control buttons of the elevator; he pressed the top one.

Next, he wandered across the roof of the building, searching for his car. When he found it he placed Lotta inside, in the back, shut the doors, stood for a time and then, reopening a door, got in behind the wheel.

He then reached the sky; the car flew through the evening twilight. Where? he wondered. He did not know; he merely kept driving. He drove on and on as the evening became darker; he felt the evening settle about him and the whole earth. An evening which would last forever.

Flashlight in hand he searched among the trees; he saw grave stones and withered flowers and knew that he had come to a cemetery – which one he did not know. An old one, a little one. Why? he wondered. For Lotta? He looked around, but the car and Lotta had disappeared: he had gone too far from them. It didn't matter. He continued on.

The narrow, yellow beam of light carried him at last to a tall iron fence; he could go no farther. So he turned about and started back, still following the light, as if it were alive.

An open grave. He halted. Mrs Tilly M. Benton, he thought; she lay here, once. And, not far off, the ornate monument under which the Anarch Peak had once rested. This is Forest Knolls Cemetery, he realized. He wondered why he had come here; he seated himself on the damp grass, felt the cold of night, felt the utter cold deep inside him: much colder than the night itself. Cold, he thought, like the grave.

Flashing the meager beam of his light on the Anarch's monument he read the inscription. Sic igitur magni quoque circum moenia mundi expugnata dabunt labem putresque ruinas, he read, without comprehension. He wondered what it meant. He could not remember. Did it have any meaning? Perhaps not. He withdrew the yellow beam of light from the monument.

For a time, a long time, he sat listening. He did not think; there was nothing to think about. He did not because there was nothing to do. Eventually, his flashlight gave out; the beam shrank to a spot and then dimmed away and vanished. He laid the tube of metal and glass down, touched his injured shoulder, felt the pain and wondered about that, too. It, like the Latin inscription, did not seem to mean anything.

Silence.

And then, as he sat, he heard voices. He heard them from many graves; he detected the growing into life of those below – some very close to it, some indistinct and far off. But all moving in that direction. He heard them coming closer; the voices became a babble.

Under me, he thought. One very near by. He could – almost – make out its words.

'My name is Earl B. Quinn,' the voice crackled. 'And I'm down here, shut in, and I want to get out.'

He did not stir.

'Can anybody up there hear me?' Earl B. Quinn called anxiously. 'Please, somebody; hear me. I want to get out – I'm suffocating!'

'I can't get you out,' he said, then. Finally.

Excitedly, the voice stammered, 'C-can't you dig? I know I'm near the top; I can hear you real clearly. Please start digging, or go tell everybody; I have relatives – they'll dig me out. Please!'

He moved over, away from the grave. Away from the insistent noise. Into the babble of all the many others.

Much later the headlights of an aircar beamed down at him. The engine of the car roared as it set down in the parking lot of the cemetery. Then footsteps, and the illumination of a large-battery light, a vast sealed headlight beam. The path of illumination swung from side to side; like a visible pendulum, he thought; like part of a clock. He waited, not stirring, but at last the light reached him, touched him.

'I figured I'd find you here,' Bob Lindy said.

He said, 'Lotta is – '

'I found your car. I know.' Lindy crouched down, shone the heavy white beam on him. 'And you're seriously hurt; you're covered with blood. Come on – I'll take you to the hospital.'

'No,' Sebastian said. 'No; I don't want to go.'

'Why not? Even if she's gone you still have to – '

Sebastian said, 'They want to get out. All of them.'

'The deaders?' Lindy gripped him around the waist, lifted him to his feet. 'Later,' he said. 'Can you walk at all? You must have been walking; your shoes are covered with mud. And your clothes are torn, but maybe the blast did that.'

'Let Earl Quinn out,' Sebastian said. 'He's the closest; he can't breathe.' He pointed to the grave stone. 'Under there.'

'You're going to die,' Lindy said. 'Yourself. Unless I can get you to the hospital. Goddam it, walk as well as you can; I'll try to support you. My car's right over here.'

'Call the police,' Sebastian said, 'and have the cop who

patrols this area sink an emergency air shaft down. Until we can get back here and start excavation.'

'Okay, Sebastian. I'll do that.' They had reached the car; Bob Lindy tugged the door open, grunting and perspiring, got him inside.

'They need help,' Sebastian said, as the car lifted and Bob Lindy put on the headlights. 'It wasn't just one I heard this time; I heard them all.' He had never heard anything like it before. Ever. So many at once – all of them together.

'In time,' Lindy said. 'We'll get Quinn out first; I'll call the police department now.' He quickly picked up the receiver of the car's phone.

The car flew on silently, in the direction of the city receiving hospital.

Voyager Classics

Neverness

David Zindell

Neverness is a romantic science fiction epic, related in evocative language that turns mathematics into poetry. It tells of a quest for knowledge of mythic proportions, spanning the universe and the human psyche.

The world of *Neverness* is intriguingly complex and filled with extraordinary beings. They include the Alaloi, who have chosen to return to the Neanderthal state, the Order of Pilots, which reworks the laws of time and physics to catapult its members through dense regions of 'thickspace', and the Solid State Entity, a vast brain made up of moon-sized biocomputers. Against this rich backdrop unfolds the story of the headstrong young pilot Mallory Ringess, who against all odds has penetrated the Solid State Entity – and made a stunning discovery.

The multi-faceted storyline blends elements of hard science-fiction, philosophy, action and adventure to create an intricate meditation on time, mortality and humanity's place in the universe.

'Spectacular world-making, a kind of reverse-coin of *Dune*, that carries sudden alarms of invention to give it all great immediacy'
The Times

0 00 712437 6

Voyager Classics

The Time Ships

Stephen Baxter

Written to celebrate the centenary of the publication of H. G. Wells's classic story *The Time Machine*, Stephen Baxter's stunning sequel is an outstanding work of imaginative fiction.

The Time Traveller is filled with bitter self-reproach at his abandonment of his charming and helpless Eloi friend to the cannibal appetites of the Morlocks, the devolved race of future humans from whom he was forced to flee. He promptly embarks on a second journey to the year A.D. 802,701, pledged to rescue Weena. But he never arrives! The future was changed by his presence – and will be changed again. Hurled towards infinity, the Traveller must resolve the paradoxes building around him in a dazzling temporal journey of discovery.

Stephen Baxter weaves together modern theories about the nature of space-time with Wells's original premise to create an intricate and mind-blowing adventure story.

'*The Time Ships* is the most outstanding work of imaginative fiction since Stapledon's *Last and First Men*, and it is the best possible contribution to *The Time Machine*'s centennial year. I'm almost tempted to say (I know this is blasphemy) that the sequel is better than the original.'   ARTHUR C. CLARKE

0 00 711792 2

Voyager Classics

Red Mars

Kim Stanley Robinson

Red Mars is the first volume in Kim Stanley Robinson's monumental *Mars* trilogy, the product of years of dedicated research and the author's fascination with the Red Planet. The result is a timeless masterpiece, the ultimate in future history.

In 2027 one hundred of Earth's finest engineers and scientists make the first mass-landing on Mars. Their mission is to work together to terraform a fozen wasteland with no atmosphere into a new Eden. But before any of the team even sets foot on their new home factions are forming, tensions are rising and violence is brewing. Before they can achieve their dreams the new Martians must struggle against their own self-destructive instincts. *Red Mars* is a gripping study of the human condition and what it takes to create a new world and a brand-new society; a tale steeped in human truths, the development of myth and a love of place that is utterly convincing in its insight into a future that could be ours.

'A complex combination of science fiction and fact, political and social commentary together with strong characterization and a brilliantly conceived plot'   *Time Out*

0 00 711590 3